CONSORT OF SECRETS

THE WITCH'S CONSORTS #1

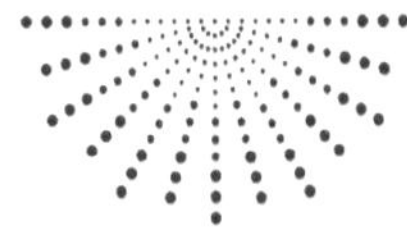

EVA CHASE

INK SPARK PRESS

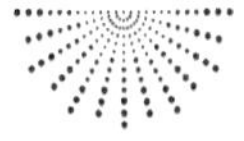

CHAPTER ONE

Rose

To a stranger, Hallowell Manor would have looked like the kind of place where dark deeds happened. You know: skeletons bricked up behind the tall foreboding walls. A madman prowling in the attic beneath the steeply sloped roof. Cheating lovers pushed from the turrets' arched windows to their death. Although as far as I knew none of those things had actually happened there.

Let's just say the house had a lot of character.

My father pushed the control on the Bentley's dash, and the automated gate whirred shut behind us. The car turned along the drive through the falling twilight. As the house loomed over us, my heart lifted with anticipation.

I wasn't a stranger, and to me this place was home. It didn't matter that I hadn't set foot on our country estate in more than eleven years. The manor and the massive property around it had set the stage for my fondest childhood memories. Through all that time in Portland, through my studies and the dinner parties and the strolls through fenced back gardens, part of me had always been waiting for the moment when I'd return here.

"That is an eyeful and a half, now isn't it?" Philomena said in her lilting British accent. She craned her neck as she peered out the window. "Just ripe for adventure."

"I'm supposed to be settling back in, not stirring up trouble," I said.

"Oh, I'm sure we can find time enough for both, Rose." She shot me the classic Phil expression: lips curved, brows lightly arched, brown eyes sparkling with mischief.

Dad parked by the garage. A couple of the staff were already hustling over to retrieve the few pieces of luggage we'd brought with us instead of sending it ahead. My stepmother let out a slow breath, her pale blue gaze fixed on the house.

"Well, here we are," she said. Her tone was so dry I couldn't tell whether she was expressing relief or trepidation.

I found it safest to care about Celestine's feelings about as little as she cared about mine—which was essentially not at all. Ignoring her comment, I pushed open the door and stepped out onto the pavement. The cool breeze of the early spring evening teased through my hair. I pushed the black tumble of those locks back over my shoulders and drank in the lush green scents of home.

The tang of fresh paint reached my nose. The staff must have been touching up the outer buildings to prepare for our arrival. The once-green slats of the garage walls now glowered a deep maroon.

Something deep in my chest twisted. The change jarred with my memories. But it couldn't stop the image from rising up in my head of the last time I'd seen the boys, standing just a few paces from where I stood now, watching a car very much like this one carry me away.

I jerked my gaze away before Dad or Celestine could notice me looking. It was the company I'd been keeping all those years ago that had prompted our move to the city. Better if neither my father nor my stepmother suspected how much those memories still meant to me.

Dad typed a quick message into his phone and tucked it into his slacks pocket. Probably letting one of the many people he did business with know he'd be available for conversation and negotiations within the hour. Celestine smoothed her hand over her sleek silver-blond bob and wrapped her slender fingers around his. He directed a quick but warm smile over his shoulder at me, and we started toward the house.

"Good Lord, it looks even bigger from out here," Philomena said, clutching her expansive skirts with one gloved hand while she braced the back of the other against her forehead. She stared up at the manor. "Are you absolutely sure you didn't forget to tell me you're a duchess or a marchioness or some such?"

I swallowed a laugh. "I promise, I'm nothing by regular standards. In witching society, I guess we're about on the level of a viscount?"

"Hmm." She glanced at Dad. "I hope you'll forgive

me for saying I *have* always thought your father would look rather tempting in a proper tailcoat and cravat."

"Ugh. I'll forgive you if you promise to never mention finding him 'tempting' ever again."

Philomena just smirked at me. It really was a good thing she was only a figment of my imagination and not someone Dad could actually overhear.

Phil's insatiable exuberance had practically made her leap out of the book she starred in during the gazillion times I'd read it in the last seven years. I hugely admired her habit of speaking her mind unfiltered. But it wouldn't have gone over any better in my society than it should have in hers, if her regency romance had been particularly true-to-reality.

Trust me, if you'd met the company I'd had in Portland, you wouldn't blame me for plucking my best friend out of the pages of my favorite novel instead. The girls from the witching families around the city had all been as alternately judgmental and fawning as my older stepsisters. As far as they'd been concerned, I was either a country rube to look down on or a Hallowell they should suck up to. Sometimes both at the same time, which had thrown more than one of them for a loop.

But they didn't matter now. I was home.

The staff had opened up the manor's broad front door. Golden light spilled down over the front steps. My gaze caught on the tiny crack that ran through the second from the bottom.

How many times, long ago, had I sat there and traced my finger along that spidery line? A voice that wasn't Philomena's swam up in my head from the past. *Are those stairs a lot more fascinating than they look, or do you figure you'd like to come have some real fun?*

My fingers curled toward the sleeve of my sweater. I had one of my ribbons wrapped around my left wrist, like always. "Rose's little fashion trend," my stepsisters had liked to comment with a giggle.

We stepped into the grand front hall. The porters hefted our luggage up the wide, velvet-carpeted staircase to the second floor. The cherry wood of the banisters and the wall paneling gleamed.

"I hope the journey was smooth, Master and Lady Hallowell," our estate manager, Meredith, said, welcoming us in. She'd come ahead with the rest of the key staff that moved with the family when we relocated from one property to another. They'd have spent all day setting the house in order for our arrival.

"And for Rosalind as well," she added with a quick wink. Now with only a few streaks of gray left in her white, braided hair, Meredith had been with the Hallowells for generations. You could say she'd raised me alongside my father.

My stepmother considered the grand front hall and sniffed. "I don't like to see a painting askew the moment I step inside," she said in the icy voice she usually used when speaking to Meredith.

She glanced around to confirm none of the unsparked staff were nearby and motioned the gold-framed artwork that had provoked her displeasure. The gesture turned into a quick flick of magic. The painting shifted straight without so much as a touch.

Celestine looked at Meredith with a slight arch of her

eyebrows, as if to remind the manager that a lesser witch like her couldn't afford to use her own magic that flippantly. "I hope the rest of the house is in better shape. Double-check the main floor rooms, will you?"

The corners of Meredith's mouth tightened only a smidge. "Yes, Lady Hallowell." Her gaze slid past my stepmother to my father, the man she considered her real employer. He nodded, but he gave her a wry smile at the same time as if to apologize.

As Meredith bustled away, a sallow, gangly figure appeared at the top of the staircase. "I've seen to it that all your office materials are as they should be, Lady Hallowell," Douglas, my stepmother's primary assistant, called down.

"Excellent," Celestine said with a wave to dismiss him.

From the depths of the house, the chime of our ancient grandfather clock rang out. Seven o'clock. A lump lodged in my throat. The familiar smell of the manor, wood polish and aged plaster, had drifted all around me, but it only made the ache in my chest deepen.

This place was home, but it felt abruptly empty.

"From what I understand, your Derek plans to arrive tomorrow morning," my stepmother said to me. "You did pack some of your nicer clothes, didn't you, Rosalind?"

"I did," I said without looking at her. Although I wasn't sure why it mattered. Derek was *my* Derek because he'd already agreed to the betrothal. In two months he'd become both my husband and my consort in magic. Spending this time on the Hallowell estate together was only meant to give us a grounding for that bond, the final step before the official ceremony we were already committed to. I couldn't imagine how horrible an outfit he'd have to see me in to back out now.

A persnickety part of me kind of wanted to experiment to find out. And to see the look on my stepmother's face.

"Well, make sure to get out something appropriate for his arrival," Celestine said.

"I'm sure Rose knows how to dress herself by now, dear one." My father patted both of us on the shoulders as if we'd been having an affectionate conversation. "I believe dinner is nearly ready. Shall we freshen up and assemble in the dining room?"

The thought of walking deeper into the house made my chest clench tighter. An excuse tumbled out of me. "I think I forgot something in the car. I'll be there in a minute."

I managed to walk at a normal pace out the door and down the steps. Then I hurried toward the gate. My fingers dug under my sleeve, unwinding the ribbon as I went.

The tall wrought-iron bars glowered down at me. I clutched the ribbon—white, the one I'd always thought of as mine among its five companions of other colors. My pulse hitched. Then I reached up and tied the ribbon by one of the hinges. Loosely, roughly, as if it might have blown away and simply gotten tangled there.

"What's that meant to accomplish?" Philomena asked, cocking her head.

I stepped back with a breath that came easier. "I'm not sure," I said. "I guess we'll see."

* * *

The leaves on the oak outside my bedroom window rustled with the rising wind. I drew my feet up under me on the armchair where I was curled up with a book. After dinner, I'd told Dad and Celestine I was heading right to bed, but instead I'd started unpacking my library.

The built-in shelves around the room were only half full. I'd gotten sucked into one novel along the way. The rest could wait.

"I'm *sure* that story can't be half so exciting as mine," Philomena said where she'd flopped down on my bed. She was slightly prone to envy. One of her very few faults, she liked to say.

"I don't know," I teased. "It's pretty good. Maybe I'll have a new favorite."

She stuck her tongue out at me.

"Oh, very lady-like." I waggled the book at her. "Haven't you always said that a girl needs a little variety?"

"In men," Phil said. "Not novels. And even when it comes to men, I did settle down with one in the end."

"I'm pretty sure that library you snuck into for your trysts had more than one book in it."

She huffed, but she was smiling. "Well, perhaps."

"Anyway, this is the only way *I'm* getting any variety of men," I said.

"Which really is a shame. You could be the talk of the ton."

"There isn't a 'ton' anymore," I pointed out.

"You know what I mean, Rose."

I did. There was a reason that for all my diverse literary interests, about half of my collection was romances both historical and modern. I was three months shy of twenty-five, and I'd never even kissed a guy. On the lips, anyway.

That kind of intimacy was supposed to be reserved for my consort, to kindle the spark inside me that would bring me my power. But I was hoping that Derek and I could generate other sorts of sparks once we were finally allowed to get down to it. The witching men were discouraged from much physical intimacy with any witch until the consorting was complete. We women would have a lot less incentive to settle down if we were getting our spark lit wherever we wanted.

Until our time ran out, at least.

"I can have plenty of fun still, when the time comes," I said to Philomena, and waved the bad boy billionaire romance I was racing through again. "This is research as much as entertainment."

"Hmm," Phil said as if she wasn't totally convinced. To be fair, I wasn't either. The couples in these books always seemed to be blown away by their attraction just looking at each other. Derek, well... He'd been the most appealing of the options I'd had. So I would make the best of it. This was real life. Passion could take time to kindle.

It wasn't as if I had a lot of choice in the matter.

Thinking about that, about seeing him tomorrow and starting the preparations for the consort ceremony, made me feel twice as tired as I'd been from the drive. I set down the book on the arm of the chair and turned off the lamp.

"All right, you got your wish. I'm leaving Claudia and her domineering lover behind for the night. Now shove over."

Phil scooted over to the far end of the bed, where she sat primly propped up against the headboard. I crawled under the feather duvet and buried my head in the pillow.

The tension inside me unraveled with each slow inhale and exhale. I was drifting away when a branch of the oak tree rapped right against the window. The wind must have picked up even more.

Then the rapping came again, more insistently. My heart skipped. That wasn't a branch.

I sat up and turned to the window. The pale moonlight outside caught on a hovering face—and the line of my white ribbon pressed against the glass.

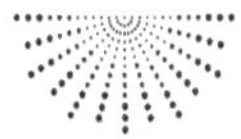

CHAPTER TWO

Rose

As I stared at the window, my heart lurched again, harder this time. Then a smile slid across the face in the night. Its eagerness struck a chord of recognition in me.

I'd left a message, and that message had been answered.

"Well, this is certainly an exciting turn of events," Philomena said as I climbed out of the bed. She squirmed with anticipation.

"Shut up," I said—only in my head, of course. You look crazy if you start talking to your imaginary friends in any way other people can hear. There really wasn't any way to turn off Phil. I'd spent so long picturing her with me that she popped up automatically now.

The figure outside the window leaned back when I approached, taking my ribbon with him. He was perched on one of the oak's branches.

I pushed up the pane. Cool night air washed over me, seeping through my thin pajamas. My pajamas with cute little black cats printed all over them. Witch humor, okay?

Rather than let myself get embarrassed about my clothes, I focused on the guy outside my window. "Hello."

The guy's smile had grown wider. "Rose. You're really back. I mean, I knew you had to be when I saw this." He held up the ribbon. "But I couldn't help checking to make sure."

Up close, I could make out the rest of his features better. Tawny waves framing an angular face, clean-shaven. A slim frame I could tell was tall even when he was crouching. It was too dark to distinguish the color in his light eyes, but they'd be a soft gray-green.

I'd actually known two boys who fit that description, way back when, but only one who'd approached every situation with upbeat enthusiasm. "Kyler?" I said. His name felt rusty on my tongue. It'd been too many years since I'd last said it.

Ky outright grinned. "Bonus points for correct twin identification even after eleven years."

His balance wobbled. He dropped his hand with the ribbon to brace himself against the trunk.

Tree-climbing hadn't been one of Ky's strong points even when we were kids. I reached to detach the screen. "Here, come in." Dad didn't go overboard with security, but there'd still be a few guards patrolling around the grounds. Better if Kyler didn't fall out of the tree, and even better if we weren't caught at all.

Ky scrambled in. I went to turn on the lamp. "Close the curtain," I said. The light would draw attention too.

"Oooh," Phil said. "A secret midnight interlude with a handsome stranger. I didn't expect our grand adventure to begin quite this quickly."

"It's not midnight," I told her, silently and obtusely. "And he's not a stranger."

The handsome part, well…

Kyler Lennox had grown up a lot from the 14-year-old boy he'd been when we'd last roamed the estate grounds together. In both inches and presence. Now that he was standing straight, he had at least half a foot in height on me, and I wasn't exactly petite at five foot seven. His eyes shone with the cheerful energy I remembered, but there was a little more gravity to his gaze than there'd once been.

He ran a hand through his tawny hair, looking sheepish and excited at the same time. My gaze couldn't help following the way his arm flexed against his fitted button-down. He might have been slim, but he was clearly not a weakling.

And now that he was here, as if he'd stepped straight out of the past into my bedroom, I had no idea what to say. I crossed my arms over the chest of my kiddy pajamas. My pulse was racing.

This was what I'd wanted, wasn't it? To bring my old friends, the boys I'd spent so many hours with all those years ago, back to me somehow? But I hadn't expected them to come quite so fast.

"You saw the ribbon," I said, for something to say.

"Yeah. I go for a cycle around town most evenings,

usually swing by the estate," Ky said. "Out of habit, I guess. It's been so long I wasn't really expecting anything."

My throat tightened. "Yeah," I said. "I... I wish I could have come back sooner. Or at least gotten in touch somehow. The way things were in the city..."

He nodded, no sign of anger or resentment in his expression. Only sympathy. "Your dad and your stepmother kept things pretty strict."

"Mostly my stepmom."

"If you want to talk about witches," Philomena inserted with a mutter. I ignored her.

"We should be back pretty much for good now," I added. "I'll probably end up traveling around some, when work calls for it or just for a break, but—I'm my dad's only direct heir. The estate will be mine as much as his soon."

But I couldn't completely explain the reasons for that. The one thing I'd never talked about with my boys was my magic. I groped for a change of subject. "What are you doing these days? As far as work goes or whatever?"

"Putting my internet obsession to good use." Ky wiggled his fingers as if typing. "I took computer science at the state college, and now I do IT work for pretty much every company that needs it in town. Which still isn't a whole lot of them, but it keeps me busy enough."

That news didn't surprise me at all. Ky had loved his computer as much as I'd loved my books, always turning up to our gatherings with some new fact he'd stumbled on while researching every topic that caught his interest. Some things hadn't changed.

"Are the other guys still around?" I asked. "Do you see them much anymore?"

I hadn't seen any of their parents yet to know for sure their families were still in town. The group of us had fallen in together because all five of the boys had at least one parent who worked on the estate. Ky and the rest had gotten in the habit of rambling around here in their free time, and then I'd gotten into the habit of rambling with them.

"Most of us," Ky said. "But we don't really hang out anymore. Except me and Seth, because, you know, family. But everyone's moved in different directions." He paused. "And Gabriel left, a few years ago. I'm not sure exactly where he headed off to. He hasn't been back since."

"Oh." That news sent a jab through my chest. Gabriel had been the one who'd pulled me into the group, who'd bound us together in his easy way. It didn't surprise me that the other guys would have drifted apart without him here.

"With a reaction like that, I definitely need to hear more about this Gabriel fellow," Philomena said.

Kyler peered at me a little more intently. "But you've been okay? Things went all right in the city?"

"Yeah. Yeah, I mean, it was boring a lot of the time. I may be even more of a book addict than I was before." I restrained the urge to glance Phil's way. "Mostly just studies and meeting people my father thought it'd be good for me to know."

Magical studies. Witching people. I wondered how much Ky could fill in those blanks. We might not have talked about magic between the six of us, but the Hallowells had always taken on plenty of unsparked employees for the everyday running of the estate. People whispered. Rumors passed around town. That was how it went.

And the second-to-last time Ky had seen me, my stepmother had used her magic on him and the other boys, if only briefly.

"I'm glad to be back," I went on. "It's really good to see you. I'd love to see the other guys again too, if there's some way I can get in touch with them..."

"I have all their numbers," Ky said, motioning to the outline of his phone in his pocket. "You can call or text me any time." He shot me that bright grin again.

I opened my mouth and then closed it, hesitating. My phone was in my purse, over there by the armchair. But— "I don't know if that's the best idea. It's probably better if my stepmother doesn't know I'm talking to you at all, considering. And I wouldn't put it past her to be monitoring my phone records. We've got this whole family plan thing..."

Ky shrugged, as if that was barely a setback. His expression turned mischievous. "I can pick you up a prepaid if you want. Something she doesn't even know about."

"I like this fellow!" Philomena declared. "He knows how to scheme."

"He's always been a smart one," I agreed with her silently. And then to Ky, out loud, "That would be great. Are you sure getting it to me won't be a problem?"

"I got here the first time easily enough, didn't I? But why don't we all meet up in town. If you can make an excuse to head over there. I can get everyone together tomorrow—we'll have a little reunion."

My voice caught. It took me a moment to force out the next words. "I—Tomorrow probably wouldn't be the best. My fiancé is arriving, so I should be here to show him around."

Ky barely moved, but his eyes flickered and his voice dropped just slightly. "Your fiancé," he repeated.

I bit my lip. It shouldn't matter. I'd never been more than friends with any of the guys. But for the six years in which we'd explored every inch of this estate together, building forts and stealing apples from the orchard and all our other childhood adventures, they'd been the closest friends I'd ever had in my life, then or since. Now Derek would have to come first.

That didn't mean I should have to cut everyone else I cared about out of my life, though.

"Yeah," I said. "That's why we're back. To prepare— we're going to be married in a couple months. But when that happens, my family will have to start respecting me as an adult, finally. And since they can't be bothered to in the meantime, what they don't know won't hurt them. I could find a reason for a stroll into town the day after tomorrow."

"All right," Kyler said. "How about noon, then? If you go to the Bluebell Café and get a table on the back patio, it's on the same alley as my dad's hardware store. We can cut through there and join you without anyone being the wiser." His eyes twinkled.

"That should be perfect." Having a definite plan made my spirits lift. But— "Your dad owns a hardware store now?"

Ky's expression turned suddenly awkward. "Well, you know, there was less work while your family wasn't in residence— It's turned out well. He mostly lets his employees run the store and he does repair work and minor construction jobs around town. He likes the hands-on work."

Of course. That made sense. I couldn't expect the world to stay exactly the way it'd been when I was thirteen. People had to move on. Like I had, at least in part.

"I'm glad he's happy," I said. "And I'll definitely be on that patio at noon in two days."

Ky gave a bob of his head in acknowledgment. He paused, and then stepped toward me, offering my ribbon.

"I think you should hold onto this," he said. "In case you need us, and you can't reach out any other way. Tie it to the gate again, and as soon as any of us sees it, we'll come wait for you—by the stone bridge on the stream. That's deep enough in the woods that no one should notice us there."

My gaze slid to the small carrying case packed with necklaces and bracelets—and the five ribbons of different colors that had been braided together with this one. The gift the boys had given to me right before Dad and Celestine had carted me off to the city. "I still have the others. I've always held on to them."

"But the more you have, the better prepared you'll be."

He smiled as he said it, but the concern behind those words—and all the good reasons he had to be concerned—hung between us. I took the ribbon from him, my fingers brushing his. The feel of his warm, dry skin and my awareness of his presence now that he was standing just a couple feet away left my nerves jangling.

He was really here. One of my boys. And what a man he'd grown up into.

"Okay," I said, looking at the ribbon instead of Kyler. "I'll remember that. Thank you."

"Always, Rose," he said.

The urge ran through me to cross that short distance between us and wrap my arms around him. To hug him with every shred of my gratitude that he was here, that he still cared, that he was bringing me back to the others. But I held myself in place, that exhilarated sensation still racing through me.

I couldn't say for sure it was only gratitude I was feeling right now. I wasn't *supposed* to be feeling anything else.

To my combined relief and disappointment, Ky backed away. "I'd better let you get your sleep," he said. His tone softened. "It's really great to see you again, Rose."

When he'd disappeared back out the window, I sat down on my bed. My heart was thumping again. Sleep? Maybe sometime next century.

"Was that one of the childhood friends you've told me about?" Philomena asked.

"Yeah."

"Hmm." She shuffled her feet against the duvet. "Are you quite certain he was only a *friend*?"

I rolled my eyes at her. "I think I can tell the difference." But that statement felt like a lie before I'd even finished saying it. I sucked in a breath. "Maybe, toward the end, there were some feelings developing that were a little more than friendly. But none of us ever acted on them. I couldn't have acted on them. A witch isn't even supposed to be friends with the unsparked. So it doesn't matter."

"It seems to me you're already breaking that rule at least a little. And *I* haven't got any special spark."

I smiled at her. "You're different," I told her. "And I only want to see them again the once, to know they're all doing okay. Maybe, when I'm lady of the house, I can change the rules a little."

As I snuggled back under the duvet, I couldn't shake the feeling that I'd just told at least one more lie.

CHAPTER THREE

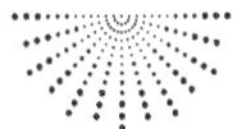

Kyler

In the bright sun shining over the town square, my late night rendezvous with Rose felt even more unreal than it had when I'd headed home last night. But it definitely hadn't been a dream. I'd held that ribbon in my hand. I'd scraped my thumb clambering up that tree.

"So you can make it, right?" I said. "Tomorrow at noon, coming in through the hardware store?"

Beside me, Jin nodded languidly, which was kind of how he did almost everything. "My schedule is pretty flexible," he said with a grin. The grin was languid too. His dark eyes had lit up a bit when I'd explained the reason I'd called this little meeting at the fountain in the middle of the square, but he seemed awfully chill about the whole "Rose returning home" news.

Of course, I couldn't remember when I'd ever seen anything really faze that guy. The way he moved through life with that perpetual dreamy expression, I'd almost have thought he was on some kind of illicit substance. Well, actually, when we were still in high school I *had* thought he must be on something, until I'd looked at every Drug Abuse Warning Signs website out there and concluded Jin didn't show any of the symptoms. He was just naturally flying high.

Our twelfth grade history teacher, on the other hand, had clearly been into some unusual recreational activities.

Seth scooped a couple pebbles off the rim of the fountain and tossed one across the rippling surface of the water. It skipped with a few *plinks* before sinking. My twin frowned at the statue overhead, a bronze woman pouring water from a bucket while perched on a horse's back. The broad cascade sent cool flecks onto my skin.

Don't ask me why anyone would go around carrying buckets of water on horseback. I'd tried to look up the history of that statue more than once, but it was one mystery that even the internet couldn't shed light on.

"You know I can be there," Seth said. "But are you sure Rose is really on board? We're risking getting her into who knows what kind of trouble all over again."

"Of course she's on board," I said, suppressing my exasperation as well as I could. Trust my brother to find the most negative way to view the situation. He might be my twin, but some days it was hard to believe we'd come out of the same womb, let alone nearly simultaneously. "It was her idea. I mean, the seeing all of us part. She didn't leave her ribbon on the gate because she figured it needed some air."

Seth gave me a baleful look. "I'm just remembering that the *last* time we got her in trouble, her family dragged her away from her home for more than a decade. If she gets caught mixing with us again, what do you think they'll do to her?"

"I don't know," I said. I'd rather not think about that. "I do know that Rose can figure out how big a risk it is and whether she's willing to take it all by herself. She's not a kid now any more than we are. Don't you *want* to see her?"

My brother glanced away. His jaw worked. "Yeah," he said, a little hoarsely. "Of course I do."

Footsteps scraped the ground behind us at a careless rhythm. I knew Damon had finally shown up before I turned around, partly because of that brash swagger and partly because of the whiff of cigarette smoke that reached my nose.

Damon flicked the half-finished cigarette into the fountain and glowered at me, as if I'd already managed to offend him without even opening my mouth. He shrugged the collar of his beaten leather jacket higher against his neck. "So what's the big news you just *had* to tell me in person, Mr. Brainiac?"

Somehow he made the idea of having a well-oiled brain sound insulting. Maybe that's why I tossed the information at him with no preamble at all.

"Rose is back."

I'd bet you could have gotten years of study out of the complex shift of emotions those three words provoked in Damon's body. The twitch of his eyes, the sudden distance in his gaze, the tensing of his mouth as his hand fell loose to his side. He let out a sound that might have been a laugh or a cry, but either way he caught it before more than a hint of it escaped him. Then he shoved his fingers back through his spiky coffee-brown hair, gathering himself.

"What's it to me?" he said, his usual cool annoyance falling back into place.

Right. Maybe he could fool the idiots he hung around with now, but he didn't really think that act worked on *us*, did he? Damon had become a lot of things in the last several years that I didn't like at all, but the last thing I'd suspect him of was indifference. Especially on this subject.

So I just ignored the tenor of that question. "She wants to see us. All of us. Well, obviously Gabriel won't be there. Anyway, she's going to meet us out back of Lennox Hardware at noon tomorrow. If you feel like showing up."

Damon's lip curled in a sneer. "She breezes back into town after all this time and wants to pick up right where we left off? It doesn't work that way."

My mind slid back to last night, to Rose's hesitation as we figured out what to say to each other. We could get past that, get back to something like it'd used to be. I had to believe it. But still... "I'm sure she knows that. And *you* know she didn't leave here because she wanted to."

"In eleven years she never got the chance to swing by for a visit and now she's here? What changed?"

My gut twisted. "She's engaged," I said. "She's come back to get married and take over the estate, is the impression I got."

For the second time, I saw a crack in Damon's front. He blinked at me for a second before shaking his head. Jin and Seth were staring at me too. I might have neglected to mention that little detail earlier.

Mostly because I'd known they'd react like this. I knew how I'd felt when she'd said those words. Even after all this time apart.

"Engaged?" Jin said, raising his eyebrows. "To who?"

I rubbed my mouth. "I don't know," I said. "Only I'd guess it's... someone like her." Someone who understood the strange things no one liked to talk about that much that happened on Hallowell grounds. Someone she could share those secrets with.

Someone very different from any of us.

Not that I'd have stood much of a chance with her compared to the other guys even if there hadn't been that invisible dividing line we never talked about between us and her. I pushed aside that uncomfortable feeling and glanced back at Damon.

"So will you be there?"

"I'll think about it," he muttered, and stalked off the way he'd come.

CHAPTER FOUR

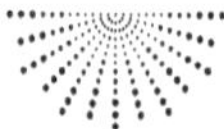

Rose

I sliced my arm through the air and pulled my hand back to my chest, closing it in a fist. My left leg swept behind me with the hiss of my sock against the polished hardwood floor. The silence of the manor's common magicking room settled back around me. I breathed in and out, slowly but evenly, the way my tutors had drilled into me years ago.

The witching forms were meant to strengthen and focus the magic inside a witch. If your spark hadn't lit yet, or had petered out, the movements didn't do anything other than provide a little physical exercise. But any witch who cared learned the patterns of motion long before they were close to taking a consort. I wanted to be able to make full use of my magic as soon as it was mine.

I leaned forward into a streak of morning sunlight. The room's only natural illumination drifted down from a few skylights on the high ceiling. No risk of any curious eyes peeking inside. Just me and the dust motes dancing with me in the air, surrounded by the wood panel walls and the lingering scent of jasmine incense.

Books were my happy place, but now that I could practice the witching forms without a tutor looking over my shoulder, this place was pretty happy too. As I moved through the shapes and stretches, my mind drifted back to all the childhood stories I'd read about great feats of magical power. Raising bridges out of the earth to cross a frothing river. Calling a rainstorm to soothe parched fields and end a drought. Casting a shield to fend off an entire army.

Not likely I was ever going to need to do anything like that, but that didn't make daydreaming any less fun.

I finished the last in the standard forms set and took a few minutes to cool down. Then I headed down the hall to my bedroom to change. Done properly, the forms could work up a bit of a sweat.

"Preparing for your grand entrance?" Philomena said, bouncing on the edge of the bed. "Oh, I can just tell this is going to be a thrilling venture."

"I'm walking into town to catch up with some friends I played with as a kid." I peered at the clothes I'd unpacked and hung in my closet yesterday. "It's not going to be that exciting."

"If you say so, Rose. I suppose that means it doesn't matter to you what you're wearing when you see them?"

"No," I said tartly, "it doesn't." But then I spent another five minutes gazing blankly at the closet. A dress would be too… dressy, right? Just to take a walk through town. But I didn't want to look as if I hadn't bothered to put in any effort at all. The sweats and tee I had on weren't going to cut it.

Phil snickered. I shot a glower her way and pulled out my best attempt at a compromise: my nicest pair of jeans and a purple cashmere blouse that would be just warm enough for me to skip a jacket. The material was so snuggly soft I always felt like I'd just wrapped myself in a bundle of cuddly kittens. A little comfort would be good for my nerves, which had already started jumping.

It was still a half hour off from noon and the walk would only take half that.

I combed my fingers through my hair in front of the mirror until Philomena started snickering again. Grabbing my purse, I headed for the door. "*You* should stay here," I told her, as much good as that was likely to do. You might think having an imaginary best friend would mean she always listens to you. Let me assure you, that is *so* far from being true.

As I started down the staircase, my pulse hiccupped. Derek was standing in the front hall, speaking to one of the cleaning staff, a slightly chubby young woman with bright red curls named Polly.

"—nothing of it," he was saying in his light voice. "I'm glad to have it sorted out."

"Of course, Mister Conwyn. Thank you." Polly blushed and then noticed me. She bobbed her head and hurried away.

Derek turned, the light glancing off his ash blond hair. When he saw me coming down, he smiled.

There was absolutely nothing wrong with Derek Conwyn, really. He had a softly handsome face with a high brow and light brown eyes that glimmered when a subject caught his interest. Looking at him from above as I descended the stairs, I had an excellent view of his broad shoulders and defined chest. He'd come up from Louisiana, where his family was based, so when he spoke it was with an appealing drawl. I couldn't complain about any of that.

The only problem was I didn't know him all that well yet. He was from a witching family, he was willing to marry into mine, he liked jazz music and sailing and dropping bad puns when a group conversation got a little tense. The rest would come now that we had more time to spend together without so much company looking on. At least, I hoped it would.

I didn't really have a whole lot of choice. If I hadn't taken a consort by the time I turned twenty-five, the spark of my magic would snuff out forever. Maybe I wasn't madly in love with Derek, but he *was* the best out of the witching guys I'd met.

"Derek," I said, smiling back and hoping it didn't look stiff. "I thought my dad was giving you the full tour."

"Oh, he got temporarily delayed with a business call," my consort-to-be said. He offered me his hand as I reached the bottom of the staircase, as if I needed help handling that last step. I took it a little awkwardly.

"He just finished up, said he'd catch up with me in a moment," Derek added. "I'm looking forward to getting a look at the full property. Would you like to join us? I'd love to hear your take on the place too." His gaze fell to the purse slung over my shoulder. "Or were you going out already?"

"I'm just going to poke around town a bit," I said. "See what's changed since I was last here. Drop in to chat with a few of the business owners who've done work for us. It's always best to keep good relations with the unsparked community."

Behind me, Philomena chortled. "'Good relations.' Is that what you're hoping to have with these dashing young men? Lots of changes to examine there. Maybe up close and in great detail."

I kept my eyes on Derek, studiously ignoring her. "Indeed," he said, the corners of his eyes crinkling. "We wouldn't want them bringing out the torches and pitchforks. We'll have lots of time for you to show me your favorite spots later. When we're both back at the house, perhaps we could take a walk in the gardens together, if we're not both walked out?"

"I'd like that," I said, meaning it. Maybe I hadn't had much choice, but I *wanted* to make this partnership work.

I slipped out ahead of Derek and my father and set off along the lonely road into town. The tall grass in the sprawling fields whispered with the breeze. Philomena had produced a bonnet out of thin air. There were some benefits to being a figment of someone's imagination, and quick costume changes was one of them.

"Are you certain there aren't any wolves or bears we need to be wary of, wandering about out here on our own?" she asked, peering toward the shadows of the forest beyond the fields.

"I thought you were eager for adventure," I said.

"Oh, quite. I just prefer my adventure without literal teeth, you know. And ideally with at least one wall between me and the wilds of nature."

"You could have stayed back at the manor."

She waggled a finger at me. "Oh, no. You're not getting rid of me that easily. I want to look over every one of these childhood friends of yours. The first one was quite a treat on his own."

I wrinkled my nose at her. "I hope you'll at least keep the commentary to a minimum once we're there. I haven't seen these guys in years. I'd like to be listening to *them*."

"We'll see," Phil said coyly. "There are some observations that simply must be made."

To be fair, I was actually glad for her imaginary company. Bantering with her made the trek pass a lot more quickly than if I'd been left to my own thoughts.

I'd never used to be allowed to walk into town on my own. Of course, I'd only been thirteen when we'd left here. Dad had never been exactly hostile about the unsparked, the way Celestine sometimes was, but he'd always reminded me to keep distance and maintain caution.

It's not that there's anything wrong *with them, you understand, little lamb,* he'd say when I'd ask him a question after reading some new book or watching a movie in which the unsparked lived their magic-free lives. *They're just different. They've never understood what we are, and they never will. So it's best we don't mingle any more than we need to.*

I wasn't sure exactly what he'd have been worried would happen to me in town on my own at thirteen. It wasn't as if anyone was burning suspected witches these days. But it didn't matter now. I'd been going around Portland without any company for the last few years, once Dad's and Celestine's nerves had settled about my interest in keeping unsparked company. It would have been ridiculous to go back to those old rules now, when I was twenty-four.

Phil and I passed a couple of farm houses and then came into the town proper. A few cars puttered down the otherwise quiet roads. The downtown area was made up of a central cobblestone square with a large fountain in the middle and a couple streets on each side with their hodgepodge of shops.

Looking around, I realized with a twinge that I couldn't actually say how much had changed. My visits here as a kid had been infrequent as well as escorted. My whole life had revolved around the estate.

It'd always been my boys coming to me.

So it really was about time I returned the favor. I scanned the signs until I spotted the Bluebell Café.

A bell over the door tinkled as I went in. The waitress by the display case of pies nodded to me, not looking at all concerned as I headed straight for the back. Picnic tables with gingham umbrellas stood beyond the screen door that led to the patio.

I stepped outside, and my pulse hiccupped for the second time that hour. The guys were already there.

Three of them, anyway, waiting around another table

off to the side. Kyler, who was standing, beamed and raised his glass to me. "Here she is!"

The guy beside him had been sitting, but he stood up at my entrance, as if I needed that formal gesture of respect. Even if I hadn't already seen how Ky had grown up, I'd have recognized his twin at once.

Seth Lennox had the same tawny hair, cropped close to his head as always in contrast with Kyler's messy waves. *His* tall frame was packed with muscle from his brawny calves to his well-built shoulders. Also as always, his face had formed that familiar solemn expression.

"Rose," he said, holding my gaze so intently I couldn't do anything except stare back. "No one gave you any hassle about coming down here?"

I shook my head. "No. No one seemed at all concerned." Why should Dad or Celestine worry about a simple stroll around town? Any normal person would have forgotten the friends of their childhood and preteens, right? Certainly any normal *witch* whose friends had been unsparked.

But here I was.

Seth's stance relaxed. "I'm glad. And—I'm glad you came down."

"Me too," I said, a lump filling my throat out of nowhere. My attention slipped away from Seth to the third figure at the table.

That guy was sitting casually, his back propped against the side of the table just beyond the shade of the umbrella. The sun lit up his golden-brown skin and the blue streaks dyed into his smooth black hair. Those were new.

The slow grin he gave me lit up his dark eyes in turn. "Our Briar Rose has returned to her castle at last," he said. "It's been too long since I've seen that pretty face of yours."

A face which was now flushing. Jin Lyang had always been a flirt. It was just a little harder to brush off those remarks when they were coming from a rather stunning man and not a still kind of gawky young teenager.

"I wish it hadn't been so long," I said. "But, you know, evil stepmothers and all." I swallowed hard and found I didn't know what else to say. It'd been hard enough figuring out how to talk to just Kyler last night. Now I had three visions from my past, all grown-up, in front of me.

I sensed Philomena lingering behind me, but for once she kept her mouth shut, as if she could tell I needed a moment or two to process. There was a reason I'd picked her as my best friend.

"You should have something to drink," Ky said, waving me over to the table.

The waitress appeared beside me. "I, um— Can I get a Coke, please?" I said.

"Sure thing, dear," she said, and hustled off.

As I sat down gingerly at one end of the picnic table bench, my gaze fell on Ky's glass. He was drinking beer. Jin had a half-empty glass of red wine beside his sprawled arm. Suddenly I felt as childish as I had in my cat pajamas two nights ago.

Well, Seth only had water.

"Where's Damon?" I ventured. "Ky said Gabriel wasn't in town anymore, but I thought—"

Jin rolled his eyes with a chuckle. "You know Damon. Thin skin, thick layer of attitude. He'll show up just late enough to make the point that coming wasn't *that* important to him."

"Oh." My gut twisted. Way back when, he'd never acted that prickly with me.

"Don't worry about him," Seth said firmly. "Whatever issues Damon has, they're definitely *his*. Ky told us you're back at the manor for good?"

I took a deep breath. "Yeah. I'm sure we'll travel around every now and then, but other than that, I'm sticking around. They've finally decided I'm all grown up and ready to take ownership."

Not that Celestine had much choice in the matter. It wasn't as if my father would have let her stop me from coming into my magic.

I glanced around the table at the guys. Ky was still beaming, rocking eagerly on his feet, and Jin still wore that easy grin. Even Seth smiled a little when my eyes met his again. My pulse skipped, but in a much happier way.

I was back. Back with my boys. It wasn't quite the same, and maybe it never would be, but I was more at home right now than I'd ever been in that house in Portland.

"What have you two been up to all these years?" I said, looking from Seth to Jin and back.

Seth swung his thumb toward the back of a store with a stack of two-by-fours outside, just down the laneway beyond the patio. "I've been helping my dad with his company. Got a degree in business management, which doesn't help as much as you'd hope with managing an actual business." His smile turned wry. "Mostly I go out and help him with the construction jobs he gets."

Philomena let out a low whistle. "With the muscles on that fine specimen of manhood, I'd bet he could do a job and a half all by himself."

I figured it was better not to pass on that observation to Seth. Even if it was accurate. "And you?" I asked Jin. My artist. We'd never had any doubt that he'd be creating some kind of masterpieces even back when we were kids.

Jin made a vague gesture in the air. "Oh, I hit the road with my dad for a while as soon as I was done with high school. Got to see a lot of the world while he was touring with the latest band. Lots of inspiration. I'm doing mixed-media paintings these days. Had a gallery in Seattle pick up a few, but mostly I sell them online. My mom even brought a couple to display at the hairdresser's so she can pitch them to the customers while she works. It's a start."

"That's great," I said, but my brain had stuck on his second-last sentence. I held my tongue as the waitress set my Coke on the table in front of me. When she'd vanished back inside, I curled my fingers around the coolly sweating glass and made myself look at Jin again.

"Your mother isn't working in our gardens anymore?"

Jin's eyes twitched, as if he'd just realized he'd made a misstep. His gaze shot to the twins before returning to me. "No," he said gently. "She, you know, after the whole thing... I'm sure it all turned out for the best."

Wait. I turned back to Seth and Kyler. "Is *your* mom still working as our pastry chef?"

Seth froze. Ky's mouth bobbed open and shut. "Well," he said, but I could already tell the answer.

A chill washed over me. "He laid them all off, didn't he? My father. Your dad didn't leave because he wanted to try something new. He had to."

Kyler grimaced. "It wasn't a big deal, really, Rose..."

But it was. Yes, Dad would have needed to reduce the staff while we hadn't been in regular residence. Maybe a pastry chef hadn't been necessary. But the house still needed at least some security, and someone to keep the gardens from overgrowing. And he'd just *happened* to lay off the parents of the boys he'd insisted I stay away from?

"Damon's mom?" I asked, my heart sinking. She'd been on the cleaning staff. "Gabriel's *dad*?" No. The Lordes had worked for the Hallowells for generations, all the way back to when our garage had been a stable instead. The Mr. Lorde I'd known had overseen everything to do with Dad's prized cars. There was no way—

Jin had lowered his head. Seth leaned forward with his elbows on the table. "It was a long time ago. We've all —we've all moved past it."

That hint of hesitation suggested maybe the "all" wasn't totally accurate. I swiped my hand over my mouth, feeling abruptly queasy. "I had no idea. I really didn't. If I had, I'd have talked to him, I'd have done anything I could..."

I never would have thought my father was capable of that kind of cruelty, punishing five members of his staff just because their kids had hung out with me a little more than he was comfortable with.

Although—had it been Dad at all or had Celestine convinced him somehow? Or snuck it by him and then when he'd found out it'd been too late to rehire them? I wasn't sure what possibility was most plausible.

"It wasn't your fault," Kyler said quickly. "I mean, we were all only kids, you included. And Seth's right. It's fine now. There's nothing..."

He trailed off, his focus shifting to something behind me. Or someone.

I turned in my seat to see a guy who was familiar and yet not sauntering over to us from the back of the hardware store.

Damon Scarsi had always been fond of leather. The jacket he had on now was more roughed-up than the hand-me-down he'd worn at thirteen, but he filled this one out better with that muscular body, so I guessed it was a fair trade-off. The sweep of his jagged dark brown hair cast a shadow over his even darker blue eyes. A few days' worth of scruff outlined his chiseled jaw.

There was no mistaking the guy in front of me for a kid now.

"Ooh la la," Phil said, producing a fan out of thin air to flap at her bosom. "Now this trip was definitely worthwhile. My dear Rose, you have *excellent* taste in friends."

Maybe—except Damon didn't look all that friendly right now. The devil-may-care stride was all him... but the slant of his mouth, half scowl and half sneer, wasn't the boy I'd known at all.

He came to a halt at the edge of the patio. I pushed

myself to my feet, feeling too awkward just sitting there. "Damon," I said.

He looked me up and down. The glance sent a shiver through my body that wasn't entirely pleasant. "So you really came back. Isn't that nice."

His stance was nonchalant, but there was heat under that cool tone. Was he... *angry* that I was here?

I scrambled for the right thing to say. "I'm sorry. About your mother—her job—I only just found out—"

He cut me off with a scoffing sound. "Words are cheap."

Philomena cleared her throat. "As a being constructed entirely of words, I must *strenuously* object."

The question fell from my mouth before I knew I was going to ask it. "What do you want me to do?"

For a second, Damon looked startled. Then his expression shuttered again. "I don't know, Rose. Why don't you give it some thought and get back to me? Or you can decide it's good enough that you saw me, and we never need to have happy times like this little get-together again."

He spun on his heel with a jerk of his head that seemed to briefly acknowledge the other guys. Then he stalked back the way he'd come. I watched him go, my chest a tangle of emotions.

Phil sniffed. "I must say, as enjoyable as that one is to look upon, I really don't care for his opinions. Just ignore him, Rose."

"Oh, you'd love speculating about what you might find under that grouchy exterior if he hadn't made the comment about words," I said in my head, through the whirl of my thoughts. My hands clenched at my sides. "And I think maybe he's right."

Dad—or Celestine—had taken away five livelihoods because of me. I had to find some way to make it at least a little right. That might be the most I could give, but it was the least my boys deserved.

CHAPTER FIVE

Rose

"You only wanted to see them again the once, isn't that what you said?" Philomena teased as I pulled on my jacket in the front hall. We'd gotten some April showers overnight, and the air outside was still coolly damp. "Just to see how they're faring?"

"Just to make sure they were doing *well*," I corrected her. "And they're not, not completely. I owe them more than they got, that's for sure."

"Mmhm. And your concern certainly wouldn't have anything to do with how delectably they've all grown up."

"All of them? Have you forgiven Damon already?"

"Five days is long enough to hold a grudge. After that it becomes unseemly, unless the matter is truly dire. And he *is* possibly the most delectable of the bunch."

"Well, you can ogle them while I see if I can make up

for the jobs their parents lost." I pushed open the door. "I'm engaged, remember?"

"Oh, *I* remember," Phil said, peeking at me coyly over her fluttering fan. "Anyway, an engagement doesn't forbid you from admiring the scenery."

I wrinkled my nose at her and headed down the walk. I'd only made it halfway to the gate when the last voice I wanted to hear reached my ears.

"Rosalind, where are you off to?"

I stopped, glancing back. My stepmother was peering out of the house. I willed my expression to stay relaxed. I wasn't doing anything wrong. I even had an excuse all lined up.

"Heading into town," I said. "I told Derek I'd pick up samples of some decorations I saw that might do for the wedding reception." The consort ceremony would be a private matter, but our wedding after would be a more typical to-do. "I was thinking of grabbing lunch while I was there too," I added, just to buy myself more time. "Unless you needed me for something here at the house?"

"No, no," Celestine said, with a smile so unexpected I had to restrain a flinch. "I'm glad to see you so interested in the preparations already. Take your time, enjoy yourself." She flipped her hand in the air. "You know I can find you if I do need you."

She had to get that little jab in, didn't she? To remind me that if she really wanted to track me down, her magic could do it for her in a matter of minutes.

Before I had a chance to decide how to answer, she'd

disappeared back into the house. "Douglas!" I heard her call out to her assistant.

Philomena raised her eyebrows. "What's she so pleased about? She looked like the cat that got the cream."

"I don't know," I said. "But I'll take it."

I dodged puddles along the gravel shoulder of the road all the way into town. When I got there, my first stop wasn't the paper-craft shop, which really did have some nice decorations, but a modest two-story house at the south end of town.

"Come in!" Mrs. Lennox's warm voice called when I knocked. I eased open the door. The mouth-watering scent of fresh-baked scones immediately filled my nose.

Snuff my spark, I'd missed that smell. We'd had a good kitchen staff in Portland, but no one who could top Ky and Seth's mom in the baking department.

I ventured through the cozy living room to the eat-in kitchen, which took up about two thirds of the first floor. "The woman has priorities," Phil observed approvingly.

But it wasn't just the woman. Mrs. Lennox shot me a quick smile of welcome as she bustled between the cupboards and the thick oak table she was setting. Beyond her, Kyler was prodding a sizzling frying pan with a spatula. He glanced over at me and grinned. "Just in time."

"Just in time for what?" I said, taking in the spread already covering the table. A basket of those scones and neat little sandwiches on rolls, a platter of fresh fruit, a pitcher of iced tea... "I was supposed to just be stopping by."

"Come on now. I can't have you back for the first time in ages and not give you a proper meal," Mrs. Lennox chided. She set down the last of the napkins and turned to face me. "What a young woman you've grown up into. You'll make your father proud, clearly."

"Yeah," I said, overwhelmed. I hadn't meant for her to go to any trouble for me. And she sounded awfully upbeat about the man who might have had both her and her husband fired. I fumbled for a less fraught subject. "Since when do you cook?" I asked Ky.

"Oh, years now," he said cheerfully, scooping caramelized onions into a pot that looked like it contained soup. "It's an awful lot of chemistry, you know. Different materials combined, subjected to heat and motion. Every dish is a new experiment."

His mother cupped her hand by her mouth. "And sometimes they taste like one too."

"I heard that!" Ky said, but he was still grinning. He motioned me over. "Here, try this out."

I squeezed past the table to join him by the stove. He'd obviously been helping with the baking too. A few of the tawny waves of his hair had a dusting of flour. There was a smudge of the stuff on his high cheekbone. His gray-green eyes sparkled as he held out a spoon to me.

When I opened my mouth to taste, he touched my jaw lightly with his free hand. My pulse skipped in the second before the spoon reached my lips. A sweetly smoky tomato flavor filled my mouth.

"That's really good," I said, making myself take a step

back in the hopes a little distance would settle my thumping heart. "A successful experiment."

Ky shot a triumphant glance at his mother. "I told you the paprika was the right call."

She waved him off. "You do what you like as long as you don't mess with my dough."

Ky gave the soup another stir and turned off the heat. His gaze fell to my wrist. "Yellow today," he said, nodding to the ribbon I had wound there. "Does the color choice have any significance?"

"Just whatever fits my mood," I said, but that wasn't entirely true. If the white was me, then the other colors each symbolized one of the guys in my mind. Yellow was Kyler: sharp-minded and sunny-bright. The thought of telling him that, of hinting at how often I'd thought of him and the other guys over all those years, made my pulse race even faster.

"I'm glad you hung on to them," he said. His voice dipped in a way that sent a flutter through my chest. Then he licked a drop of soup off his thumb, drawing my eyes to his lips and the flutter lower in my belly.

Okay, more distance was definitely in order. I swiveled toward the table, just as the front door rasped open and another two people strode in.

Right. The table was set for five. "We're here," Mr. Lennox called buoyantly. Seth was just behind him, his sweat-damp T-shirt clinging to his torso in all the right places.

They must have just come back from a construction job. Spark help me, I wasn't sure an ocean of distance would cut it with these twins on either side of me. Where was Phil's fan when I needed it?

Seth stopped in his tracks when he saw me, his eyes widening. "Rose." His gaze moved past me to his brother and narrowed. "Ky?"

Kyler shrugged with an innocent expression. I'd texted him first on the burner phone he'd gifted me with last week, checking about dropping by to see his mom. And Ky had suggested I not mention the visit to his twin. Of course, when I'd gone along with that, I'd assumed I wouldn't even be seeing Seth for the omission to matter.

"Get in here," Mrs. Lennox said. "Let's have this soup of Kyler's while it's hot."

"Are you sure this is a good idea, Rose?" Seth asked.

I'd forgotten how grim he could be. What was it Gabriel had used to teasingly call him? *The killjoy.* I waved off his concern. I was here now. "It'll be fine, worrywart. I told my stepmother I'd probably have lunch in town anyway."

The food was, of course, spectacular. I ate faster than I really should have. Then, stuffed and still enjoying the lingering tartness of the buttermilk scones in my mouth, I grabbed my purse to get on with the real reason for my visit.

"I brought these," I said, pulling out two letters of recommendation marked with the official Hallowell seal. I handed one to Mrs. Lennox and one to her husband. "I dated them this year because I figured that would be more useful. If you're ever looking for the kind of work you did for my family again, hopefully they'll help."

"Oh, sweetheart," Mrs. Lennox said, looking over hers. "You really didn't need to do this."

I shook my head. "I wish I could do more. I don't understand how you could have been let go without even any severance..." I paused, the question I had to ask sticking in my throat. "Was it my father who asked you to leave?"

"You were all already off in the city," Mr. Lennox said. "Meredith passed on the news. Not at all happy about it herself, of course."

So it could have been Celestine's or my father's orders. I'd have to ask Meredith. "I know you're already doing other work, but if there's any other way I can help, please let me know. When I'm officially head of the estate here, I'll be able to offer some financial compensation—"

"No, no, don't even think about that," Mrs. Lennox said. "We're in a good place now." She tapped her lips. "If you'd really like to do something, you could bring that fiancé of yours I've heard about into town and have yourselves some of the pie I bake for the Bluebell Café. And talk loudly about how good it is." Her eyes twinkled the same way Ky's often did. "I'm just getting started with the baking-on-commission and a little nudge in the right direction couldn't hurt."

"Of course," I said. "I'm sure I can gush over it with completely honest enthusiasm."

"All I'll say is, if you ever need anything built or repaired on the estate..." Mr. Lennox smiled.

"You've got it," I said. Although that would have to wait until after I had more authority there too. Celestine might not be suspicious of my occasional jaunts into town yet, but she'd definitely notice a familiar name if I recommended a "new" hire.

And also if my errand and lunch took much longer. I got up from the table. "I'd better be getting back now. Thank you so much for lunch."

"Any time, dear," Mrs. Lennox said.

Seth followed me to the front door while the rest of his family launched into clean-up. He looked down at the floor, rubbed his mouth, and then raised his head to meet my eyes. Standing over me like that, he seemed almost larger than life, but like a sentinel, not a threat.

"Where are you off to now?" he asked.

"Just to run a couple of errands. My excuse for coming into town." I gave him a half smile. "That reminds me—did Mr. Lorde, Gabriel's dad, move away too? I wanted to stop by and see him, find out if there was anything I could do for him, but I couldn't find him in the listings. The way he was treated seems like the worst of everyone, after how long he'd..."

I trailed off at the tensing of Seth's expression. My chest constricted. "What?"

Seth opened his mouth, closed it again, and finally came up with some words. "None of us knows exactly what happened. It wasn't something we really wanted to ask Gabriel about. His dad got into... I guess you could say a dark mood for a while after. He never really came out of it. The day after we graduated..."

"*What?*" I said when he hesitated again. My stomach had already knotted.

"The official word was he was shot," Seth said quietly. "It's generally known that he did it himself."

"He killed himself."

"Rose—"

My jaw clenched, my eyes going hot. "He gave his whole life to my family, to the estate, and then we just cast him aside. And then..."

"Rose." Seth set his solid hands on my shoulders and looked at me until I raised my eyes to meet his. "It isn't your fault. You had nothing to do with it. I promise you, Gabriel never blamed you for it for a second. Even in the middle of it—you know, it was his idea for us to go try to find you in Portland a couple summers after you left."

"You did what?" I said, momentarily distracted from my horror. They'd come looking for me?

Seth chuckled, glancing away. "Well, it didn't go exactly as planned. The bus we took broke down right at the city limits. And then for some reason we couldn't get a cab to stop for us. We started to walk, but we all got this feeling that we really shouldn't be there... It was strange, but at the time, we started to worry we might get you in more trouble than we'd realized if we kept trying."

His gaze slid back to me with a hint of a question. A feeling they really shouldn't be there. That sounded like the sort of magic a witch might use on the unsparked, to stop them from realizing there'd been any magic placed on them. Had Celestine found some way to block them from the entire city? No, that would have been too much effort. But she must have had someone keeping an eye on things who'd noticed them heading out, and made some hasty temporary preparations.

Had Dad known about *that*?

"I never knew about that either," I said.

"I didn't figure you did. Look, Rose..." He squeezed my shoulders—gently, despite the power I could sense ran through those brawny arms. "I came over here because I wanted to tell you that I didn't mean to give the impression that I don't want you around. It really is great that you're back. All of us think so. Gabriel would too if he were here. But the last thing I want to do is to bring problems your way just by seeing you."

My heart squeezed as I gazed back into his solemn gray-green eyes. "I know, Seth. I do. I promise, I've been staying out of trouble for the last eleven years—I've got plenty of practice. And if I slip up, it won't be your fault."

"I'd rather nothing happened that had to be anyone's fault," he muttered. He released my shoulders, his hands grazing the sides of my arms just briefly as he dropped them. "Are you okay?"

I dragged in a breath. My mind was whirling, but that wasn't *his* fault. "Yeah. I will be. Thank you for telling me the truth."

"Don't blame yourself, or I'll wish I hadn't." He gave me one of his rare smiles, warm as the sun's first peek from behind the clouds after a long rain. "You look after yourself, all right?"

"I always do," I said breezily, but as I stepped out of the house, my pulse was racing again.

"Well," Philomena said, appearing on the lawn, "if there's more where that came from, I'll be first on board."

I rolled my eyes at her. "Let's go get those decorations."

* * *

Coming up on the estate's front gate, my legs balked. I hadn't been gone *that* long, but the thought of Celestine catching me and deciding she wanted a little more information about my whereabouts made my gut clench. Especially after the stories I'd just heard from Seth.

Well, there were easy ways to avoid notice. When we were kids, the boys had shown me the spots it was easiest to scramble over the wall. Once I was on the grounds, she'd have no way of knowing when I'd returned.

I circled the estate to the east, following the wall. There. The old hawthorn tree was still hunched where it'd always been, one of its lower branches brushing the stones. I tucked my purse securely behind me and clambered up.

As I reached for the top of the wall to haul myself up and over, that unwanted voice again reached ears. Damn. By trying to avoid Celestine I'd run right into her.

I set my hand against the hawthorn's trunk to catch my balance, planning on dashing back to the gate. Then the words her cool voice was saying made me hesitate.

"But it can be done? A binding component can be incorporated in a subtle enough way?"

I froze, perched on the branch. The voice that answered my stepmother was familiar too. I'd know that rough and raspy tone anywhere—Master Cortland, one of my former tutors.

"It will take some more research before I can answer definitively. But yes, I believe it should be possible."

"Excellent. Then get to work on it, and report back to me as soon as you have those answers."

"I'll attempt to be prompt, Lady Hallowell."

Their footsteps faded away. My fingers curled against the gritty stone.

A binding component? Incorporated into what? She was talking about a magicking, obviously, but for what use?

An icy shiver ran down my back. I hadn't even known how hard she'd worked to control my life back when I was a teenager. I'd thought she'd eased off when we arrived in Portland, but clearly that wasn't completely true.

So maybe a better question right now was, a magicking to use on whom? And what were the chances it *wasn't* me?

CHAPTER SIX

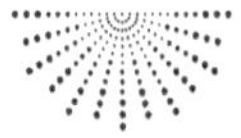

Rose

I grimaced, bracing my elbows against the top of the picnic table on the Bluebell Café's back patio. "I'm sorry. I shouldn't be coming to you with this. But you're the only people I could come to that my stepmother has no influence over."

"It's fine, Rose," Kyler said. "Of course we want to help, any way we can."

He, Seth, and Jin were sitting around the table in much the same positions we'd all taken that first reunion. But the tone of this get-together felt much more serious. And I was pretty sure Damon wasn't joining us even for a brief appearance. He hadn't bothered to answer my text.

"It could have nothing to do with you, or your fiancé, or your father, right?" Jin said in a soothing voice. "Maybe she wants to, I don't know, bind the drapes or the hedges or something. She wouldn't really tie one of you up, right?"

I wet my lips. I was already skirting the line of what I should and shouldn't tell these guys. But Celestine's magic had bound them once, if only in a literal sense for a minute or two. They knew she had power.

"Maybe," I said. "But I think she'd know how to do something that simple on her own. This sounded like it has to be a more complicated... scheme. More of a metaphorical binding? Or she wouldn't need outside advice."

"If you don't think you're safe there, Rose—" Seth started, and then hesitated. Because what could he suggest? That I run off to their house and hide away there? Leave my father and Derek wondering where the hell I was? If my stepmother meant me harm, trying to hide wasn't going to work. She could track me down with her magic if it came to that. She'd reminded me of that just yesterday.

"I hope I'm just being paranoid," I said. "It just was too much to try to think through on my own."

Philomena was hovering behind the twins, her expression more solemn than usual too. Even she could tell this wasn't the situation for jokes. And as much as I liked to pretend, I wasn't *really* any less alone with her company.

"What would you like us to do?" Jin said.

I dragged in a breath. "Nothing—nothing big. But she was talking to James Cortland, who lives in that property on the edge of town? If you could just... happen to swing by there, whenever it's not too inconvenient, to keep an eye on what he's doing. And keep an ear out for anyone talking about what he's doing. If you see my stepmother visiting him or get the idea he's up to anything that seems strange, even if it's small, just text me. I can take things from there."

"That sounds easy enough," Kyler said. "I can set up some spiders to watch for any online activity too. We'll keep watch."

Seth and Jin nodded too. I smiled at them, but the gesture felt weak. "Thank you. So much. I wish I didn't have to ask you for anything."

"Hey," Seth said firmly. "Ky is right. We're happy to be here for you."

We all got up. The guys headed back to the hardware store's back entrance. Philomena sashayed closer to me as I ducked through the café.

"Three heroes, all looking out for you," she said, attempting a cheerful tone. "You've come a long way from the Portland wallflower."

"It's not like that," I said. But it wasn't her comment that had brought an ache into my chest. I crossed my arms, rubbing them in the April damp outside. The churn of gray clouds overhead suggested it was going to rain again soon.

There wasn't meant to be only four of us. The ache was the hollowness of something missing. Someone. Damon had drifted away. Gabriel was who-knew-where.

It was Gabriel we really needed. Gabriel would know how to make any challenge feel conquerable. He'd smooth whatever chip Damon had on his shoulder with a few perfectly modulated remarks and the unshakeable confidence he'd brought to everything.

But we didn't have him, and I had no way to reach

him, not with my spark unlit. When we'd been forced to part ways, when the boys had given me those woven ribbons, I'd given them a gift too. Pages torn from the book that had been my childhood favorite, *The Lion, the Witch, and the Wardrobe*. Pages I'd thought would keep me connected to them in some way. But not with no magic at my disposal. I scowled at the concrete sidewalk.

When I reached the estate, Meredith was out in the front yard, talking to one of the garage staff. Maybe the man who'd taken Mr. Lorde's place. My lungs tightened for a totally different reason. I still had one very important question to ask our estate manager.

I dawdled by the front garden until Meredith finished her conversation. She started toward the manor, and I moved to intercept her. She stopped before I reached her, folding her worn hands in front of her.

"Rose," she said. "You look like you need something from me."

Her smooth face was as calm as always. My gaze twitched to one side and then the other to make sure no one else was close enough to hear our conversation. "Meredith, I want to know—right after we left here, eleven years ago, you were instructed to fire certain members of the staff. Who gave you those orders—who picked the names?"

The manager's thin eyebrows arched. The wind ruffled the white and gray strands of her hair. "Your father told me as he was packing up that we'd need to reduce staff. But the list of names, those I was specifically requested to let go, those came from your stepmother. I assumed with his approval."

One of the knots in my stomach released. It hadn't been Dad then. Celestine had wormed her way in there too, carried out her bizarre vengeance without him realizing. But the pain in my chest sharpened at the same time.

If she could do that, ruin five people's livelihoods and one person's entire life over their children playing in the forest with me... What else would she be willing to do just to get her way when it came to *my* life?

A rush of hopelessness swept through me. I clenched my jaw against it.

"Rose?" Meredith said softly. "Is this about—"

"Don't worry about it," I said. "It doesn't matter." The less I told her, the less chance Celestine would see our long-time manager as some kind of threat too.

I pushed forward, past the house, through the back gardens, into the forest that sprawled across most of our tens of thousands of acres. My legs moved of their own accord, drawn by some internal pull that I couldn't explain.

Twigs crackled under my feet. Bushes rasped against my jeans. I kept going, and going, at a relentless pace, until a clot of trees and vines filled the space in front of me.

I stopped with a gut-punch of recognition. Then I stepped closer, easing aside the swaths of hanging vines. Beneath them were stones—old stones, but still solid. The stones of twin towers that stood with an arch between them, like some sort of ancient gate.

Stones carved with witching glyphs.

Gabriel had found this place just a week or two

before I'd been torn away from the estate. He hadn't understood the towers' magic, but I thought he'd felt their power all the same. Even the birds quieted their song near this structure. The wind dipped as if bowing in respect.

I closed my eyes, letting the quiet stillness settle over me. My body began to move into the forms it knew by heart. The calling of power, the casting of power. The gestures that should have channeled the energy of my spark through my limbs and out to do my bidding.

Except I didn't have the light of my spark yet. I only had my ordinary self and a piercing ache of hope. So it was the hope I grasped and pushed out into the universe with every curve of my arm, every shift of my feet.

Somewhere out there was a young man. A young man with dark red hair and bright blue eyes and an air of assurance I'd never seen anyone or anything disturb. Maybe after all this time he'd held onto the token I'd given him. Maybe someday I could trace my way back to him, now that we'd lost him.

Let him hear this. Let him feel this call, somehow, through that little gift that had meant so much to me. By the spark that wasn't yet mine, please, let him.

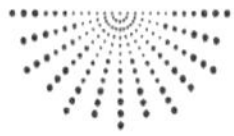

CHAPTER SEVEN

Damon

Intimidating the people around this town was so easy it was almost painful. Seriously. Get a few guys together wearing slightly scruffy-looking clothes, hang out on a street corner just shooting the breeze, send one glance at a straight-laced jerk passing by, and he's scurrying over to the other side of the street in two seconds flat.

So easy it was almost painful, yeah, but I did get a kick out of it at the same time.

"Pathetic, right?" Brad said with a scoffing sound. He rubbed the side of his partly shaved head. His leather jacket clinked with the various chains he had hanging off of it. He'd gotten the jacket after eyeballing mine. I was pretty sure he'd added the chains as some kind of a statement that he was even tougher. As if what you wore had anything to do with that.

"They wouldn't have a clue what to do if we tried

anything *really* scary," George said, scratching the scruffy beard on his knobby chin. "Walk through their neighborhoods swinging some pipes around, they'd all be pissing their pants."

"That'd be quite the sight." I grinned, imagining it.

Brad stuffed his hands into his pockets and sighed. "I need some more smokes. When's the next shipment coming by, Damon? I could really use a cash top-up."

"Silvio said soon," I said. "But it's supposed to be a big one. They'll need us for a few days to get all the sorting done. How much do you need until then?"

He shrugged. "I guess I've got some KD at home to eat. Mostly I just want the smokes."

"I think we can manage that." I tipped my head and sauntered down the street, glancing through the windows of the parked cars as I went. The town was small and quiet enough that hardly anyone except the occasional tourists locked their doors. I wasn't going to shake up the status quo by outright taking off with one—that would just be dumb. But a quick dip into someone's change stash was no big deal.

There. "Cover me," I said. Brad and George shuffled closer to obscure the view from the laundromat we were outside. I tugged the door open, dug into the mess of quarters and dollar bills some sap had left in the cup holder, and shoved the door shut again. As we hustled off, I handed the cash to Brad. "Enjoy yourself."

"Smooth, man," George said. *He* never bothered trying to one-up me. The awe got on my nerves sometimes, though.

"Soon as we get that next paycheck, I'm swooping in on that Melinda girl," Brad said. "Just you wait."

I snorted. Melinda was a clean-cut girl who worked at the dentist's office. "Like she's ever going to go for a guy like you."

"One night. You'll see."

"Sure. Well, I've got a thing. I'll catch you two bozos later."

I gave them a wave. Brad offered his middle finger in return.

I sure as hell wasn't going to tell those idiots where I was going, which was to check in on Mom. I didn't care about much around here, but I'd be damned if I was going to turn my back on the woman who'd raised me.

I climbed up the rickety back stairs to her apartment on the second floor of the divided townhouse. After a quick knock of warning, I pushed open the door. "Hey, Mom, I brought some—"

My mouth snapped shut in shock. It wasn't just Mom sitting at the formica table that marked the division between the tiny kitchen and the almost-as-tiny living room. Rose was perched across from her. Rose Hallowell with her pert little ass in that nicked chair, her dainty feet on the cracked linoleum tiles.

"What the hell are you doing here?" I demanded.

"Damon!" my mother said, her face blanching.

"It's okay, Mrs. Scarsi," Rose said. She pushed back her chair and stood up. "You just think about what I said and let me know, whenever."

She turned that angelic face of hers toward me. Jin

always liked to call her Briar Rose, but if we were talking fairy tales, Rose was all Snow White. Ebony hair, pale skin, ruddy lips. Lips she was biting right now, sending a rush of heat I didn't like at all through me. And those dark green eyes, holding my gaze, cautious but not even slightly apologetic.

"Come on," I said brusquely. "We'll talk outside."

Rose followed me down the steps onto the patchy back lawn. Such a far cry from her family's perfect gardens the sight of her standing on it made me grit my teeth.

"I'd have told you I was coming if you'd been answering any of my texts," she said. "I got the impression you didn't want to hear from me."

"I don't," I said. "And that includes not wanting to see you in my mother's apartment."

Rose crossed her arms over her chest. Which of course emphasized the curves of her breasts in a way it was very difficult to ignore. My hands balled at my sides.

She tossed back her hair. "It is your *mom*'s home. She didn't mind me coming."

"I don't care. There's no reason for you to be here."

"I think I had a pretty good reason."

"I don't think you're really in a place to judge."

Rose sighed, her expression softening. "And I don't really want to fight. Damon, you're obviously mad at me. I don't even really know why. But if it's about your mom getting fired—which I know was completely unfair—I'm trying to make that right by coming here."

"It isn't your problem anymore, angel," I said with an edge of sarcasm. "You have no idea how things have been since you've been gone. You've got no business interfering."

Couldn't she see how little she belonged here? Couldn't she see how little she mattered to me? I wasn't some dumbass thirteen-year-old chasing along at her heels anymore. I could be fucking dangerous if I needed to be. I drew myself up taller, letting the muscles in my arms flex.

Rose didn't look remotely impressed. She just looked sad. "I'm trying," she said. "That's all. And..." She ducked her head before meeting my eyes again. "I missed all of you, all those years I couldn't be here. I missed *you*, okay? You can act like a jerk as much as you want, but that's still true."

My heart squeezed despite myself. I kept my voice gruff. "Well, great. Don't expect me to return the sentiment."

"I didn't." Her shoulders drew up. For a second she looked almost breakable. Our Rose had never really been fragile. But suddenly the question was spilling out.

"That thing you were worried about, when you wanted us all to meet up the other day—did you and the rest of the crew get it sorted out?" I wasn't going to admit how often I'd wondered about that since I'd seen the text.

"Not exactly. But it's okay if you don't want to get involved." Rose sucked in a breath. "Look, Damon... We don't have to be friends again, but I hate feeling like you see me as an enemy. If there's any way we can talk it out, or I can make things up to you, just tell me. I wouldn't ask for anything more than that."

Friends. *Friends.* When she looked at me like that, all

I could see was the girl I'd been in love with back then in the woman I couldn't help wanting—wanting her mouth against mine, our limbs tangled together, her voice moaning as I made her feel more than I'd bet that fiancé of hers ever had.

But she hadn't been mine back then, not really, and she sure as hell wasn't now.

"Good," I made myself say. "Because I've got nothing to give."

"Okay. I'm sorry." She offered me a small smile. "You know how to get in touch if you change your mind."

She slipped away around the house, and it was like she took all the sunlight and warmth with her. My throat constricted with the urge to call her back. I clenched my jaw and smacked my fist against the side of the steps. Then I hissed at the pain that radiated through my knuckles. Very smart, Damon.

I marched back up to my mother's place, but I couldn't shake the angel's voice echoing in my head.

I'm sorry. I missed you.

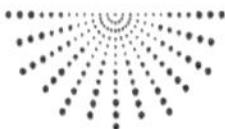

CHAPTER EIGHT

Rose

My gaze skimmed over the same page I'd been pretending to read for the last ten minutes. I tugged the wool blanket tighter around me, ignoring its scratchy texture against my neck. The air in the manor's library wasn't that cool, but I was playing my role to the fullest.

And it was because of that role that I couldn't concentrate on this book, even though reading normally came as easily to me as breathing. My heart was thumping too fast, my thoughts too scattered. I kept listening for someone to come fetch me. We were meant to be going to visit one of Dad's friends for dinner any time now. But I didn't plan to be around for that.

Footsteps sounded outside the door. I started to straighten up, and then thought better of it, hunching over instead. I rubbed my eyes with the back of my hand to redden them.

The door whispered open. It was my consort-to-be who stepped inside.

"Here you are," Derek said. "Nose in a book?"

Something about his dry tone made me bristle. "It's a good one," I offered, and coughed.

His gaze drifted through the room with its vast array of mahogany shelves, all of them packed with books of various sorts. "Well," he said, "it is an awful lot of paper, isn't it?"

It took me a second to find my tongue. Was that really all he saw in here? "Not much of a reader?" I asked.

He shook his head. "So much out in the world to see. I'd rather experience it myself than read about what someone else did. Or some total lies an author made up."

Philomena had grown bored with my sick act, but at that she popped out from behind one of the bookcases. "Pardon me? *Lies*? I really must take exception."

"Me too, Phil," I said in my head. And to Derek, out loud, "I guess I like that I can experience things second-hand that I never could on my own."

"If I can't do it myself, it can't be that worthwhile," Derek said, with a grin that was probably supposed to be charming, but right then only came off as smarmy.

"How could you not know your fiancé deplores books?" Phil hissed at me.

A good question. I hesitated, gripping the one I was holding tighter. I'd simply never brought it up with him, had I? The novels I loved had always felt like something private, little friendships I didn't want others intruding on. I'd *never* had anyone to share my love for them with, and I hadn't been about to start revealing that side of myself to the Portland witching elite. And even after a couple weeks in this house together, Derek still felt partly like a stranger.

He knew I'd been working on committing old records to computer for the primary Archive of witching folk. He'd asked a few questions that had seemed genuine enough when I'd mentioned I was gathering material to try to compile a more comprehensive modern history of our community. What had he really been thinking?

I shook off those thoughts. We had plenty of time. Maybe I could get him to come around. It wasn't as if any of the other eligible witching men I'd met had been avid readers anyway.

"I was instructed to bring you out to the car," Derek said, still grinning. "Shall we go?" He offered his elbow.

I made a show of coughing again, louder this time. Then I swiped my hand across my forehead. "I don't think I can come to the dinner after all. I was feeling a little under the weather this morning, and it's gotten worse fast. I was hoping that doing a little reading would perk me up, but... it'd probably be best if I just go to bed."

Derek's grin faded. "I'm sorry to hear that. Should I ask your father about getting you a doctor, or something from the pharmacy?"

I shook my head. "I already took something for my fever. It's just taking a while kicking in."

"Well, I could at least escort you to your room."

"I don't hear him offering to stay back and keep you company," Philomena muttered as I swayed to my feet, pretending my legs were weak. "He should be down in the kitchen throwing together some chicken soup for his lady love."

"I'd be willing to bet Derek has never cooked any kind of meal in his life," I told her. "I mean, neither have I."

She huffed, but she stayed silent as my consort-to-be led me out into the hall. He glanced around on the way to my bedroom, with a brief shake of his head.

"This old building is awfully stuffy, isn't it? When the house is ours, we can see about doing some renovations. Bigger windows, knock down a few walls to open up some of the spaces more."

I bit my tongue to hold in a pained sound. "My dad had the kitchen updated not long before we last left residence here," I offered. But I loved the maze of rooms and the way the sunlight streaked through the narrow windows.

"That's a start. Plenty of time to consider the possibilities."

The comment echoed my own earlier thought so well it made me feel a little queasy. How much was he waiting to change about me and my situation?

"Thank you," I said when we reached my door, letting go of Derek's elbow. "Please give my dad and Celestine my apologies. Hopefully I'll be feeling better tomorrow."

"Relax and get some rest," Derek said. "You look like you need it."

"Well, I'm quite sure *that* last comment was completely unnecessary," Philomena muttered as soon as we were alone in my room.

"He didn't mean anything offensive by it," I said, sinking onto the edge of the bed. "And I was *trying* to look sick."

"A gentleman shouldn't remark on such things."

"Standards are a little different in the twenty-first century, Phil."

"And what was all that talk about wrecking this gorgeous house?" she continued, ignoring me. "He's been here two weeks—does he believe it's his already?"

My throat tightened. "It will be, once we're officially partnered."

"Oh, Rose." Phil sighed. "I've tried not to say anything, because friends should support each other's decisions, but—"

No. I didn't want to hear this right now. "Phil," I interrupted, trying to stop her.

She barreled on. "He isn't right for you, darling. He isn't right at all. He doesn't care about your opinions and he mocks the very idea of reading stories. He'd rather go meet some strangers who might offer some influence than make sure you're happy and well. And that's just in the last ten minutes! I can't stand by and keep quiet when I can only imagine that marriage making you wretchedly unhappy."

"I *know*," I said, hands balling against the duvet. "I don't want to marry him. I have to, Phil. I have to, or I'm going to lose my magic."

She faltered. "Surely there must be *some* way—"

I shook my head with a jerk. "I waited and waited, hoping the 'right' guy would come, and now I'm out of time. Who would have been better? Vincent Canterbury, who spent more time looking at my boobs than my face? Carlton Hewer, who wasn't capable of talking about anything except race cars and whiskey? The selection of eligible witching men is a little limited. So Derek is what I get."

I lowered my head, blinking hard. My eyes had gone hot. Philomena came to stand beside me. I swore I could really feel her rest her hand on my shoulder.

"You're absolutely sure?" she said softly.

"Yes. Every tutor I've had, every text on the witching way was completely clear. The spark must be properly kindled by a witch's twenty-fifth birthday, or the seed of it dies. You can't ever get it back then. I met a woman once, the cousin of one of Dad's friends, who'd lost hers... You could still the pain of it in her eyes."

I took a shaky breath. "I'll be okay. Derek and I just have to get to know each other better. We'll make some compromises. And if I give it a real go and in a few years it's still not working... I don't *have* to stay with him."

Of course, even once my spark was kindled, I needed a consort to keep it lit, to replenish my power as I used it. If I didn't have Derek, I'd need to take another partner, or go without my magic all the same.

The sound of a car engine starting carried through my window. I pushed myself off the bed, willing all those fraught feelings to leave me.

A Hallowell witch didn't wallow in self-pity. Especially not when she had a secret mission to carry out. At least that mission could distract me for a little while.

The base on the second of my built-in bookcases was a tad loose. I eased the board open and snatched the prepaid phone Kyler had given me from the gap behind it. My thumbs darted over the keypad as I sank into the armchair, entering the numbers I'd already memorized to send a group message. I'd been deleting all our conversations after I'd read them, just in case one of the cleaning staff stumbled on the phone.

Okay, they just left, I wrote. *Let me know when they go past you, Jin.*

Already on watch, he replied. Jin's studio had a view of the road Dad's car should be heading down. When he spotted them, I'd know they were well on their way.

Well away from here, so they wouldn't catch me.

Are you sure you can manage the climb? Seth asked.

There you go being a worrywart again, I wrote back. *It's no problem. I eyeballed the ledge from outside—it's nice and wide.*

Let us know as soon as you make it back, he answered.

I might as well get ready for the climbing part of the plan. My window was already open. I wiggled the screen out of the frame like I had the night Ky had visited me and set it on the floor.

An alert pinged. Jin had checked back in. *Just saw the Bentley zooming by. Good luck, Briar Rose!*

My lips twitched into a smile at the nickname. I shoved the phone into my pocket and clambered onto the windowsill.

The house's architecture wouldn't have made a climb from the ground very easy, but the design included a wooden protrusion that ringed the second floor. When I'd looked before, I'd thought it was at least half a foot wide. Now, glancing down at it, I had to admit that "nice and wide" might have been overstating the situation. I'd be able to stand on it, but it wouldn't hold much other than the balls of my feet.

That was enough. The room Celestine used for her business affairs was only a couple over from my bedroom. I didn't have far to go.

I eased myself out and settled my feet on the ledge. It held firmly enough. Leaning into the side of the house as tightly as I could, I edged one foot over, then pulled the other foot after it. One scoot, and another, and another, leaving my bedroom window behind.

The breeze licked past me, tossing my hair. My pulse skittered. My fingers tensed against the cool slats, attempting to grip their edges.

Almost halfway there. I reached the next window, the bedroom that would have been my stepsister Anastasia's if she hadn't married off into some other witching family a few years back. Stopping, I clutched the windowsill for a minute to rest my tensed muscles. Then I pushed myself onward.

To my relief, I found that Celestine had left her office window halfway open. Bracing my elbow on the sill, I prodded the screen with my other hand until I managed to pop it free. I flinched at the clatter as it hit the floor.

No one came running. After hanging there frozen for a moment, I scrambled inside.

My stepmother's office was about the same size as my bedroom, filled with similar built-in bookshelves and a few cabinets and a big desk that was so barren I had to wonder if she ever used it. Celestine worked as a stockbroker for a bunch of the witching families, moving their money here and there to make it grow. Sometimes even giving the market a little magical "assistance" in a particular direction, from the comments I'd heard her make.

I'd never asked her much about the job. She thought the stuff in here was important enough, though, that she kept the door magically locked at all times and had to admit the housekeeping staff personally, watching them as they worked. I guessed that made sense, when she was dealing with people's fortunes.

I wasn't sure exactly what I was looking for, but whatever shady activities she'd gotten into, I had to assume this was the most likely place for her to be keeping evidence. Well, this or her private magicking room, but that was entirely windowless, so there was no way I was breaking in there.

I prowled from cupboard to cupboard, opening binders, checking inside boxes. Everything I found appeared to be related to her business.

Here. One drawer in her filing cabinet offered a slew of private documents. Medical records, real estate documentation, financial reports... I skimmed everything quickly until my gaze caught on one large number on a bank statement.

Just a couple months ago, Celestine had transferred fifty thousand dollars out of one of her personal accounts.

What the hell could that have been for? I didn't remember hearing mention of anything that would have cost even a tenth that much. Actually, she'd been making a fuss about how she was needing to be careful with money to save up for my wedding celebration. And if she'd already spent tens of thousands of dollars on *that*, I was sure I wouldn't have heard the end of it yet.

The recipient was identified only as a different account number, so that didn't help me. I stared at the paper for a few minutes, gnawing at my lower lip. It might have nothing to do with anything. But if Celestine was throwing around that kind of money in secret... Just thinking about it set me nerves on edge.

Who was she paying off—and for what?

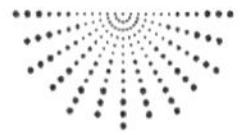

CHAPTER NINE

Rose

Kyler's apartment was up a narrow flight of stairs beside the fish and chips place it was perched on top of. The smells of fried batter and vinegar followed me up.

I paused under the dim light fixture, my fingers curling into my palm. I hadn't visited any of the guys in their own homes before now. The thought of it made my heart thump faster. But what Ky and I were going to be discussing, I wanted to be sure no one else overheard. I hadn't even wanted to send the information to his phone. If my stepmother ever had proof that he'd helped me poke around in her finances... I *really* didn't want to think about that.

"Well, go on," Philomena said. "You've already been fretting over this for two days. If it goes on much longer, I'll start growing gray hairs."

"You are never going to turn gray," I said, but I did knock on the door.

Ky opened it a few seconds later, grinning when he saw me. "Come in, come in," he said with a sweep of his arm.

Stepping inside, I felt immediately at home. Which was strange, because the space was pretty chaotic. The open-concept kitchen area was all clean lines and stainless steel. The living room attached held a futon with big cedar arms and moss-green cushions, a shabby-chic coffee table, and a matching cabinet stuffed full with a huge TV, sound system, and various other electronic devices. At least a dozen pieces of art, ranging from the size of my hand to the size of my outstretched arms and in nearly a dozen different styles, hung on the pale gold walls.

But it felt like *Kyler*. So much boundless enthusiasm for so many things, jumping from one area of interest to the next as a new thought struck him. Full of bright warmth underneath. As he motioned me to the couch, I caught a whiff of lemon that suggested he'd done some equally enthusiastic cleaning for my visit. Then the sweet cedar scent of the futon's frame smoothed over that tang.

"Quite the place," I said, taking it all in.

Ky laughed. "I know what I like. And I like a lot of things." He pointed to the entertainment cabinet. "Battling pixelated monsters." Then to the walls. "Exposing myself to visuals I don't totally understand." To the furniture. "Supporting this town. Everything in here I got locally. Which does mean you've got to be a bit flexible when it comes to style. Especially when some of it was donated by my clients."

My eyes had been drawn to one particular painting, one of the larger ones. Swaths of different shades of blue and purple bled into each other across a canvas, broken by streaks of what looked like clear glue and scraps of red fabric.

Ky nodded to it. "Not surprised you like that one. I had to buy something of Jin's, of course."

"It's nice," I said. There was something hypnotic about the fall of the colors, as if they were pulling the viewer right into the image.

"I think so, even if I haven't got a clue what it's supposed to mean," Ky said cheerfully. He plopped down at one end of the futon and grabbed his laptop off the coffee table. "All right. Let's get cracking on that mystery of yours."

I sat down next to him and brought up the photo of Celestine's bank records that I'd taken on my phone. "Here," I said, zooming in on the item that had caught my attention. "Can you figure out who she sent this money too?"

Ky took the phone from me. He scanned it with a low whistle. "That's an impressive chunk of change all right. Let's see. Yeah, I should be able to trace this." He glanced up at me, and his face turned slightly pink. "I, uh, may have gone through a rebellious stage in my later teens when I taught myself how to hack into any database I wanted to. The harder the firewall, the better the payoff."

My eyebrows rose. "So I'm dealing with some kind of criminal mastermind, huh?" I teased.

His grin came back. "I didn't actually do anything criminal. Just proved to myself I could and left everything as I found it. And what about you? Pulling stealth maneuvers like a super-spy, keeping it totally cool with your stepmom afterward. No one suspected a thing, right?"

Now I was blushing. "Not as far as I could tell. As I've tried to reassure Seth at least twice a day."

Ky chuckled. "Aw, my brother can't help it. That's just how he operates. He hates problems he can't just step up and solve with his hands."

And here I'd come barging back into his life. I rubbed my mouth. "Yeah, I guess I brought some big ones back with me."

"Hey." Kyler waited until I raised my eyes again. "Maybe he worries, but don't let yourself think for a second that he's not overjoyed that you're back. Your presence here is a net gain, Rose. I promise. We've all kind of drifted apart, but you're bringing us back together. And I think we're better off that way, you know?"

The affection in his tone and his gaze made it suddenly hard to breathe. I fumbled for something to say. "Damon doesn't seem to think so." The way he'd talked to me when he'd found me in his mom's apartment—my gut still twisted when I remembered it.

"Damon..." Ky exhaled sharply. "He's had a rough time of it. I don't even know the half of it. But it's still not your fault. I do know his mom struggled to get enough work after—after she lost the job on your estate. And his dad, who knows where he is? But Damon just got really angry in general. He did a bunch of stupid stuff at school, got expelled halfway through senior year—after a ton of warnings... And the company he's been keeping lately is pretty sketchy. But that's on him, and he knows that, deep down."

"Maybe too deep down for it to make a difference?" I muttered.

"Oh, no. He's not that far gone." Ky paused and shot me a conspiratorial smile. "He'd blow a gasket if he knew I told you this, but you know what? I don't really care about him being pissed off. He texted me the other day. Saying he wanted me to keep him updated, if whatever issues you were having took a turn for the worse. If we started doing anything to help."

"Oh." The knot in my gut unwound. I sagged a little on the futon. Maybe I'd gotten through to Damon last week after all. He cared at least a little. "Thank you for telling me. It's good to know."

"He'll come around completely," Ky said. "Even he knows what we had back then—it was something pretty special."

"Yeah." The way Ky was looking at me left me groping for words again. Then he turned to his computer.

"All right. Let's see what secrets we can uncover."

His fingers started flying over the keyboard. I didn't understand the process he had to work through, so I found myself just watching him as I leaned against the back of the futon.

I'd never really thought about the lovely speckling of

the faint freckles on his face, denser along the prominent cheekbone and then more scattered across the slight hollow below. His eyes, I could see when I was this close, were speckled too, the foggy gray-green flecked with shards of a more vivid green. And they seemed to shine when he focused this intently on a task.

"Here we go!" he said. He made a quick gesture with his hand. I leaned closer to see the screen—but not too near. When I closed that distance, every inch of my skin woke up to his presence. A hint of a smell that had to be him reached me, lightly musky with a hint of mint.

"So," Ky said, motioning at the screen, "that first transaction you saw was actually your stepmother moving her money from a joint account she has with your father to a private account that's only in her name. *Then* she transferred it again to a... Cora Conwyn. Does that name ring any bells?"

My lips parted. My heart had been beating a little fast before, but now it was outright thumping.

"Derek—my fiancé," I forced out. "Cora is his mother." The lady and head of his witching family, until one of his sisters claimed that role.

Ky's eyes widened. "And you didn't know anything about your stepmom passing on this money to her? This isn't, like, some wedding tradition or something?"

"Not one I've ever heard of." If it was, there'd be no reason to keep it secret. Snuff my spark. "Why would she be paying his family all that money? There's got to be something going on that she's not telling me." Or Dad, if she'd bothered to transfer it to a separate account before giving it to her intended recipient. She must have told him it was for something else. Which meant whatever it was, it was something he wouldn't approve of.

My chest clenched. Kyler grasped my hand. "Rose," he said. "It'll be okay."

"How can it be okay?" I demanded. "My stepmother is having secret discussions about special... techniques, she's paying huge amounts of money to my fiance's family in secret, she's hiding all of it even from my dad."

"But now we know. We'll figure it out from here."

"I can't even prove it! There's no legitimate way I could bring this to my dad." I waved at the computer screen. "He'd believe her over you. It's not like I can explain how you figured it out."

"So we'll find more proof. Rose." He raised his other hand to touch the side of my face, bring my gaze back to his. "We can do this. *You* can do this. Look at how much you've been able to unravel already."

My breath came a little steadier as I stared back at him. "How can you be so sure?"

He gave me a crooked smile. "Because I know you. And I don't believe there's anything you *can't* do, especially when you've got us behind you."

The gentle contact of his fingers against my cheek sent a wash of heat through me. The faith and admiration in his expression seared right through to my soul. I'd like to say I couldn't have helped what happened next, but I probably could have stopped myself. It's just that right in that moment I didn't want to.

I leaned across those last few inches and pressed my lips to his.

Ky's breath hitched. His fingers slid back into my

hair. His lips were warm and the kiss he offered in return so tender and—

A jitter of energy shot up from the center of my chest, right behind my rib cage. No, not just a jitter—a spark. A flash of magical electricity, so heady it tingled right up to the roof of my mouth.

I jerked back, my body suddenly shaking. How could that—it wasn't possible. Ky didn't have a witching bone in his body. He couldn't have lit my spark.

And yet I could still feel it, sizzling faintly behind my sternum.

"Rose," Ky said, his voice rough, and I snapped the rest of the way back to reality. Ky didn't have a witching bone in his body, no, and I had no business kissing him anyway. I was supposed to be getting married in a month and a half's time to *Derek*. If I screwed that up, I might as well kiss my magic good-bye. What the *hell* had I been thinking?

I scrambled to my feet. "Thank you," I blurted out. "For the—the computer stuff. I have to go."

I snatched up my phone and bolted for the door before I could do anything even more stupid than I already had.

Philomena caught up with me at the bottom of the stairs. "You couldn't have interrupted that?" I asked. "Yelled 'Fire!'? Thrown something at my head?"

Her smile was both bright and strained. "I've never been one to stand between a woman and what she truly wants."

"I want my magic," I said.

The tingle of energy inside me had already flickered out. Had I even really felt it?

It didn't matter whether the sensation had been real or my imagination. I couldn't do that again. I couldn't let one kiss distract me. All I could focus on right now was uncovering the rest of my stepmother's plans before it was too late.

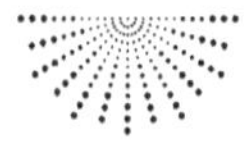

CHAPTER TEN

Jin

Rose by mid-morning sunlight was my favorite Rose. The soft glow brought out the pink in her pale cheeks and the gloss in her black hair. Seeing her in it made my fingers itch for a paintbrush or a stick of oil pastel.

Of course, there were other Roses I'd never seen. Rose by twilight. Rose when she first opened her eyes in the morning. Those might be even more arresting.

I'd have liked to see them all. But I'd take what I got, which was mid-morning Rose.

"I wish I had something better to offer," she was saying as we ambled down the street to my studio. She'd just finished visiting with my mother, trying to make up for what her family had done wrong eleven years ago. "If I'd known back then..."

"It's fine, Briar Rose," I said before she could go on. "Like the fairy tale, right? You were asleep, unknowing, and now you've woken up. What matters is what you do now. That stuff from the past, you can't let it drag you down."

She groaned. "Easy to say, not so easy to do."

I knew the shadows in her eyes had as much to do with present concerns as anything way back then. "How have things been going with your stepmother?"

"Oh, you know..." She made a face at the ground. "I'm still playing along, acting like everything's fine. That's all I really can do until I figure out more about what's going on. I just need something obvious I can take to my dad. Once I have him on my side, I'll be fine."

"And your fiancé?" I asked.

I didn't have anything against the guy exactly. Or I wouldn't have, if he'd made Rose happy. But I was pretty sure he didn't. Every time she or anyone else mentioned him, her mouth tightened, just for a second.

Like it did right now. "I'm acting like everything's fine with him too," she said. "I have no idea if he even knows about the payoff, after all. It didn't go to *him*. His parents might be manipulating him like Celestine is trying to manipulate me. If that is what she's doing."

"You could postpone the wedding until you have—"

"No," Rose broke in sharply. "Jin, I can't. There are parts of the situation you don't understand."

Parts she wasn't willing to tell me. It was all right. I could give her that space, like we always had. But when she looked that downcast, I couldn't just leave it.

"I'm sure there are," I said. "But I'm also sure that there's a way out of any bad situation, even if you can't see it right away. So keep looking, all right? And we'll look with you."

"I know you will," she said, and I got the smile I'd been hoping for. Maybe it wasn't as relaxed or as happy as she deserved to feel, but I could keep working on that.

I'd closed my little gallery space for the morning. I unlocked the door and motioned Rose in with a little bow. Her lips parted as she ventured inside, taking in the same mingled smells of oils and acrylics, glue and gesso, that I was. Our feet clattered loud against the floor in the quiet.

"Wow," Rose said, turning around. "These aren't all yours."

A couple dozen paintings and mixed media pieces scattered the white walls. Five sculptures posed on display stands spaced around the room. I'd wanted to capture the feeling of all those great modern art galleries I'd gotten to visit over the years around the world, squeezed into miniature form.

"Only about a quarter of the pieces are mine," I agreed. "I take works on consignment from local artists across the state. The place doesn't get a lot of visitors, but I've made it into a few guide books, so we get some tourists stopping by. And people from around here come by more often than you might think."

I didn't sell enough to fully justify the space, but my dad covered half the costs, and I had no problem taking advantage of that generosity. It was his way of apologizing for not being around half the time.

"This is yours," Rose said, pointing to a red-tinged piece with an arching bridge.

The corner of my mouth twitched up. She could recognize me in my work already, huh? "There's a lot of Paris in that one," I said.

"And this?" She motioned to a jumbled city street streaked with blue.

"Berlin."

She raised her eyebrows at me. "You've gotten around a lot."

I grinned back. "My dad thought it'd be good for me to take some time after high school, broaden my horizons. And the band he was substituting bass for was on a world-wide tour. I got to tag along for some pretty wild adventures. Lots of material to draw from."

Rose wandered deeper into the room and paused by another work of mine. Fragments of glass pressed into the blues and greens gleamed under the overhead lights. She stared at it for a moment and then looked at me.

"This is the stream on my estate."

I nodded. She swiveled on her heel, scanning the room, and found the other one in just a few seconds. A stone wall draped with vines, lit with the shifting colors of a clouded sunrise. Those were just the two I had out on display.

"I still get a lot of inspiration from those times, too," I said. "There was... something really special about that time, wasn't there? The way we all bounced off each other but somehow kept a perfect harmony." For six years the six of us had roamed Rose's property together, and I couldn't remember a single fight that had lasted beyond one visit.

"Yeah," Rose said softly. "I miss that."

The words hit me with a punch of emotion so sudden I didn't even think before saying, "Me too."

Maybe that was true. But like I'd said to her before, there was no point in dwelling on what was gone. What I wanted was a Rose as bright and lively as she'd been back then. How could she think she was bound to whatever jerk her family had set her up with?

I stepped closer to her and gave a strand of her hair a playful tug. "I'd like to paint you sometime, you know. Not that I have much hope of doing you justice."

She laughed. "I don't think I'm quite *that* stunning."

"Ah, that's just because you haven't seen yourself through someone else's eyes. The line of your cheek... The angle of your jaw..." I traced a finger down her face. "It's calling to be put to canvas, I'm telling you."

A hint of a glow came into her face then. It took all my self-control not to keep trailing my hand downward to take in the other curves of her body. She was taken, and I could respect that.

But maybe I'd already overstepped a boundary. Rose blinked, and the glow faded. She backed up a step, looking around the gallery one more time.

"It's gorgeous," she said, with more distance in her voice than had been there before. "I'll have to come back when I've got more time to take it in. Today I've been away long enough as it is. But thank you for showing me."

I got a flash of a smile and then she was slipping out the door. As I watched it swinging shut, a strange ache welled up in my chest. As if I'd just lost something I couldn't live without.

That was ridiculous. The only thing I *needed* was my

art. Nothing good came from tying your happiness to any person other than yourself. I wanted to enjoy Rose's company and for her to enjoy mine. I wasn't looking for more than that—not from anyone.

But as I headed up to my apartment over the gallery, the uneasy ache remained.

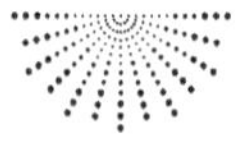

CHAPTER ELEVEN

Rose

"My goodness," Philomena said, strolling past the bookcases. "I don't recall facing an interrogation when *I* intended to get married. Which, I'll remind you, has happened at least half a dozen times."

"This isn't my idea," I told her silently. To the high witching figures across the library table from me, I gave only my most polite smile. The scrutiny of the pair who'd come to conduct my and Derek's pre-consorting interviews made my skin itch, but the comforting smell of books all around me eased my nerves a little.

The woman of the pair tapped the end of her pen against the table. "Rosalind Hallowell, do you confirm your intention to take Derek Conwyn as your consort and husband, bringing him into your family and giving him your name?"

"Absolutely," I said, hoping my smile hadn't just gotten too tight. It wasn't as if they could tell I'd just been kissing another guy four days ago... or that I'd wanted to kiss a totally different guy yesterday. I could keep all that guilt and all my doubts squashed down. I had to.

The man nodded with an expression that seemed inappropriately grave. "I see from your father's records that you've received extensive tutoring in the forms and symbols of magical practice. Do you feel prepared to take on the power of your spark? Any concerns you'd like to discuss?"

"More than ready," I said. I probably would have felt ready with half the training Dad had insisted on. "I have no concerns at all." Well, other than the fact that my spark had seemed to react to a guy with no magical heritage at all the other day.

But the more distance I got from that moment with Kyler, the more sure I was that I'd been wrong. The excitement of my first real kiss had simply *felt* like what I imagined the lighting of my spark might.

It wasn't as if I could ask these two for their opinion on the subject anyway.

"And what career path do you see for yourself once you're fully settled into witching life?" the woman asked.

That was an easier topic. "I've already been helping commit to computer and organize the records of the official Archive," I said. "My supervisor there has said they'd be happy to take me on in a role of more responsibility once I can bring my magic to bear. And I've been working on a private project, compiling a history of modern witching."

This time, both of my questioners nodded. "There may be work for you along that line to serve the Assembly more directly," the man said. "It would be a shame to see the power you can expect to wield put only to our history rather than our present and future."

A tingle raced through me at his words. *The power you can expect to wield.* I knew that was why Dad insisted on the training. The Hallowell blood—which had run from his grandmother and his mother into him, his mother's only child, before he'd passed it on to me—was strong with the spark. But hearing a member of the Witching Assembly, the governing body over all those of witching descent, made it feel even more certain.

"I'll be interested in hearing about the possibilities," I said. "I think it's important to have clear records of both our past and what's happening now."

That answer earned me a couple of muted smiles, which was more than I'd gotten so far. The Assembly witches were always so dour. Maybe I didn't want to become one of them through my work after all.

"Another matter we always consider at this stage," the woman said, shuffling her papers. "Have you given any thought to when you'd begin having children?"

Moldy cinders, that was the last thing I wanted to be thinking about right now. Being tied to Derek not just through ceremony, but bearing his children... I'd set that idea aside until I'd gotten my head and my heart in better order.

"I believe we'd give it at least a few years," I said. "So we have a chance to strengthen our bond and I'll have adjusted to my spark. What's the rush?"

"Indeed," the man said. "We do find a waiting period before progressing to the next stage of the relationship is wise. Just remember that when you are ready, you'll need to register your intent with the Assembly before you perform the magic to engage the quickening."

"Of course," I said. I *couldn't* get pregnant unless I brought my spark to the task. One of the little quirks of witch physiology, which Meredith had told me once was for our own protection. *Children are the loveliest thing in the world, but a pregnant woman is a vulnerable woman. And there've been many times when we witches faced far too much danger to make that decision lightly.*

"Speaking of rushing..." The woman paused, fixing me with a steady look that held what appeared to be genuine concern. "I must remind you that in every case recorded, if a spark isn't fully kindled by a witch's twenty-fifth birthday, it won't kindle at all. I understand you've left your consorting rather late. Your plans appear to be on track, but you'll want to ensure they stay that way. Even if you feel your spark lighting some, if you've started to become close to your intended—nothing is set until the consorting is complete."

I gave her a tight smile. "I know," I said. "Thank you."

"Well, it sounds as if everything is in order, then." The man stood up. "Thank you for your time, Miss Hallowell."

That was obviously my cue to leave. "Thank you for seeing us," I said with a respectful bob of my head, and left while they were gathering their things.

I ended up in the breakfast room, nibbling on one of the mini muffins that had been left over from our meal, when Derek came in. My back stiffened automatically. I inhaled deeply, willing myself to relax.

What I'd said to Jin was true. Derek might be as much a pawn in my stepmother's dealings as I was. Whether I believed that or not... I couldn't throw this engagement away until I was sure. Not when my entire life as a practicing witch was on the line.

He came to a stop beside me and gave me a smile that looked genuine. "Being asked personal questions by total strangers," he said. "Always my favorite thing."

I had to laugh. "Tell me about it. Well, at least that part of the formalities is over."

"I hope you had only good things to say about me."

"Naturally," I said, but the truth was they hadn't really asked me much about him at all, had they? Had they questioned him all that much about how he saw me?

Probably he was just joking. I offered him the sparse plate of muffins, watching his face. So he didn't like books, and he hadn't been the *most* considerate of my pretended illness, but I hadn't seen any signs he was in on some conspiracy against me. I'd never come across him talking to my stepmother outside of our regular family conversations.

Philomena paced at the other side of the room with brisk steps and twitches of her huge skirt. "I'm not certain about this, Rose."

"I'm not going in blindly," I said. "I won't marry him unless I'm sure he isn't part of any scheme. But until I know one way or the other, I can't afford to push him away."

She huffed. "I don't like him either way."

"I know," I said. "But... I might not have been his first choice in partner either, you know."

Derek plucked up one of the mini muffins and tipped it to me as if in a toast. "To our consorting and our marriage."

I held up the last bite of mine. "To us."

Of course, as soon as I'd swallowed that bite, I couldn't think of what else to say. In the last three weeks of walks and meals and drives admiring the countryside, we'd pretty much exhausted all possible small talk—and an awful lot of mid-sized talk too.

What did you talk about with someone who wasn't interested in about half of the things you were, and wasn't supposed to know about the other things you'd been up to? Who might be up to things *you* wouldn't be happy to know about? "Say, have you been plotting with my stepmother lately?" wasn't going to cut it.

Maybe I could get at his true feelings about our impending partnership in a less direct way.

"Are you starting to feel settled in here?" I asked. "I know it's got to be pretty different from where you grew up."

Derek chuckled. "The weather's certainly different from New Orleans. But I'm an adaptable sort. I think I'll do fine here."

"You don't mind having to make that big a change?" As a witching man with sisters, he'd have known he couldn't keep his last name and his family property, but he might have intended to stay in Louisiana in the absence of extra incentives.

He tucked his arm around my waist, so smoothly my nerves only jumped a little. The corners of his light brown eyes crinkled with his smile. "I think what I'll have here with you more than makes up for anything I'm giving up."

He lowered his head, close enough that his intention was clear but slowly enough that I could have pulled away from the kiss. Consorts-to-be often continued to hold off on much physical intimacy before the ceremony, which would encourage a passion for each other, but getting a little cozy at this committed stage wasn't discouraged. My pulse skittered, but I held myself in place.

I could get a taste of my real spark, and that might give me all the answer I needed. So I tipped my head and let Derek meet my mouth with his.

His lips slid against mine, coaxing mine apart with an ease I wouldn't have expected. Who had *he* kissed in the past to learn how to do that? I gripped his shirt for balance, the closeness of him and the heat of his mouth making me abruptly dizzy.

But doubt stayed clenched tight around my heart. And not a hint of a glimmer lit inside me. My chest felt as hollow as a reed.

I eased back from him, my pulse thudding. Derek smiled at me again, looking pleased. I tried to mimic his expression, as if that kiss had given me exactly what I'd been looking for.

As if it hadn't been a complete and total failure.

CHAPTER TWELVE

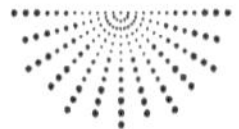

Rose

As estate manager, Meredith had an office to herself, a small room at the back of the house. Of course, she was so busy overseeing the rest of the staff that she was rarely in it except for first thing in the morning, when she went over the day's itinerary, and last thing at night, when she filed away any results of that day's work. So it was already pitch black beyond the window when I knocked on her door.

Another April storm had kicked up, the wind howling past the manor's walls. Loud enough that Meredith didn't hear me until I knocked a second time, a little harder. She glanced up and saw me through the gap where the door stood slightly ajar.

"Oh, Rose! Come on in, honey."

Her office was warmer than the hall. A space heater was humming in the corner. I leaned against the cabinet next to it, soaking up its warmth, while Meredith finished sorting through the last batch of receipts and work forms. With a twitch of her fingers, she brought her magic to bear on the bottom of one paper and then another, affixing her magical signature to the documents that required it.

Then she turned to me, leaning her sturdy frame against the desk. Even at the end of the day, her hair remained neatly pinned in her braid, not a white or gray strand out of place.

I wondered if she used a little magic to hold it there, the same way she encouraged her face to stay smooth. She looked no older than Celestine, who was around fifty, even though I knew Meredith had to be at least a couple decades older. It had always seemed impolite to ask that sort of thing. Meredith was as much a witch as I was, but being from a lesser family, she'd ended up running ours instead of starting her own. Two generations from cradle to consorting.

She did have a consort and husband of her own—Anton, who served as Dad's accountant. And she'd always been my best source for witching info when I had questions Dad was too busy to answer or I was too embarrassed to ask him about.

"What's on your mind?" she said now with a knowing look.

I bit my lip. "I was just curious... How do you know for sure that your spark will light with someone? Does the consorting ceremony *make* it happen, or..." I trailed off, uncertain how to express what I wanted to without saying more than I did.

Meredith gave me a gentle smile. "It's a confusing

time, isn't it? So much anticipation, but also so much to worry about. You can be sure your spark will light with Derek, Rose. He's a witching man, and the ceremony will align your hearts and passions to provoke the kindling."

"So it's just the ceremony that makes it happen?" I said. "I just—I know that Dad and Celestine were, er, close before they officially became consorts, and Celestine kept her magic even though she lost her first husband years before. And there's always that talk about how the men should be careful about who they give their intimacy to *before* the consorting."

"Well, that's where it gets complicated," Meredith said. "It's not all one thing or another. Where there's mutual attraction, the man's energies can light and sustain the spark without any formal binding. The more powerful your emotional bond, the easier you'll kindle too. But immediate passion is hardly necessary. Sometimes it's better without. There's no shortage of tales of young witches getting swept up in dalliances with some tempting man only to find that excitement runs dry before long."

"So it's okay if you're not feeling... swept away?"

She nodded. "You want sure and steady. Build up that light over time, with growing affection. The ceremony will help you open up to each other."

"Does that mean you didn't feel your spark until you completed the consorting with Anton?" I said, on the verge of relief.

Meredith laughed lightly. "Oh, no, child. Even a little affection can give you a flicker, if you give it the opportunity. Not enough for any major magicking, of course, and it fades much faster than after you're properly kindled." She cocked her head at me. "Are you considering getting a head start on your relations with Derek? If you're feeling ready, you may as well start laying that groundwork. You can still take things slowly."

"I don't—I don't know," I said. My thoughts were stuck on that one thing she'd said. *Even a little affection can give you a flicker.*

I'd felt at least a little affection for Derek in that moment, despite my doubts, hadn't I? Thinking of him giving up his home to be here with me?

So if nothing had sparked, not even a flicker... I resisted the urge to hug myself. Maybe I'd gotten my answer after all. That would have to mean *he* had no affection for *me*. Not a shred.

He'd talked as if he did. Smiled at me as if he did. It could have been my fault, with all my suspicions of him... or all of that was a lie.

The pond our forest stream fed into looked just the same as it always had when we were kids. I slowed to a stop as I reached the edge. Minnows dimpled the otherwise-still surface of the water. Sparrows chattered in the trees, and sunlight poured through the gap in their foliage across the mossy bank.

Jin was already there, the sun making the blue streaks in his hair stand out even brighter against the black. He was leaning over, trailing the end of a stick he'd picked up through the mud between the moss.

"You've always got to be sketching something, don't you?" I said with a smile. I set my hand against the cool granite surface of the boulder at the edge of the pond— the one I'd used to duck behind to shimmy out of the clothes I'd hidden my bathing suit under, way back when. The boys would have simply tossed off shirts and pants and jumped in wearing their underthings.

Jin grinned back at me, and my face warmed. Hmm. Maybe it wasn't such a great idea to be thinking about my guys, even all those years ago, mostly undressed. My emotions were jumbled up enough as it was.

"What can I say," he said, twirling the stick. "It's an obsession. I'll cop to that. But as obsessions go, you've got to admit there are a lot worse."

"Okay, that's fair," I said, propping myself against the boulder. "Although maybe calling it just an 'obsession' is downplaying the situation a little. Didn't you travel around, like, half the world chasing inspiration?"

"I guess so. But I didn't really have to. Finding it all over the world was just more fun than trying to get it all in one place."

"Uh huh." I couldn't help raising my eyebrows. "And is that a policy you apply to all sorts of areas of your life? Suddenly I'm imagining you leaving a trail of broken hearts all across the globe."

Jin's dark eyes gleamed with amusement. "I won't say there's no truth at all in that either. But I swear I've never made promises I didn't intend to keep."

"Always a gentleman, even when you're being a ladies' man?"

"I don't know any other way to be," he said with that

flirty smile. I wasn't sure if he meant the gentleman part or the ladies' man part—maybe both.

Curiosity prickled at me despite myself. "None of those girls kept your interest long enough to make any promises?" I asked.

"Well…" Jin cocked his head. His tone turned a bit more serious. "There are places and people that give you what you're craving in the moment, right? And that's a pretty wonderful thing. The ones that give you something so essential it becomes a part of your soul… That type is a lot harder to find."

His gaze caught mine across the pond for a beat longer than felt completely casual. A warm tingling spread down my chest. He meant the estate, of course. The estate had worked its way into his soul. Not *me*.

Didn't he? My hand dropped to the ribbon I'd tied around my wrist this morning. Deep purple, as rich as Jin's unwavering passion. I'd picked it as if wearing it would help me tap into my own feelings, or at least figure out what the hell they were.

Jin waved his stick in the air, breaking the moment. "Look at me, turning into a philosopher! When I get into a serious mood, you know it's probably time to start ignoring me." He winked, but he still couldn't quite seem to look away.

I swallowed hard, trying to think of how to answer him, and other voices carried through the trees. I turned, not sure if I was glad for the interruption or regretting it.

Seth and Kyler had come together. They came to a stop between me and Jin at the edge of the pond. And suddenly my heart was thumping for a completely different reason.

I hadn't seen Kyler since I'd kissed him. He clapped his hands now with his usual energy, but his gaze twitched away from mine a moment after ours met. Yep. This was plenty awkward. I didn't have any idea how to smooth that weirdness over either.

"Looks like we're all here," he said. "I told Damon, but who knows whether he'll show."

I grasped for a topic that was safer than hook-ups or illicit kisses. The reason we were here in the first place. "You said Mr. Cortland is out of town right now—how did you find that out?" Ky was the one who'd sent the text to the group announcing that fact and prompting this meet-up.

"One of the clients I do IT work for is the post office," Ky said. "I saw a temporary mail hold come in for James Cortland. Nothing to be delivered for a ten-day stretch. Usually people only do that if they're going on vacation."

He gave me a hopeful smile before his gray-green eyes twitched away again. Somehow that made me look at his lips. Which reminded me that I kind of wanted to try another kiss with him. Argh.

I was the one who'd suggested we meet in person to talk the situation through, partly because I'd hoped seeing the guys would help me sort out my feelings. So far I was only feeling more muddled. So much for that plan.

Seth ran his fingers over the short tawny waves of his hair. Ky's twin was the one who'd suggested we meet *here*. He felt I'd already risked too much coming into town as often as I had.

"Since it doesn't seem smart to make any decisions based on assumptions," he said, "I've taken a couple drives past the house. There's no car in the drive. The second time I went right up and knocked on the front door, and got no answer." He spread his hands. "It does look like he's gone."

Watching him move those solid arms through the air was making me feel all kinds of weird too. Rose, get a grip. Two kisses and my hormones had gone haywire. Maybe all those romance novels had finally oversaturated my brain.

"I could double-check," I said. "I have a history project I've been working on—I could tell my dad I'm thinking of paying a call on Mr. Cortland to see if he has any records I could use. Dad's probably been in touch with him enough to be able to warn me that he's away. But then what?"

Jin looked up from where he'd been tracing patterns in the pond with his stick. "I think the idea is we sneak in there somehow. Take a look around, see if there's any evidence showing what your stepmother asked for his help with. Right?" He glanced at the twins with one eyebrow arched.

Seth grimaced. "I wouldn't normally say breaking and entering is a good idea, but... If we could do it without actually *breaking* anything, and we wouldn't be stealing anything, just looking..."

"How easy do you think it'd be to get in there?" Ky asked, looking at me steadily for the first time. "Is there anything we need to worry about other than, er, regular locks?"

Anything magical, he meant, without knowing exactly what he meant. I sucked in a breath, considering.

Master Cortland understood magic—studying it and teaching its theory and techniques was his trade. But like all witching men, he'd only been a witness to it, never the caster. His wife and consort had passed on a few years ago. Regularly warding the house to prevent entry wasn't remotely practical for someone who couldn't adjust those wards if they happened to *want* to let someone in from time to time.

Even we didn't ward the estate like that, only rooms like Celestine's office that she felt needed special protection. Too much hassle to constantly manage a barrier like that when there wasn't any real need.

"I don't think so," I said. "But it's not like regular locks will just open because we want them to either."

Wouldn't it be nice if that kiss with Derek had lit up my spark? I could have used a little magic right now. Of course, the thought of kissing *him* again to try—and possibly being reminded all over again of the affection that didn't exist between us—made my stomach clench. This expedition wouldn't just be an attempt to reveal my stepmother's treachery, but his as well.

"I'm sure I can look up—" Ky started.

A twig snapped in the woods nearby. I flinched, spinning around. There was no reason for anyone to come out this way, but if one of the staff had randomly taken a stroll deep into the woods at just this time...

I started to motion the guys back behind the boulder.

Then I caught a glimpse of the approaching figure through the trees, and my hand dropped to my side. My pulse hiccupped, but not out of panic.

Damon halted at the edge of the clearing. "So here we are," he said in a cool tone. His hands were dug tight in the pockets of his leather jacket and his eyes stayed narrowed when he glanced around our gathering. "I figured I might as well see the place again just once."

His posture was guarded from shoulders to feet, but I couldn't help smiling. "I'm glad you came."

He shrugged, keeping his distance from us, and scuffed his sneaker against the mossy stones. Kyler eyed him for a moment as if waiting to see if Damon would say anything else. When the other guy didn't, he launched back into planning.

"Like I was saying, there have to be ways to break in without actually *breaking* in. I can find instructions for anything online. Look up some lock-picking videos, do a little practice at home, and we're good to go." He waggled his fingers with a grin.

Seth frowned. "I know you're the master researcher, Ky, but do we really want to stake our lack of criminal records on you learning how to become an expert lock-picker in a couple of days?"

"Why focus on the lock?" Jin said breezily. "There might be a window we can open. He might not even lock the doors in the first place. Most people in town don't."

"No, I'm pretty sure Mr. Cortland would," I said. "Especially if he's gone for ten days." He might not want to overdo the security, but he didn't want just anyone wandering in there either. "I guess there could be—"

"For fuck's sake," Damon broke in, rolling his eyes. "You guys are hopeless. *I* can pick a lock. Does that solve everything?"

We all stared at him. Another smile tugged at my lips, but I didn't give in to it in case looking too eager would scare him off. "It does if you're going to come with us," I said.

Damon sighed. He bowed his head, the jagged line of his dark brown hair falling to shadow his eyes. "I guess I'm in, then," he muttered. But he looked up at me through that shadow right after, as if he wanted my smile after all.

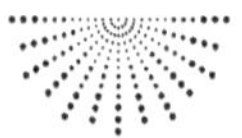

CHAPTER THIRTEEN

Seth

"Well, that's the whole house," my brother said, sounding frustrated. "I can't think of anything we didn't check." He stood in the center of James Cortland's dining room, hands on his hips, light brown hair askew from bending to peer behind cabinets and under side tables. Right now he was glowering at the antique maple buffet as if he could force it to give up some secret through sheer force of will.

Given the strength of Kyler's will when he put his mind to something, maybe he wasn't totally wrong to try.

Jin replaced the painting he'd glanced behind with a careful thump against the wall. "There's still the grounds," he pointed out. The old Victorian house had a yard about as big as one of the town blocks. Nothing on the same scope as Rose's estate, but a sizeable property.

"I don't think we should go wandering around out there," I said. "People drive by here going to and from town all the time. There's too much chance we'd be seen."

"And what the hell are the chances this geezer buried his evidence in the garden or something?" Damon said, his lips curling disdainfully as he took one last look around the room. "He'd probably be too afraid of getting dirt under his fingernails."

The house was incredibly well kept. I'd seen a pretty wide range of homes during the renovation projects I'd worked on with my dad, but I couldn't remember any other building I'd been in with the furniture so orderly, not a speck of dust anywhere, not even a spot of mildew in the bathroom. Even though the place had been shut up tight, the air wasn't stuffy, just dry and faintly bready-smelling.

Rose's hand had come to rest on the top of the maple table, which was just as solid and polished as the buffet. Her expression was distant. She was trying to think of something we might have missed, I guessed. She'd been counting on us finding *something* here. Something that could either reassure her or confirm her stepmother's intentions.

My only memory of Rose's stepmom was the day she'd barged in on our little gathering in the woods, years and years ago. The flash in the woman's eyes that had looked almost electric. The sharp clamp of the air around my body when I'd tried to reach for Rose. I hadn't been able to move, not a finger, not my mouth to shout, until after the woman had already dragged Rose away.

My stomach clenched. We hadn't been able to do

anything for Rose back then. We had to come through now.

"I guess we're done then," Rose said finally. "It makes sense, if he's involved in anything shady, that he might not keep any evidence even in private." But her brow was still knit. She'd expected more than this. "The longer we're here, the more chance we'll get caught. We'd better get going."

We slunk through the shadowed rooms to the back door. Damon had, true to his word, disengaged the lock on it with just a couple of metal rods. At the time Jin had made a joking comment about new skills he'd developed, and Damon had retorted with a glare and a mutter about how *some* people had to make the best of bad options, and no one had said anything more about it after that.

Now Damon strode out first, hardly pausing to check that the road outside was clear. Jin squeezed Rose's shoulder and said in a jaunty tone, "More mysteries still to uncover. But they don't stand a chance with the bunch of us on the case, do they?"

I couldn't help noticing the flush that had crept into Rose's cheeks at his touch.

My brother gave both her and me a playful salute. "I'll keep at it on the data side of things. See you soon."

They slipped out. Rose brushed her hand through her hair as we waited for them to disappear down the road. We'd figured it was less noticeable if we didn't all cross the yard in a pack. But now I had no one to distract me from her.

She tested the lock to make sure it would engage when we shut the door behind us. "He'll come in the front anyway," she said, as if to herself as much as me. "We left everything else the way it was. Even if the lock doesn't quite catch, he'll probably just figure he didn't set it properly before he left."

"It looks to me like the door will lock just fine," I said. After all the buildings I'd worked on in the last five years, I should at least be able to comment on that factor with certainty.

Rose glanced up at me. The sun was getting low outside, and in the dimming light her dark green eyes looked almost as black as her hair. A soft, liquid black that I could almost see the worries behind. God, this close to her I could smell her too, a delicate freshness that made me think of spring lilacs.

Before I knew it, the words were tumbling out. "You go on ahead. I want to stay and do one last sweep of the place. I'll make sure it's locked up when I leave."

Rose blinked, startled. "Are you sure?"

"Yeah. I'll feel better knowing we covered everything twice."

She nodded with a grateful smile that almost unknotted my stomach all on its own. Then one corner of her mouth quirked higher. I had the urge to brush my thumb over that dimple.

I had the urge to do a hell of a lot more than that, if I was being completely honest.

"Are you still glad I'm back?" she said. Her tone was lightly teasing, but something in her gaze told me she wasn't just kidding around. "Now that I'm getting you into all sorts of potential trouble?"

I did touch her then. There was nothing in the

universe that could have stopped my hand from rising to rest on her waist, just for a moment. To revel in the warmth of her skin seeping through the fabric of her shirt. "Not a single regret," I said. "You need me, I'm here."

The heat between us rose by a few degrees as we looked at each other. I made myself drop my hand. Rose stepped back with a breath that sounded slightly shaky.

"I'd better let you get to it," she said. "Stay safe. If you think you need to get out of here, just go."

"Of course," I said.

When she was gone, I stood for a moment in the back hall, getting my bearings. What the hell was I even doing?

A good question. One I asked myself way too much these days. I didn't really want to be here, in a house we'd broken in to. I didn't really want to be most of the places I found myself most days. Construction wasn't exactly my calling; it was just the easiest way to make ends meet. Because I had no idea what else I'd be better off doing.

I was sure of one thing, though. Even if this situation was crazy, even if I never said a word to her about how I felt, I'd do anything to protect Rose. That had always been true, and somehow the eleven years she'd been gone hadn't shaken my instinctive devotion one bit. One solid thing I could hang my hat on.

So here I was.

I moved back through the house slowly, methodically, as if I were here to inspect its construction for flaws, not searching for hidden evidence. Everything looked the same and as innocuous as it had the first time. I slunk through the upstairs rooms, suppressing my discomfort as

I edged around the guy's bed. Even if he were scheming with Rose's stepmother, walking around in some stranger's bedroom was more intrusive than I'd ever have wanted to get.

I found nothing there anyway. I headed downstairs again, ready to give up. But as I came into the front hall, my gaze slid over the wood paneling along the side of the staircase—and paused.

The spacing of those slats in the middle didn't totally make sense, did it? I stepped closer, running my fingers over the panels. The slats were set almost as if to support a hinge. But why would there be a hinge here unless...

I crouched down and pressed the oddly sized panel hard. It clicked and swung open to reveal a narrow compartment on the other side. A few books with cracked leather covers lay in a stack there, a newer-looking notebook on top of them. Holding my breath, I picked up the notebook. I had to squint to make out the words.

The pages were filled with starkly neat handwriting that matched the house's impeccable interior. Something about pests in the back garden, something about the weather, something about a boat. The notations around those subjects didn't make much sense to me—arm positions and degrees and "direction of flow"—but they didn't seem to have anything to do with Rose's worries, so I kept skimming on. The dates in the top right corners were from before Rose had returned anyway.

About halfway through, I hit on the last pages with any writing. The top of one of them said *CH – binding*. The date was from just a couple weeks ago.

CH. Celestine Hallowell?

My heart thumped faster. I pulled out my phone. In the dim light I wasn't sure the camera would capture all of the light strokes of the pen, so I started typing up everything Cortland had written. A vine. A dagger. A backwards stream of water to channel "the flow." Something about "the consort harmony."

I still had no idea what he might be planning. I just hoped it'd mean something to Rose when I sent it to her.

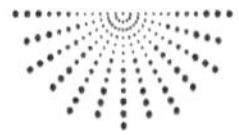

CHAPTER FOURTEEN

Rose

My sharp inhale cut through the quiet in my bedroom. I almost dropped my prepaid phone. But instead I kept staring at it, tensed where I'd sat on the floor to retrieve it from under the bookcase. My gaze scanned the words Seth had written a second time.

CH and *binding*—these notes had to be on the same matter Master Cortland had been talking to my stepmother about. What were the chances he'd been investigating bindings in some other way that related to those initials?

The rest of the remarks Seth had related word-for-word were vague. Brainstorming, I guessed. *A vine split and retied. A dagger brought to bear? If water is streamed backward it may channel the flow against the tide. The consort harmony—an alteration. Reversing polarities? Tangle one and then the other.*

Mixed in were little asides in brackets like *as per HV* and *consult YSN for confirmation.* Books or fellow academics he was gathering information from, presumably. I had no idea how to decipher those. But the fragments of a picture were enough.

My stepmother wanted a binding. A binding that had to do with my consort ceremony, unless she had some secret daughter who just happened to be undergoing that partnering at the exact same time. Something to do with reversing it or turning the connection against itself? What did that even mean?

"Rose?" Philomena ventured. She settled into the armchair beside me and peered down at my hunched form. "What's the matter?"

The enormity of the situation clogged my throat. It was real now. It was utterly real. "My consorting," I said. "Celestine isn't just meddling with my marriage using money—she's trying to change the actual ceremony somehow."

Not a chance it was to my benefit, either. Even if I'd been inclined to give my stepmother the benefit of the doubt, which I wasn't, daggers were only used to aid focus in more complicated magicking that involved severing or separation—or outright violence. None of which were factors anyone would welcome at a consorting.

"I've always said she's the worst kind of witch," Phil said. "So what are we going to do about it?"

"I don't know." All I had was Seth's second-hand report. He'd left the notebook behind in Master Cortland's house—as he should have. Who knew what chaos would result if my former tutor discovered a book like that missing?

But if I understood what Celestine was trying to accomplish better, I might be able to interrupt her magicking. I pushed myself to my feet. "I think I'd better start asking some more questions."

Meredith had been out back when I'd returned to the house, checking the new planting in the gardens. I darted to the stairs and down, my gut still twisted tight.

"Rose!"

My father's voice carried from the doorway of the front living room. I stopped halfway down the hall and turned. He was smiling when our eyes met, but his expression fell as he walked closer to me.

"Is everything all right, lamb? You look upset. And you were running off in quite the hurry."

My lips parted and then pressed shut again. An ache formed at the base of my throat. I wanted to tell him. Wanted to see his hazel eyes fill with affectionate concern, wanted to hear his warm baritone tell me he'd see that the problem was solved.

When it'd been just the two of us in our family, no matter how busy he'd gotten with his work, I'd been able to turn to Dad for anything. The nights when the boys had been home and Meredith off-duty, he'd been my whole world. Reading stories to me in the library. Sneaking down to the kitchen with me to grab that last slice of pie to share.

But Celestine had started to worm her way into our lives when I was ten, and nothing had been quite the same since.

Whatever he saw in her, he cared about her enough to have promised her his loyalty. Anything else, anything she wasn't involved in, I could have trusted he'd be on my side. But this?

I needed enough proof to make *him* sure, beyond any doubt. I needed there to be no way for Dad to argue that I was simply making unfair assumptions. When I had that, he'd have my back completely. I just didn't have it yet.

I swallowed hard and forced a smile. "Everything's fine. I just remembered a message I forgot to pass on to Meredith. A little distracted with everything going on, you know."

Dad chuckled. "Of course. Well, you'd better hurry and find her then."

To my relief, I found Meredith in the gardens where I'd expected. She was scowling at a couple of newly planted lemon trees at the end of a bed of flowers. "These were meant to go on the other side," she said as I came over to join her. "Well, the boys will just have to dig them up and move them over tomorrow."

Evening was falling—the gardening staff had gone home for the night. I pitched my voice low so no one could hear from an open window. "Meredith, there's something else I need to ask you about."

She turned to me, her pale eyebrows rising. "Go ahead, Rose."

With the number of strange questions I was coming to our estate manager with, she was going to start wondering if I'd developed some sort of psychosis. I wavered and decided I was better off playing along with that idea.

I clasped my hands in front of me. "I just—I guess it's nerves. With the consorting so close. I can't help worrying about things that seem silly. There isn't any way that the ceremony can be... adjusted, to, I don't know, change the outcome somehow, or hurt someone..."

Meredith shook her head. "You've spent too much time holed away with all those books. I promise you any story like that is only a fairy tale, child. It'll be your stepmother conducting the ceremony. I know the two of you haven't seen eye to eye all the time—and the Spark knows I've had my share of complaints—but you must know she wouldn't mean you outright harm."

I didn't know that. Not at all. But this was exactly why I couldn't talk to Dad. If even Meredith reacted like this, to a question without any accusation—

I focused on the other part of her answer. "Books? I don't actually remember reading anything about mixed up consorting."

"Oh, I'm sure you did when you were younger. Your father collects everything, and you read everything." She let out an amused huff. "Clearly some idea got stuck in your head somewhere. But the ceremony is all very straightforward. You'd have to really be trying to get it wrong. So set your mind at ease, you hear?"

I ducked my head. "Sorry to bother you."

She waved me off. "Oh, badger me whenever you want. I'm glad to talk your head out of the clouds as needed."

I didn't think she'd have been very happy if she'd known I'd taken her advice and then headed straight to the library. Philomena reappeared beside me as I trailed my fingers over the books' spines, scanning for the section I wanted. Dad's system of organization wasn't entirely intuitive.

"Do you know what we're looking for?" Phil asked.

"Witching stories. Our legends and that sort of thing. There've been some collections gathered over the years when people got around to writing them down. It sounded like that's what Meredith was talking about."

My hand stilled over one shelf. *Tales of the Witching Past. Witching Folklore. A Compilation of Witching Stories.* "Here we are."

"And what are we looking for *in* these?" Phil leaned her head over my shoulder as I pulled the first volume off the shelf.

"Any stories that have to do with consorting," I said.

I glanced over the first book's table of contents, shoved it back into the row, and grabbed the next. "The Autumn Consort." That could be it. I flipped to the right page and skimmed the story.

Nope, this was a romantic tale about a young witch meeting her great love just before she reached the dreaded age of twenty-five. A little too close to home right now, and not at all useful. I put that one back and moved on.

I'd paged through at least ten books when I found it. "A Twisted Consorting," the title said. My pulse hitched as I found its starting point.

The story was about an orphaned witch taken in as a girl by a sadistic low-family couple who wanted to use her for their own ends. The man dissolved his consorting with his wife and persuaded the orphan to partner with him. Fine, fine, none of that related to my situation.

Then I reached the part where the woman of the couple conducted the consorting ceremony for her former partner and her adopted daughter. *When the glyphs were drawn, she drew a dagger through the symbol of the spark. Then, as she drew the energies of the consorting between the two, she twisted the ties back on themselves, locking the girl's spark to her husband's will. Her magic kindled, but only with his blessing could she call on it. And if he demanded and she tried to refuse, the pain of a dagger's cut would slice through her chest.*

I lowered the book, my stomach churning. It was too easy to imagine being trapped like that, forced to bend my magic to someone else's will...

But it was just a folk tale. Meredith had said they weren't true.

Of course, Celestine hadn't been sure what she wanted to do was possible either. That was why she'd gone to Master Cortland in the first place.

An icy prickle ran down the center of me as my gaze lingered on the story's title. "A Twisted Consorting." On an impulse, I flipped back to the front of the book. This one's title was *Witching Tales of the Yesteryear*.

Something about those words felt far too familiar.

My fingers tightened around the book. I nudged the other volumes on that shelf so the gap wasn't obvious. Then, tucking that one under my arm, I hurried to my bedroom.

"Did you find it?" Phil said. "Do you know what that witch has up her sleeve?"

"Maybe," I said. I'd wanted answers, but now I almost hoped I hadn't found one. I shut my bedroom door, locked it, and retrieved my prepaid phone from beneath the bookshelves. My nerves jittered as I brought up the notes I'd saved from Seth's now-deleted texts. The second I laid eyes on them, my heart sank.

There it was. The reference right next to Master Cortland's note about the dagger. *Via WTOTY/ATC.* The letters couldn't be clearer. *Witching Tales of the Yesteryear/A Twisted Consorting.*

I didn't know where he'd gotten the other ideas for Celestine's "binding," but that one had come from a copy of the same book I held in my hands right now.

"She wants to bind my magic to Derek's will," I said. My voice shook as the words spilled out. "So I can't use it without his permission, and if he wants me to use it, I have to."

Philomena's eyes widened. "And she *can* accomplish that?"

"Master Cortland told her he thought it would be possible."

My imaginary best friend made a disgruntled sound. She stalked from the bookcase to the end of the bed and back, her skirts rustling against the floor. "And what do you think your fiancé knows about all of this? A spell like that wouldn't do her much good if he didn't agree to use it."

That question jabbed even deeper than my initial revelation had. I dragged in a breath, a burn forming behind my eyes.

"You're right. He has to know."

I pressed my hand to my temple. My consort-to-be was conspiring with my stepmother to take control over my magic. Just because he wanted to? That was so much worse than simply not liking me all that much. You'd have to *hate* a person to do that to them, wouldn't you?

Was there any possible explanation? Celestine had sent that money to his family—she could have told him anything—maybe he thought the binding would help them somehow?

It didn't really matter what the explanation was, though. One thing was perfectly clear.

The words popped out. "I can't marry him. I can't take him as consort. Not if he was willing to be a part of this, for any reason."

"I can't marry him." The words popped out before the thought had even solidified in my head, but I knew they were true. "I can't take him as consort. Not if he was willing to be a part of this, for any reason." Even if I could expose Celestine's scheming and put a stop to it, how could I ever trust Derek again?

"Well, fine. I didn't think you should marry him anyway. Call off the engagement!" Phil let out a little cheer.

"And then what? I don't have anyone else. I only have two months left before I turn twenty-five." Could Dad arrange a new consort for me that quickly—one I'd be able to tolerate spending my life with—when it had taken so long just to find Derek? A few of the tears that had been threatening spilled out. "Phil, I think I'm going to lose my magic."

The power I'd been training my whole life to take.

The spark I'd been longing to feel light inside me since I was a little girl. I'd lose that.

I'd lose my home. A magic-less witch couldn't inherit. The estate would go to one of my stepsisters, I guessed. I didn't even know where I'd go.

A magic-less witch was nothing. Worse than nothing.

"No," Phil said firmly. "You're not losing anything. I refuse to allow it. We just have to consider the situation thoroughly."

"There's nothing to consider," I said. "I need a witching man as my consort, to complete that magical bond and show my commitment, or my spark will never light."

I paused, a memory tugging at me. Except... maybe it had lit, just a little, once already. With a man who had nothing to do with witching at all.

CHAPTER FIFTEEN

Rose

I knew how a seduction was supposed to work. I'd read enough of those scenes in the copious novels I'd devoured.

Put on some slinky clothes that showed off however much cleavage was just slightly inappropriate for the time period. Primp hair and dab on some alluring perfume. Then head over to that guy ready to knock his socks off.

What those books hadn't generally mentioned was how awkward you could end up feeling wearing clothes both fancier and more revealing than your usual casual blouses and jeans. Or how easy it was to overdo it on the perfume when you pretty much never wore the stuff.

After several changes and a lot of hasty wrist scrubbing, I was here. Standing in the stairwell beneath Seth's apartment, one of the two that sat on top of his dad's hardware store. Smelling mostly of my usual soap, but at least I didn't smell *bad*. The silky V-neck blouse and somewhat more modest skirt I'd finally settled on still felt out of place on me, but nowhere near as out of place as the dresses I'd considered, so I'd call that a win.

But I was having an awful lot of trouble convincing my legs to climb those stairs.

"I look okay, right?" I said to Philomena.

She tipped her head with an amused smile. "You look lovely, Rose. My little girl, all grown up."

I rolled my eyes at her, and she giggled. Then she swatted me with her fan. "Well, are you going up there or not?"

I dragged in a breath. "Do you think I'm doing the right thing?"

"Darling, I think the only one who can answer that is you."

"I have to know. I can't make any decisions if I don't know."

"Well, there you go. Consider how many men I've kissed just to find out if I found the experience worthwhile. You've got much more urgent reasons than I ever did."

Even though she was only in my head, it was comforting having her there with me. Which was why it stung a little for me to say, "All right. I think you'd better give us a little, ah, privacy."

"Why, of course. A lady wouldn't intrude." She fluttered her fan and her eyelashes. "But I do want to hear *all* the details when I see you next."

I was doing this. Yes, I was. One step, and then another, and then another. My hand settled over my opposite wrist, where I'd wrapped today's ribbon. Green, for Seth's steadiness and strength. I could use some of that for myself right now, oh yeah.

My heart thumped faster. Those stairs passed by far too quickly. Just like that, I was stopping in front of the apartment door.

He was going to think I'd gone crazy. Or pity me. Or—

No. I'd seen the way he looked at me when we were alone in Master Cortland's house. I might not be experienced, but I was pretty sure I could recognize desire when it was written all over someone's face.

When I felt it echoing through me at the same time.

I raised my hand and knocked.

At first there was nothing on the other side. Then hesitant footsteps brushed across the floor. Seth eased open the door.

He was wearing glasses I'd never seen before. Rounded rectangular frames, a glint of glass over his gray-green eyes. Eyes that were blinking at me in confusion.

"Rose?" he said. "Why are you— Did something happen? Are you all right?"

"I—" I started, and my throat closed up. The sense of just how not all right my life was right now hit me in a way it somehow hadn't before.

"Come in," Seth said, guiding me with a hand on my shoulder. "Sit down. If there's anything I can do to help, you know I will."

I didn't think he was the slightest bit prepared for the kind of help I was going to ask for. But first things first.

Everything in Seth's apartment looked as if it'd been

chosen for function or comfort over style. Nothing on the walls except a set of coat hooks in the hall and a pot rack in the kitchen. A set of weights stood in one corner. The boxy sofa and tables filled the living room's space efficiently. The rug was the perfect beige to swallow just about any stain.

But when I sank onto one end of the sofa, I found the cushions were enjoyably cushy. I shifted my weight, settling right in.

Seth took the other end of the sofa, turning to face me. I couldn't help staring at his face. "When did you start wearing glasses?"

"Oh!" He took them off and set them on the coffee table next to a sports magazine he'd left open. "I just need them for reading. I guess I'm not the twin you'd expect to see in glasses, huh?"

My lips twitched upward. "I guess not. But I like them."

Had his neck just turned a tad red? He gestured toward the kitchen. "Do you need anything? I can get you something to drink."

I shook my head. "No. That's all right. Thank you. Just give me a second."

He watched me gather myself. His gaze skimmed briefly down my body, over the bare skin above the neck of my blouse, the curves it accentuated beneath. The skirt I'd picked was riding just a few inches up my thighs from my knees. He schooled his eyes upward a moment later, but his Adam's apple bobbed. He'd noticed.

But the efforts I'd gone to felt suddenly horrible. I didn't want to try to tempt him into anything he wouldn't have done if he were thinking clearly. I wasn't here to *trick* him. The guy sitting across from me was my friend, one of my closest friends, before anything else. He deserved honesty.

I tugged my skirt closer to my knees. "The information you found," I said. "I figured out what it was for. It's... It's hard to explain. I guess you could say my marriage was being planned as a trap. So obviously I'm not getting married anymore."

Seth's face darkened. "Your fiancé was in on this too?"

"He had to be. I don't know exactly how much, or why—" I made a jerking motion with my hand. "It doesn't matter."

"How are you going to handle it?"

"I still have to figure that out," I admitted. "I think I need to get proof, maybe go back to the house and take that notebook... But that's not why I'm here."

Snuff my spark, this was the hard part. Maybe I should go back to that whole seduction scheme? It suddenly sounded a whole lot simpler. I squared my shoulders, bracing myself.

"There's something I need to know. And to find out, I need to... er... kiss someone. Possibly do a little more than kissing too. Not too much." Argh. That had come out even worse than I'd feared. Was there a crack in the floor I could disappear into for the next century or so?

Seth's mouth had fallen open. He snapped it shut, but he didn't seem to know what to say to that.

I bit my lip. "I got the impression that maybe... you might be up for that? And I definitely wouldn't mind—

that is, I'm definitely attracted to you, so I figured it would probably—" I groaned in frustration and dropped my face into my hands. "I'm sorry," I said, partly muffled. "This conversation went a lot more smoothly when I only had to picture it in my head."

Seth laughed, and I thought I heard a little of the tension leave him with that sound. Maybe honesty had been the right call after all.

"It's okay," he said. "I'm just—I didn't expect—Well." He stopped and sucked in a breath. "I don't totally understand. You can't tell me what it is you're trying to find out with this... experiment?"

"I don't know if I could explain it properly." I raised my head tentatively. "But if it works... maybe I could show you."

He nodded. His expression turned serious again. "Why me?" he said. "You know any of the other guys, they'd jump at the offer."

Would they? Maybe I did know that. Kyler hadn't made an indication he wanted to repeat that kiss, but then, the last time I'd seen him I'd also still been engaged and committed to that partnership. And Jin seemed up for just about anything. But there was a reason I'd come here with this request and not to either of them.

"I'm not totally sure what I'm doing," I said. "I know in *theory*, of course—believe me, I have plenty of theory— but in actual reality, not so much. I know I can trust that if I get too caught up, you'll be looking out for me at least as much as I should be. Probably more, knowing you."

The intentness of Seth's gaze sent a warm tingling over my skin. Yeah, getting carried away might be a real problem tonight. "Clothes stay on?" he suggested, his voice gone rough, and somehow that made the suggestion the sexiest thing I'd ever heard, even though it was a restriction rather than a proposition.

"That sounds like a good line to draw," I said, suddenly breathless. I had to remember why I was doing this.

Seth just looked at me for a moment longer. My face started to heat. He held out his hand. "Come here?"

I scooted across the sofa to him, my heart beating so fast I was scared it was going to shatter. What if this didn't work?

What if it did?

Seth touched the side of my face, so close now the heady smell of him, like sun-warmed bronze, washed over me. I had the sudden urge to lean in and lick my tongue up his neck, to see if he tasted that way too. To find out what sound he'd make if I tried it. Heat spiked low in my belly just at the thought.

"You're sure?" he said, the question sounding almost pained. But I knew if I said no, he'd move away, no matter how much he wanted this. Thankfully I didn't have to.

"Completely," I said, and tipped my head to offer him better access to my lips. Seth's fingers tensed against my cheek. Then he leaned in and pressed his mouth to mine.

Kissing Seth was nothing at all like kissing his twin, maybe in part because I'd let him take the lead rather than catching him by surprise. But everything about the kiss was utterly Seth. Firm and yet gentle, strength radiating from his body as his arm slid around me with the utmost care. I pulled myself even closer, my legs sprawling across his lap. His breath stuttered against my mouth. He kissed me again, harder but somehow still tender.

Every inch of my skin, every nerve running beneath it, felt as if it were glowing with pleasure. And deep in the center of my chest, that flickering sensation I'd felt with Ky sparked into being again.

Exhilaration rushed through me. My spark. It was lit. I wasn't letting it stop at that small burst of light this time. I wanted more.

I looped my arm around Seth's neck. My other hand gripped the sleeve of his shirt. He adjusted the pressure of his mouth, softly encouraging, asking for entrance rather than insisting on it the way Derek had. My lips parted to deepen the kiss, and the spark inside me flared brighter.

Seth's fingers traced up and down my side, trailing heat in their wake. I let my tongue slip between his lips tentatively. His teased out to meet it. They tangled together until I felt as if I were trying to devour him, or maybe him me, or both at the same time. Either way I was happy to be along for the ride.

The flare inside me danced higher, but it still wasn't enough. I wasn't halfway sated. I twisted my body toward Seth's caressing fingers, letting them graze my breast. His chest hitched. As we kept kissing, his hand shifted to cup my breast completely. His thumb stroked over the side, sending shivers of pleasure through my sensitive flesh. Then it reached right up to the tip.

My nipple pebbled under the flick of his thumb. I

whimpered, kissing him again. Pressing into his touch. Seth groaned.

"Rose," he murmured, that one syllable so full of joy and longing it sent an answering wave of emotion through my body. The flame danced inside me, its power vibrating in time with the thump of my pulse. And just like that I knew, as well as I knew how to walk or speak, that it was there for me to use.

I drew back from Seth just slightly, my breath still ragged, and made a small flick of my fingers. A soft glow burst above my palm, shining and dancing like the spark inside me.

Seth stared at the conjured glow, his face softening with awe. "What is that?"

My lips curled into a giddy smile. "It's magic."

CHAPTER SIXTEEN

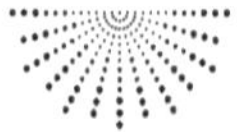

Rose

If you'd glanced into our breakfast room any given morning, the four of us would probably have looked like a happy family. Dad and Celestine on one side of the elm-wood table, Derek and I on the other, fine china all around and the scents of buttery rolls and herbed scrambled eggs filling the air.

Of course, if you stopped to watch a little longer, you'd notice that not a whole lot of talking went on during those breakfasts. Derek would remark on the weather and the food and I would say something agreeable in return, Dad and Celestine might briefly discuss some business around the estate, but mostly we just ate in our own little bubbles.

The morning after I'd snuck out to see Seth, my bubble felt particularly close to bursting. The glow of my spark had already almost entirely died out. Until it was fully kindled by a consort ceremony, any magic that sparked inside me would seep right back out of me like water through a sieve. But a glimmer of that power still danced in the middle of my chest.

A glimmer that had been kindled by an unsparked, non-witching man. How was that even possible? It went against everything I'd been taught. Not a single historical or modern witching record I'd read had mentioned such a thing.

Of course, it could be that this glimpse of magic was deceptive. Maybe affection between a witch and an unsparked man could bring a brief flicker, but never more than that. Never a proper consorting.

There wasn't any way or anyone I could easily ask. Imagine all the questions they'd start asking *me* if I brought up the subject.

More distracting, though, were the questions I still had about two of the three people I was dining with. And the schemes they were making against me.

As I chewed and swallowed my eggs and toast, I tasted only blandness. "Pass the salt," I said on autopilot.

"Of course," Celestine said with a glitter in her eyes. She swiveled her wrist, and the salt shaker sailed along the table to drop in front of me. My back tensed.

A little show of her power—for me? To remind me that she still held the magic here, I guessed. Little did she know.

I scooped up another forkful of egg and studied my stepmother and my fiancé. Just how allied were they in this binding Celestine was planning? Could I catch any sign of their secret understanding?

So far I still hadn't seen a hint of it. Derek smiled at

Celestine when she offered him the cream for his coffee, but he smiled at everyone like that—me, my dad, the server who brought a fresh pot of coffee, that cleaning staff girl Polly who was gathering dishes as they were cleared of food. They didn't say anything to each other except when Derek mentioned a music festival a few towns over he was thinking of taking me to, and my stepmother made a comment on the best route there.

I watched the morning light gleaming off my once-fiancé's bright hair, and my heart squeezed. Was there *any* chance he could be even slightly absolved in this? I might not have ever been thrilled about the idea of marrying him, but he'd ever seemed cruel. Celestine was unshakeable, I knew that, but if there was any appeal I could make to convince him to turn on her...

I turned back to my plate. By this evening I might have enough proof to go to Dad on my own. Better to focus on that.

"It'll just be four days, and then I'll be here right through the wedding," Dad was saying. I realized I'd tuned out the conversation.

"Four days?" I repeated.

He gave me an amused smile. I could almost hear him teasing like he'd used to when I was a lot younger than now, *Off in your own world again, my little lamb?*

"On Thursday I have to go to Cairo on business. I wish the timing hadn't worked out that way, but..." He spread his hands.

My stomach tightened. So if I didn't come up with proof in the next two days, I'd have to wait almost another week before I could turn to Dad.

I couldn't retrieve my proof any earlier. Damon was the one who could get into Master Cortland's house, and Damon had curtly informed me that he was busy with "actual work" until late today.

I gulped down the rest of my breakfast without tasting it at all. Derek got up when I did. He caught up with me as I wandered toward the doors to the back garden.

He slung his arm around me with a proprietary confidence that set my nerves on edge. It took all my willpower to stop my back from noticeably stiffening. I might be willing to give him the benefit of the doubt, but that didn't mean I wanted to get cozy, not ever again. Whatever Celestine was planning, he had to be mixed up in it somehow.

"Off on another of your walks?" he asked.

"Some fresh air and pretty scenery always seems like a good way to start off the day," I said. I didn't want him to offer to join me. Or maybe I did, so I could try to pry for proof in other ways? My stomach twisted, my emotions torn.

Derek let go of me, and what I felt then was definitely relief. "I have a few work things to catch up on," he said. "But don't forget this afternoon we're supposed to decide on—what is it? The tablecloths? The name card designs? And then perhaps I can challenge you to another game of chess."

"Perhaps this time I'll win," I said, with a laugh I had to force. I breathed easier the second I put a door between us and ventured into the gardens. The moment I could feel safe dropping this charade and seeing the back of him, the happier I'd be.

"Ugh," Philomena said with a shudder, appearing beside me. She was carrying a dainty parasol that she was enjoying twirling more than she was actually using it to keep any sun off her head. "Good riddance to him."

My feet carried me on into the woods. As the trees closed around me, the rustling of the brush and the calls of the birds covering any sounds from the house behind me, my nerves settled more. I needed to be settled— settled and calm and ready for whatever came at me.

I wasn't exactly surprised to find myself approaching the old towers hidden deep in the estate grounds. The deeper stillness around them drew me right up to their vine-draped stones. I dragged in the scents of fresh earth and newly grown leaves. The spark inside me flickered again. Just a tiny sliver of magic left. If I didn't use it, it'd fade by the end of the hour.

Without really thinking about it, I let my body move into the forms I'd drawn with my body the last time I'd been here. A call to the one still not with us. Gabriel would have known what to do if he'd been here, wouldn't he? He'd always been unshakeable.

Was he even still carrying the torn page I'd given him more than a decade ago? It probably hadn't been half as significant to him as it had been to me. It wasn't as if I could have told him how I'd hoped it would keep me connected to him. I wasn't even completely sure how it would work now.

But I reached out to that snippet of story I'd given him, sending my last glint of magic into the air, to wherever he might be. As the glimmer left me, my chest went fully dark. The way it had always been until last night, other than that incredibly brief moment with Kyler. But now I felt the hollowness so much more sharply. Philomena watched me from the edge of the glade, rotating her parasol slowly and giving me my space.

I didn't really want to head back to the house yet. Idly, I brushed at the lichen that had covered the etchings on the stones. So many glyphs carved here. What had this symbolic gate been used for before it had been abandoned?

The etchings I uncovered twined glyphs for connection and communication, defense and loyalty. Then my fingers stumbled over a patch of stone that had been crudely scratched. I paused, my forehead furrowing.

"What's wrong?" Phil asked.

I traced the bits of stronger lines I could make out where other symbols had been carved. "It looks like someone purposely gouged out some of the carvings," I said. "Destroyed them."

Phil's eyebrows shot up. "Why on earth would anyone do that? Is this heap of rock really that important?"

"It's more than a heap of rock," I said, rolling my eyes at her. "I think it must have been used for some magical purpose... a long time ago."

"A *very* long time ago," Phil put in.

I tugged aside the vines, ducking under branches to get at more of the stones. Farther around the first tower, I found a few more etchings that had been scratched out. Someone had gone to a lot of work to hide part of this structure's meaning.

My gaze rose to the crumbling peaks of the towers. They stood about ten feet tall. I'd climbed higher than that in trees as a kid.

Before I could second-guess the impulse, I grasped onto the lower branches of one of the trees that surrounded the tower. My muscles twinged from lack of practice as I hauled myself upward, but I managed to scramble from one branch to the next. The trunk was just narrowing to the point that I was getting a little nervous when I reached the tower's ragged top.

"I hope you don't mind if I just wait down here," Philomena called after me. "I think tree climbing is a little more excitement than I'm up for today. I am wearing one of my favorite dresses, after all."

"All of your dresses are your favorites," I reminded her.

"Well, that's the only way to properly live one's life, isn't it?"

"That's fine," I said. "I'm not even sure *I* should be doing this."

I peered over the rough stones. The tower wasn't just an empty cylinder. A set of narrow stone steps wound down the inside in a spiral, down to a soil-strewn floor mostly swallowed by shadow. The lines of more etchings caught sunlight and shadow along the walls all the way down. All of them appeared whole.

Whoever had scraped away the ones outside hadn't made it this far—or hadn't realized they'd need to.

"Well, what's up there, then?" Philomena's voice followed me. "I might not want to climb trees, but that doesn't mean I'm not curious."

The corners of my mouth curled up. "There are stairs inside. I'm going in."

I swung one leg and then the other over the crumbling stones at the top and found my balance on the steps. The air felt a few degrees cooler simply easing inside that darker space. I edged down just far enough to make out the carvings here.

"Still alive?" Phil inquired.

"Yep," I called back. "Nothing too exciting yet. Just more etchings."

These ones weren't all glyphs. A few, like the ones below, were scattered across the stones, along with others I hadn't seen on the outside: passion and power, trust and loyalty, openness and cohesion—how did those two even work together? But the rest of the etched images were closer to pictures, though rough ones. Figures standing with arms raised or held out to each other or linked by the hands. Most of them were pairs, with a flame carved inside one's chest. My heart leapt.

These were pictures of consorting. Witches and their partners. But then...

My gaze stuck on one image that showed a woman with a flame filling her entire chest. Not one but three other figures stood around her, reaching toward her in the start of an embrace. I stared at it, my breath catching in my throat.

"Oh!"

"What?" Philomena said. "Don't leave me dying with

anticipation down here, Rose."

"There's... there are pictures of consorts. I think. But some of them..."

"Some of them *what*?"

"Some of the witches appear to have more than one. Consort, that is."

If that etching in front of me was meant to represent one woman with three consorts, no wonder her spark flared so brightly. But taking more than one consort would never be allowed, if it even worked that way. There were only so many witching families, only so many witching men. If some witches had taken multiple partners, too many others would be left without. And once you'd bound your spark to one consort, no other man could light it, even a flicker.

"My goodness," Phil said. "That sounds rather exciting."

"Well, they're not *doing* anything in the pictures, if that's what you're thinking."

"Hmph. That is a bit of a shame."

I stared at the etching. Who had carved this, and when? I didn't remember ever reading a story, even one of those questionable folk tales, where a witch took additional consorts. Could you bind your spark to more than one man simultaneously?

That picture wasn't the only odd one either. As my gaze darted down, I spotted another that showed a woman with two consorts, a second with three, one with four, and—was that witch surrounded by *seven*? Holy Spark, I couldn't imagine how anyone could keep up with that number of partners.

But at the same time, a tingling warmth crept through me, pooling at the base of my belly. Even if I couldn't imagine it, something about the idea did feel rather... appealing.

Time seemed to have stilled around me with the air and the sounds of the forest. I was only broken out of that dazed reverie by the crunch of footsteps somewhere beyond the tower walls. Real footsteps, not Philomena getting restless.

My pulse stuttered. Bracing my hands against the gritty stone, I eased up to peek over the top of the tower.

A man was walking through the woods, circling the towers and the arch between them. Tall and gangly, with hair not quite as dark a chestnut as my father's and a face much more sallow—oh, it was Douglas, Celestine's assistant.

Normally he acted as her ambassador of sorts, going off to meet with clients when she couldn't be bothered to. What was he doing prowling around in the woods? And why here? He almost looked as if he were specifically checking for any signs of recent trespassing.

A scrap of rock broke free under my clutching fingers and slipped from my grasp. It tumbled onto the stairs with a soft rattling. Douglas's head jerked up, and I yanked mine down. I held there, lungs clenched, praying he hadn't seen me.

"Hello?" he called. When I didn't answer, he let out a huff of breath. "Damned squirrels."

I didn't move again until the sound of his footsteps had retreated beyond my hearing.

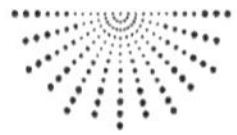

CHAPTER SEVENTEEN

Rose

Damon was waiting in the thin evening light by one of the last houses at the edge of town. When he saw me coming, he flicked the glowing butt of his cigarette into the gutter. He didn't say anything, just lifted his shoulder in a *Let's go* gesture and started walking down the country road that passed Master Cortland's property about five minutes outside town.

I fell into step behind him on the narrow shoulder. A hint of nicotine smell wafted off him, mingling with the battered leather scent of his ever-present jacket. The gravel rattled under our feet. I shrugged my own jacket, thin and cotton, tighter around me against the cool dampness of the breeze.

The other guys were waiting to meet up with us after, but we'd figured for a quick in and out mission, it didn't make sense for everyone to come.

I felt a little awkward just walking in silence and

looking at Damon's leather-clad back. I weighed my words, wondering how to start a conversation without hitting on a sore spot accidentally.

"You said you were working today," I went with finally. "What kind of work are you doing these days?"

Damon made a scoffing sound. "Not anything you'd approve of, angel."

The nickname should have been sweet, but the way he said it made it sound like an insult. I glowered at his back. "I don't think you know what I'd approve of. You've hardly talked to me at all since I've gotten back."

"How much do you really think we have in common to talk about? You're off in that big house with everyone catering to you... Most of us don't have lives like that."

"I know," I said. Even I didn't exactly have a life like that. But I wasn't going to argue that mine hadn't been a lot easier than Damon's. "That doesn't mean I don't want to hear what you've been through."

He kicked at a larger pebble. "Which part? Watching my mom get beaten down trying to find work so she could put food on the table for me? Getting kicked out of school? Fencing stolen goods to make ends meet?"

"All of it, I guess." My curiosity was stirred now. "Is that what you do? Steal stuff?"

He made a noncommittal sound. "You watched me pick my way past a lock yesterday, didn't you? Some of us don't have a whole lot of choices. We do what we have to."

I wouldn't have pictured the boy I'd grown up with considering stealing his only option. "Who do you steal *from*?" I couldn't help asking.

"Don't worry," he said. "I'm not casing your joint. I don't even do most of the actual stealing. There's a guy who brings stuff to a warehouse, and I help with the... distribution, I guess you could say. But maybe if I make a good enough impression, I can move up. Get out of this freakin' town. Get my mom out too."

He put on this whole show of not caring what anyone thought, but he clearly cared about her. And he must have cared at least a little about me, or he wouldn't have been here doing this favor.

"I *am* sorry," I said. "For how things went after we left for Portland. Your mom deserved better than that."

"Yeah," Damon muttered. "She did." Then, after a pause, he added, "I know you didn't have anything to do with that."

Just hearing him admit it felt like a major victory. I drew up beside him as we reached Master Cortland's property. It was easy enough to hop chain-link. Damon landed first and offered me his hand, but I ignored it and jumped down on my own. The corner of his lips quirked up.

"Still don't like to admit you could use a hand, huh?"

I raised my eyebrows at him. "Look who's talking."

That shut him up as we crossed the yard to the back door. He pulled out the metal picks from the cloth case he was carrying and knelt down by the keyhole.

"You don't really need to be here, you know," he said as he adjusted the rods. His eyes narrowed with concentration. "No point in you getting the heat if we get caught."

"You're only here because of me," I said. "It'd hardly

be fair if you got in trouble and I didn't. *I* can take responsibility for my decisions, even if my family doesn't seem to have the greatest track record there." I glanced around, watching for headlights along the darkening road. "Anyway, there might be something in the compartment Seth found that he didn't realize was significant and I would."

Damon hummed under his breath with what could have been agreement or skepticism—it was hard to tell. Then the lock clicked over. He pulled the door open and swept his arm for me to enter ahead of him. "Ladies first?"

"Why thank you," I said, with as much elegance as Philomena could have mustered. Which actually wasn't that much, given her temperament. Elegance wasn't really her style. As Damon closed the door behind us, I hurried to the front hall by the staircase.

Now that Seth had described it, it was easy to see the odd panel out, only half as wide as the others. I crouched down and pushed it the way he'd said. The panel popped open easily, revealing the notebook and the other books he'd mentioned.

A couple of glyphs marked the inside of the door—connection and power. If they'd been meant to keep it locked, the magic on them must have faded. I checked the other books Master Cortland had stashed with the notebook.

Was he using these for his research for my stepmother or some other project? I wavered and then scooped them all up. He'd notice someone had broken in from the missing notebook, so why not take everything?

"All right," I said to Damon, kicking the panel shut. "No point in hanging around. Let's get out of here."

We strode back toward the door. I'd just reached the threshold when the notebook on the top of the stack burst into flames.

A yelp broke from my mouth. My hands jerked, tossing the books onto the kitchen floor. They fell with a thump. The notebook hissed, its cover already disintegrating, the pages crumbling into ash. The other books had flared up too. A sharp smoky smell filled the room. Damon's jaw had dropped.

"No!" I dropped down, swatting at the flames, but they were already flickering out of their own accord. Leaving nothing but the burnt husk of the notebook. My proof, seared away. A choked sound escaped my throat.

"What the hell?" Damon said.

I drew in a shaky breath. "He had a protection on them." Master Cortland must have had a spell laid to prevent any witching items from leaving the house. A wise move, actually, when he couldn't work magic himself. A general catch-all could be laid down to last a long time—and it would prevent even him from bringing anything that would reveal us beyond that boundary, even if he were coerced somehow. Destroying the evidence immediately.

But the glyphs on the cupboard... I spun and checked the doorway. There they were, the same ones, faint but visible if you knew what to look for under the layers of paint. Shit. My heart stuttered. "There might be an alarm connected to those protections. Come on. We've got to get out of here."

Damon grabbed my arm. We bolted across the yard together.

"He's on vacation, right?" Damon said between sharp breaths. "That's what Mr. Braniac said. Even if he comes racing back, he can't get here right away."

"Maybe," I said. "But Mr. Cortland might have someone local on call just in case." He had plenty at stake too. If the Assembly found out he was helping someone pervert a consort ceremony... There'd be hell to pay.

We scrambled over the fence and dashed down the road toward town. We'd just reached the first proper street when laughter echoed from up ahead.

Damon reacted with instincts that must have been honed from the Spark only knew how many petty criminal dealings. He snatched my elbow and jerked me into the shelter of a narrow walkway between one of the houses and its garage. We pressed against the rough shingles, watching the couple go by.

They looked like totally normal people. Meandering along hand-in-hand. Definitely not in a hurry to investigate a magical break-in. The panic gripping me eased off just a little. I glanced at Damon.

"I'm pretty sure we didn't need to hide from those two."

He let out a huff of breath. "You never know. Better to get out of the way than end up handcuffed."

The space was so narrow that his chest brushed mine with that breath. His fingers were still curled around my arm, firm but not rough. The heat of his body radiated over me. I swallowed hard, and his gaze slid from the street to meet my eyes.

I wasn't the only one affected by our closeness. For a moment we just stared at each other, Damon's pupils dilating into the deep blue of his eyes. My breath was still a bit ragged from the run, and I was finding it awfully hard to catch it. We could have walked right back out there, but that would have meant pulling my gaze away from him. Which felt somehow impossible.

"Thank you," I said quietly. "For helping me tonight, even if it didn't work out. You didn't have to do that. You never had to do anything for me, but you did, a lot."

Damon shifted, his hand trailing down my arm to my wrist. His touch sent a pleasant shiver through my nerves in its wake. "Don't think I'm going to roll over and play nice just because you butter me up, angel."

I grimaced at him. "I'm not trying to butter you up. I'm just saying what I'm honestly thinking. Isn't that what you want—honesty?"

A soft, strangled noise worked its way out of his throat. He tipped his head forward, his forehead almost grazing mine. His mouth just inches from my lips.

"There's so much I fucking want, Rose," he murmured with a rasp. A full-out shudder of longing shot through me. But he didn't bridge that last short distance. "More than you could handle."

"I always kept up with you before," I said. "All of you."

A hint of a smile touched his lips. "Yeah," he said. "I'll give you that." He inhaled deeply. "I missed you too."

He pushed away from me the second the words had left his mouth, so abruptly I almost thought I'd imagined them. But I definitely wasn't imagining the flush that had colored the back of his neck above his jacket collar. He motioned for me to follow him with a jerk of his hand, not bothering to look back. I shook off the chill he'd left behind with me and hurried after him.

The farther we went into town, the more my immediate fears faded. I didn't think anyone would be able to tell *who* had been in the house. Maybe Master Cortland would be able to make a guess if he determined why we'd been after his notebook, but that would only lead him to me, not the guys. I'd just have to deal with him when it happened. It'd be difficult for him to prove anything without revealing what I'd been trying to steal and getting himself into a heap more trouble.

The other guys were waiting down the alley by the back of the Lennox Hardware store. The café's patio was closed, but we weren't here for an extended chat anyway. The others had just wanted to be ready to act in case I needed anything else.

My heart sank, seeing them waiting. I held up my hands as we came into view to show how empty they were. Seth frowned, and Kyler's eyes widened. Jin straightened up off the wall he'd been leaning against and ambled to meet us.

"Not as simple as you were hoping?" he said with a crooked smile.

"No," I said. "We couldn't get the books. There was..." I trailed off, my gaze veering to meet Seth's. A fresh flicker of warmth shot through me, just remembering his hands and his mouth on me last night.

He had some idea now. He hadn't pushed for

answers, and I hadn't offered many, but he knew I had more power than he would have once thought was possible. And that other people, people like me, had that power too. But I hadn't revealed that much to the other guys yet.

"There was a sort of trap," I settled on. "It wouldn't let the books leave the house. I know that sounds weird—"

"*Fucking* weird," Damon muttered.

"It's okay, Rose," Ky said before I had to go on. "You don't have to explain. We get it."

Jin rested his hands on my shoulders, his thumbs rubbing over the muscles there with just enough pressure to release the tension I hadn't realized was coiled inside them. "One way didn't work," he said in his usual relaxed tone. "So we move on to something else."

I didn't know what else. For a second there, all I really wanted was to lean back into him and forget all the uncertainties ahead of me. His hands moved from the base of my neck to the peaks of my shoulders and back again, the gentle caress flooding me with even more warmth.

How was it possible that I wanted all of these guys so much? I wanted Damon gazing down at me like he had right before he'd told me he'd missed me. I wanted Seth's careful strength pressed up against me again. I wanted to rediscover the taste of Kyler's mouth, to stay long enough to see how his eyes would light up at *my* touch.

It hung all around us like a hum in the air. I wanted all of them—and I could almost taste their desire echoing back at me. What was the point in trying to deny it? That was just the way it was. Maybe the way it'd always been, only our feelings had grown from childish affection to the deeper, headier emotion coursing between us now.

And I didn't have the slightest idea what to do with that knowledge. I wanted them, sure. But how could I have any of them? They were unsparked and I was a witch—a witch who still needed a fully-fledged consort. I wouldn't even have the brief flares of magic they'd given me if I passed my twenty-fifth birthday without my spark properly kindled. The seed inside me would die and leave me with nothing but that terrible hollowness.

Maybe there was a chance—maybe it could work—but how could I risk my entire magical future just to find out?

CHAPTER EIGHTEEN

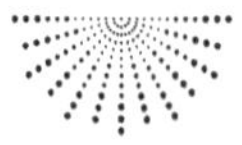

Kyler

A cloud streaked past the rising moon, but I didn't think I could blame that for the shadow that crossed Rose's face. For a moment, standing there between the four of us in the alley, she looked so hopeless my heart wrenched.

"Mr. Cortland should be gone until after tomorrow," I blurted out. "That's the last day he had his mail held for. We could go back, try some other way—"

Rose was shaking her head. "The books are—we can't take them. Consider them gone. And nothing but the actual books would have been enough proof to accuse a man with the standing Ma— Mr. Cortland has, in my community."

Jin's hands stilled against her back. I tried to ignore the way that simple contact ate at me.

She'd kissed me. So briefly, but it had been the best fucking thing I'd ever felt in my life. And then she'd run.

She'd been upset and reaching out for comfort, and afterward she'd realized what a mistake she'd made. She looked so much more comfortable with Jin touching her than she had when she'd dashed for my door.

I wasn't supposed to think things like that. She was still engaged, even if she meant to end it. But God how I wished I could have believed it'd be me she'd turn to, and not every guy here before me, if she was ready to move on.

"How do you think we should go on from here?" Jin asked.

Rose rubbed her mouth. "I don't know. Maybe I can find out more from my stepmother, or my fiancé, somehow. There's got to be proof on their end, somewhere, or they'll slip up. Or we'll think of something else."

"We'd better go our separate ways for now," Seth said, his gaze intent on her. "The longer you're out here with us..."

My twin was right. The last thing Rose needed right now was to get caught running around with us, to give her stepmother ammunition against her. But just for a second, like a punch to the solar plexus, I hated him. I hated the way his words had made her eyes shimmer with affection. I hated Jin, for his hands now simply resting on her shoulders as if they belonged there. I hated Damon, for the glance she shot his way as if his reaction mattered that much to her.

But mostly in that moment I hated me. All the facts I had at my fingertips, all the data I'd dug up, and what good had it done her? What had I accomplished, really, that would actually help her get out of this mess we'd uncovered? I'd hacked into banks and spied on confidential mailings for her, and she was still just as trapped by her stepmother as before.

As eleven years ago when she'd been dragged away from us nearly for good.

Rose nodded and sucked in a breath. She blinked, the lamp out back of the hardware store catching on a glint of moisture in her eyes. The way she was looking at us... I couldn't help thinking it was as if she believed she might not ever see us again.

She moved as if to step away from Jin, but then she spun around and wrapped her arms around him. His face blanked with surprise, but only for an instant. He hugged her back, tipping his head beside hers. The squiggle of jealousy in my gut squirmed deeper.

Damon started to turn away and head off. Rose detached herself from Jin and grabbed Damon's sleeve. "You'll survive this," she told him, and pulled him into an embrace. Damon's back stiffened, but his face seemed to wobble at the same time, that mask of indifference vanishing. He closed his eyes almost reverently and tugged her closer. Rose's hand fisted in his jacket as if she never wanted to let go.

But she did. She released him, and Seth was already stepping forward to meet her. Something about the confidence with which my brother drew Rose into his arms made my throat tighten. When had he gotten so comfortable with her?

I stood there awkwardly, the last of the bunch. Rose squeezed Seth's broad shoulder and then turned to me, because of course she couldn't leave me out. I couldn't imagine she had an unkind bone in her body.

She stepped toward me tentatively, and I extended my arms, abruptly unable to even meet her eyes. Embarrassed by how every particle of my body was jittering with eagerness at this chance to hold her, even if it meant so much more to me than it did to her.

I didn't draw the hug out, just embraced her quickly and then pulled back. Rose's hand groped after me for a second as if she'd meant to hug me even tighter. My gaze leapt to her face with a skip of my heart. Was that... *pain* flashing through her expression?

As if it'd hurt her that I'd barely accepted the embrace. As if it had meant something to her, more than just a token gesture.

I opened my mouth, but my tongue tangled. There was no glib comment that could turn back time.

"I hope I'll be seeing you all soon with better news," she said, hunching her shoulders in her jacket. Then she was slipping away between the stores before I could figure out the right words to fix my mistake, which was feeling more and more colossal by the second.

* * *

A request for me to press the START button blinked on my TV. I picked up the video game controller, but the computer-generated enemies looming on the screen just made my worries niggle deeper.

There were too many real enemies threatening people I cared about. I hadn't heard anything from Rose in almost two days, and as far as I knew neither had the other guys. At least a dozen times I'd picked up my phone ready to just text her some mindless message like, *U OK?* And then stopped myself when I remembered the look on her face when I'd pretty much rejected her embrace.

With a groan, I flopped over on the couch. Would it really be so hard to say something? Apologize, tell her I hadn't wanted to overstep, and if anything I'd wanted to hold her too long, too tightly...

What if I'd just imagined that hurt, though? Wishful thinking? It wouldn't be the first time. I didn't have the best track record with girls. The last thing she needed was me hassling her about that when the marriage she was supposed to be planning was in the process of imploding.

My gaze came to rest on the one work of art on my wall that hadn't come from anyone in this town. The little metal etching sent to me all the way from New Brunswick in Canada, from the one girl I'd had more luck than I deserved with. Marian.

It had been such a cliché. We'd started talking in the middle of an online game and somehow enjoyed each other's conversation so much we'd just kept going after we beat the boss—who, for the record, we'd completely pulverized. Chatting on our headsets had turned into video chats and... more than just chatting. I'd called her my girlfriend. She'd called me her boyfriend. I hadn't gone a day without seeing her face. We sent each other gifts like that etching on my wall.

But then, in the middle of trying to plan our first trip to really meet, it had all fallen apart.

"There was some other girl, wasn't there?" she'd said over Skype, what seemed like out of the blue. "You said you've never really had a girlfriend before, but there was someone."

"What?" I'd said, but even in my confusion my mind had leapt to Rose. It just did. Even years after she'd left. I didn't know what had happened to her. None of my internet searching had reassured me she was okay. Of course I couldn't completely let her go.

But I hadn't lied. Rose hadn't been my girlfriend. Not even close.

"There are those things you never quite talk about," Marian had said. "I can see you stopping yourself and editing stuff out. It's not like I mind if you've been with other people before. *I* have. I just want to know you're being honest with me."

"I am," I'd said. "There's nothing important. Some of the stuff from when I was younger, it's just... complicated."

"Too complicated to tell me about?"

"I guess there are just secrets I don't feel are mine to share," I'd said, which had felt like a weak excuse even as it came out of my mouth.

"Secrets you're keeping for a girl you don't see anymore?" Her expression had shuttered. "Or do you still see her?"

"No," I'd protested. "I haven't seen her in years—"

And just like that I'd admitted it.

It might not have mattered. Maybe I could have figured out a way around that admission. But something in my face or my body language must have given me away. Marian had watched me and asked, ever so carefully, "And if she came back, would you still be talking to me?"

The correct answer, clearly, would have been an instant, "Yes, of course, don't even worry about it." The problem was, it wasn't all that clear to me. I liked Marian a lot, yeah, but part of my heart was still tied up in the girl who was woven all through my childhood and early teen memories, the girl who'd be a woman now. So I'd hesitated.

We hadn't broken up right then, but I knew that was what had done it. The conversation about meeting up had faltered. A few days later, Marian had emailed me to say she didn't think we wanted the same things. And I hadn't even blamed her for it.

Lying here now, staring at the metal etching, resolve balled in my stomach. I'd never let go of Rose, had I? Not really. Not even when I'd had another girl right in front of me. Not until she'd been reaching out to me.

What was *wrong* with me? The girl I'd never stopped caring about was back, and I might as well have slapped her in the face two days ago.

If I lost her, it might be my fault this time.

No. Screw all those stupid insecurities. If she didn't feel that way about me, she didn't feel it. But she had to at least know how much she meant to me.

I sat up and reached for my phone.

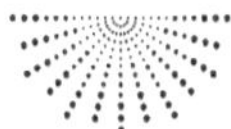

CHAPTER NINETEEN

Rose

The moment after Dad left the house, a porter in tow with his luggage, a quiet descended in the hall. The three of us who'd come to see him off didn't seem to know what to say to each other all of a sudden.

Derek ran his hand over his ash blond hair. "Well, I have a property to gather some details on for work, but I expect that'll only take a couple hours, if you wanted to do something later this afternoon." He gave me a gently questioning look.

Mouldy cinders, I had to offer something. "Maybe we could..." What to suggest that didn't make me cringe? I'd have offered a stroll into town, but then we might run into one or more of the guys, and I couldn't be sure how I'd handle myself then. Or how they'd handle themselves, if it happened to be, say, Damon. Derek and I had already taken so many turns through the garden he probably had every flower memorized. The thought of being confined in a car with him had me suppressing a shudder.

Oh! "You mentioned that concert recording you wanted to show me," I said. "We could dust off the DVD player." And watching TV meant I could do more observing him and less trying to think of things to say.

"Sounds like a plan," Derek said. He leaned in to give me a kiss, so abruptly and so unexpectedly my head flinched to the side. His lips brushed my cheek.

I blushed with a flip of my heart that wasn't at all pleasant. I had to make *some* appearance of still seeing him as my consort-to-be, or he or Celestine or both of them would realize something was very wrong.

"Sorry," I said with a quick smile. "My nerves are all over the place this morning. Didn't see that coming."

Derek chuckled as if it didn't matter. I offered my lips to him, and he gave them a peck that didn't provoke too much of a cringe. For the first time in my life I was grateful that my stepmother was around, so he didn't go for anything more.

Celestine had stepped to the side to watch Dad's car leave for the airport through the big picture window in the living room. As Derek ambled off, I edged closer to her. If Master Courtland had discovered the attempted robbery, I had to think he'd have told her. Did she know yet? Did she suspect it'd been me? I'd been careful sneaking out yesterday evening, but I couldn't assume I was safe.

I waited until the car was out of sight before I opened my mouth. My stepmother turned in the same moment and startled as if she'd forgotten I was there. "Rosalind," she said with a twitch of her hand over her glossy bob. "I'm sure we'll get along until he returns."

As if you could call what we did at any time "getting along." She did seem to have a bit of an agitated air about her. I cleared my throat. "I was just wondering, do you know if Master Cortland will be back today? I was thinking it'd be a nice day for a walk over there if he's home."

Did her eyes widen slightly at that question or was I just imagining it? Her lips pressed flat, but that was pretty much Celestine's standard expression.

"I don't keep that close accounting of his schedule," she said. "I only heard he was going to be away for some time. You could always call the house and see, you know."

"Right," I said, with an apologetic dip of my head. "I'll do that."

Except I absolutely definitely wouldn't.

"What now?" Philomena murmured, appearing next to me as I headed up the stairs. "Shall we tie them to chairs and interrogate them with hot pokers?"

"Have you been getting caught up in stories that aren't yours?" I asked. "Where did that come from?"

She grinned. "Oh, it's just something my older brother used to threaten me with when I was getting up to a little too much secret mischief. He was just joking. At least, I think he was..."

"Well, I think going straight to physical torture might be a little extreme." And also it wasn't as if I could have gotten a direct advantage over Celestine while she had her magic and my spark was dim. I bit my lip.

In the upstairs hall, Meredith was just ducking into

her office. Without really knowing what I intended to do, I meandered over.

I stopped in the doorway, watching our estate manager as she gestured at one of her filing cabinets. A drawer slid open and a folder jumped out. "There you are," she murmured, grabbing it.

She bent over the papers, her pale hair drifting across her smooth face. A lump rose in my throat. Meredith had been the closest thing I'd had to a mother most of my childhood. I couldn't even remember my birth mother, who'd been taken by a sudden and aggressive cancer when I was a toddler. But she was still my father and stepmother's employee. What could I tell her that would make this whole conspiracy sound believable?

She turned and raised her eyebrows at the sight of me. "You'll give me a heart attack, standing there so quiet, Rose," she said with a little laugh.

"Sorry," I said. "I was just wondering..." Could I ask if she'd noticed Celestine and Derek talking at all when I wasn't around? No, that might sound as if I suspected them of some kind of intimate dalliance. I restrained a shudder at the thought. Maybe I could ask about Derek's activities as if I were trying to arrange some romantic surprise for him?

Before I could decide, the floorboards creaked down the hall. I glanced over. Celestine had just come up the stairs. Our gazes locked, and then hers slid from me to the room I was standing outside of. A prickle ran down my back.

I couldn't ask *anything* with my stepmother watching.

"Never mind," I said to Meredith. "I think I've remembered on my own."

I headed for my bedroom as if the answer to my question was there. As soon as I'd closed the door behind me, I let out my breath.

"Maybe the guys have thought of something," I said to Philomena. Not that it seemed very likely. If *I* couldn't solve this witching problem, how could they, so far outside it?

"Or maybe you just want to talk to them more than anyone here. That's all right. I don't blame you." Phil gave me a playful smirk.

I wrinkled my nose at her, but she wasn't entirely wrong. When I dug the prepaid phone out from its hiding place, my spirits leapt at the sight of a text alert on the screen.

It was Kyler, and not news, just checking in. *You've been quiet for a bit. Everything all right over there?*

He'd sent it to me directly instead of in a group conversation with the other guys. I wasn't sure what to make of that. I wasn't sure what to make of his reaction to me the last time I'd seen him in general. He'd acted like he couldn't stand to hug me. I'd thought...

Well, obviously whatever I'd thought, I'd been getting away from myself. It wasn't as if I needed all the guys to be head over heels for me. It wasn't as if I even knew what I could do about the three who seemed to return at least some of my feelings. But Ky's response had still stung.

Laying low, watching for any chance to gather more info, I wrote back. *Sorry for the silence.*

His text had been from late last night, but he answered mine immediately. *Don't worry about it! Now I've got my peace of mind.* He added a winking emoji. There was a pause, and then the app showed him typing again. A new message popped up a minute later. *Actually, can we talk? In person, ideally? I can come to you.*

My breath caught. *Okay,* I said. *Tomorrow morning, by the pond again? Around 10am?* Derek was meant to drive out to see one of the properties he was considering pitching then, so at least I wouldn't have to worry about making excuses to him. Although... *Unless you have to work.*

My schedule is flexible! Ky wrote back at once. *10am tomorrow it is.*

* * *

I took a roundabout route to the pond, in case my stepmother or the staff happened to notice me heading into the woods. During the walk there, I didn't hear anything but the usual whisperings of the forest.

The air was dry and the sun beaming this morning, but last night's rain had left the ground between the trees squishy. I trod carefully as I approached the pond. If I ended up sinking up to my ankles in mud, that would prompt some questions.

I heard Kyler before I saw him. A periodic plinking as he tossed pebbles into the pond. When I emerged from the trees, he was leaning against the boulder with a handful of stones. He shot me a smile and threw another, making a face as it hit the surface and promptly sunk.

"There's a whole formula for it, you know," he said brightly. "Skipping stones? The best velocity and trajectory and— I could tell you all that. But I can't seem to follow it well enough to make the damn things actually skip."

"Well, when it's your arm, there's muscle control involved, right?" I said. "I don't know how you'd even judge exactly how fast you're moving. Obviously what you need to do is invent a machine with the process fully automated."

His smile came back, stretching into a grin. "And what a great contribution to society that would be." He dropped the rest of the pebbles, brushed his hands together, and straightened up. "Rose," he said. He looked at the ground and then back at me. Something in his gaze made my heart thump. He opened his mouth, hesitated again, and then simply said, "Oh, fuck it."

With two strides of his long legs he'd crossed the ground between us and brought his hands to my face. His kiss was determined but careful, as if to give me room to move away if I didn't want it.

But I did. A giddy joy rushed through my body. I leaned into him and kissed him back, hard, my pent-up desire bubbling up. My spark sprang to life in an instant.

Ky tipped his head to end the kiss, but he stayed where he was, his hands framing my face, his hot breath tickling over my tender lips. "Rose," he said again, like a prayer.

Giddiness was still tickling through me alongside the

flicker of my spark. "Is that what you came here to tell me?" I said with a smile.

Kyler chuckled roughly. "I was worried, after the other day— I didn't want you to think— I didn't mean to push you away."

"You did kind of give the impression you needed more distance," I said.

"I know. I assumed, after how quickly you left that night at my apartment—and, I mean, when you have the other guys..."

An ache surrounded my heart. "I didn't leave that night because of you. I thought I was still going to marry my fiancé then. I was upset with myself for forgetting that promise, for giving in to my feelings."

"So you do have feelings?" Ky said, his tone turning playful. "For me? Because I definitely have a lot when it comes to you."

A laugh slipped out of me. "So many I don't know what to do with them, Ky." My mind turned over the words he'd said a moment ago. *When you have the other guys...* My throat tightened. He knew, then. "Does it bother you that it's not just you?"

He shook his head. "Why wouldn't you want any of them? All of them? Doesn't matter to me, as long as you know I'm here for you too."

"You don't think it's strange? I don't know if I could ever just decide between you." I paused. "I wouldn't want to."

"It's always been all of us," Ky said. "That's how we're at our best. Maybe it makes more sense like this."

My thoughts drifted to those images I'd seen carved

inside the stone tower. The witches with their multiple consorts. Maybe it hadn't been strange to some distant ancestors of mine either.

But those consorts would still have been witching men, wouldn't they?

The tension in my throat came back. I wanted to burrow my head in the crook of Ky's neck and drown myself in the musky, minty smell of his skin, but that wouldn't change what was true.

"I don't think I can have any of you, though."

He pulled back a little farther so he could more easily meet my eyes. "Why not? You said before that this marriage isn't so easy to get out of—what's really going on, Rose?"

My instinct was to deflect and change the subject, like I'd always had to when we got close to any witching subject. I stopped myself before those words could come out.

I'd told Seth. I'd *shown* Seth. Maybe not in extended detail, but enough. The guys all knew at least a little.

Ever since I was a little girl, my father, Meredith, every tutor had drilled into me that a witch never showed her magic, never talked about her magic, with the unsparked. But my guys were more than that.

"Kiss me again," I said, "and I'll show you."

Ky looked a little puzzled, but not enough to stop him from lowering his mouth to mine. I tipped my head, my lips sliding against his, the shiver of that pleasure racing down into my chest and making that glimmer of a spark flare a little brighter.

When Ky drew back, I curved my arm, summoning

up that hint of power. Then I twisted my wrist and cupped my fingers. One of the pebbles he'd gathered lifted off the ground and flew into my hand.

Ky's eyebrows rose. He stared at the pebble on my palm and then at me. A grin broke across his face. "Amazing," he said.

His appreciation emboldened me. "I'll be able to do a whole lot more than fling around stones," I said. "But only... I'll lose every chance I have of coming into my power if I don't take a consort in the proper ceremony by the time I'm twenty-five. Which is two months from now. And I need a consort who comes from a family line that shares that kind of power."

Ky was silent for a moment. I could almost see his thoughts darting by behind his curious eyes. He knew how to put the pieces he had together.

"I helped you do that somehow," he said, motioning to the pebble. "Like this consort of yours would? But I'm not—I'm just ordinary."

"You," I said firmly, "are anything but ordinary. But you're not... You're not my kind."

"Are you *sure* that's what you need?" Ky asked. "If it could work a little bit with someone like me..."

"I don't know," I said. "But that's what I've always been taught. And if I ignore what I thought I knew, and it turns out I'm wrong... There'll be no way to get back my magic."

CHAPTER TWENTY

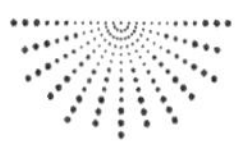

Rose

D̶ad's library had at least thirty volumes on witching history and folklore. Not one of them contained any mention of a witch taking an unsparked partner as consort. Or taking more than one consort at the same time.

I frowned as I slid the last one back into the shelf.

"You know I hold books in high esteem," Philomena said, strolling around the bookcases. "But not *everything* can be found in one."

"It doesn't make any sense," I said. "If it *ever* happened, you'd think someone would have told a story about it."

"Hmm." Phil fluttered her fan. "It depends on who was writing up those stories, and how much they wanted anyone to know, don't you think? That's your specialty, isn't it—organizing and archiving? Choices are made, and not always by people who want the full story told. It horrifies me sometimes, the amount of truth that was written out of the texts of my time."

My stomach knotted. She had a point. Every book cautiously published and distributed for the witching community had to go through a rigorous vetting process by the Assembly. And of course the stories collected were edited by the collector. What I'd done with those I'd gathered for my own modern history project was simply removing repetitive bits, but that was because authenticity mattered to me. And the stories I'd gathered were accounts committed to paper, possibly already edited by the teller or by those who watched over us.

I couldn't say any of the other witching people involved in our record keeping or governance had an agenda to keep information like this secret... but I couldn't say they didn't either.

Any editing out might not even have been done by someone currently around. Those towers and the drawings in them had looked hundreds of years old. All it would have taken was one or two people in a position of power back when witches had started to commit the stories of the past to paper, and any aspect of that past they'd disliked could have been struck from the record. A few generations of strict enforcement of one rule or another, and no one would be the wiser.

It could be no one living even knew there was anything to hide at this point.

The Assembly's archives might have even more books on the subject, older records that hadn't been printed widely. Dad would have their catalogue of entries around somewhere... Meredith would know where it was.

I headed to her office, even though chances were fairly slim she was there in the middle of the day. I hadn't seen her since our brief conversation yesterday, but that wasn't totally unusual, given how much running around the estate she did.

I knocked and then, when there was no answer, tried the door just in case. It swung open—and I froze, my jaw going slack.

The desk and the filing cabinets were still there. But the desk was bare, the photo of Meredith with her husband when they were young gone, her glazed clay pen holder and the usual scattering of papers too. The few pieces of art she'd picked out and hung on the walls had vanished. Even her *chair*, that leather beast with the wheels so she could roll it out of the way with a shove, was missing. The whole room felt too empty, too uninhabited.

What the Spark's name had happened here?

I spun around and found Celestine in the hall outside her own office, watching me.

"Did you need Meredith for something?" she asked in her cool voice. "I'm afraid I had to let her go. It'll take a few days to arrange a new manager. In the meantime, whatever your concern was, I suppose you can take it to the appropriate staff."

My heart stopped. "What do you mean, you 'let her go'?" I said, only just managing not to sputter.

Celestine's eyes glinted icily. "She was no longer a good fit for our household. It isn't wise to hang on to staff for purely sentimental reasons."

"She was just here yesterday," I protested. "You can't

just fire her. When Dad finds out—"

That was why she'd done it now. Dad wasn't around to argue, and he wouldn't be back for another three days. A shiver ran down my back.

"Your father will understand perfectly when we discuss my reasoning," my stepmother said. "He has given me equal authority over this estate, and I will make use of that when I feel I need to."

She hadn't even given me a chance to say good-bye. She must have timed it perfectly so that I wouldn't see it happening—late at night or early in the morning. Sending Meredith off like a stray cat that'd gotten too familiar, not like a loyal employee who was practically a member of the family and had been for generations.

Heat welled up behind my eyes. I strode forward, raising my hand in a demanding gesture. "You have to know where she's gone to. I want a way to contact her, and—"

Celestine whipped her hand through the air. A magical force slammed into my legs, forcing me to a halt. I swayed to keep my balance.

"Do not approach me like that," Celestine said, her voice lowering, now frigidly cold. "We won't be speaking on this matter again."

My feet wouldn't move. There was nothing I could do. I gritted my teeth as a sense of helplessness washed through me, blinking back the threatening tears. She'd made her point. I didn't need her seeing just how upset I was.

My stepmother swept past me in her silk day dress and glided down the stairs without another word. With a swivel of her wrist, the force holding me released. My legs wobbled. I caught myself against the wall with a sharp inhale and swiped at one tear that crept out.

What was I going to do now? With Dad on his trip and Meredith gone, there was no one left in the house I could count on at all. And Celestine had just demonstrated how willing she was to use her magic against me.

My gaze rose to the door to Derek's room, down the hall. I'd been focused on looking for proof among Celestine's things, but maybe he wouldn't have been as careful. He didn't have magic to help him cover his tracks.

He'd gone out to meet a friend for lunch. I had time. And if he came back and found me, well, I could pretend I'd been waiting to surprise him or some love-struck story like that.

His door opened easily. I crept inside and shut it behind me.

"Not much for neatness, is he?" Philomena said with a sniff, looking at the rumpled duvet on his bed.

A whiff of the spicy spruce cologne Derek wore lingered in the air. My feet whispered across the floorboards as I slipped farther inside.

Nothing stood out on the shelves or the dresser. I peeked under the bed. Tested the baseboards in case one was wobbly like the bottom of my bookcase. Opened his closet and rummaged through his clothes: slacks and khakis, sweaters and polo shirts and button-downs.

Where my shelves held books, his held vinyl records and binders with business notes and architectural sketches. I was flipping through one of those, my chest clenching around the growing possibility that I might leave this room with no more evidence than I'd come in with, when the floor in the hall outside creaked. The knob rasped.

My pulse skipped a beat. "On the bed!" Phil suggested with a breathless laugh. "Sprawl yourself out, get a come hither look ready—"

Her mouth snapped shut. "Come on," Derek's voice said on the other side of the door—and a soft feminine murmur answered, "Are you sure?"

He wasn't alone. My heart outright lurched. I threw myself at the first shelter I could think of: the closet.

I tugged the closet door shut behind me just in time. A giggle carried into the room. I knew that sound.

Polly, from the cleaning staff. Nausea washed through me. What were they doing? He couldn't really be—with one of my family's employees, in my own home, while I might be right down the hall...?

A rustling of clothes and a sigh filtered through the closet door. Apparently he could. Oh, snuff my spark, no, I didn't want to witness this. I drew my knees up to my chest, hugging them.

I'd known Derek couldn't care much about me, I'd known my stepmother had roped him into her schemes one way or another, but it hadn't occurred to me he'd flaunt his lack of caring this blatantly.

"Again?" Polly said. "It doesn't seem completely right..."

Her protest was cut off by a startled breath and the

squeak of the mattress. Then a gasp of what could only be pleasure.

Derek chuckled. "I should be allowed to have a little fun, don't you think? Have you seen my wife-to-be? My God, you'd think it'd kill her just to give me a kiss. A man has needs."

My face burned. I swallowed thickly, clutching my legs now.

"And you have needs too, don't you?" he went on, his voice slyly seductive. More clothing rustled. Polly whimpered encouragingly. "Why shouldn't we take care of those together? Lord knows I'd rather have a girl with real curves on her than some waifish thing."

A waifish thing like me?

Philomena sank down on the floor across from me, her skirts enveloping my feet. "Don't you dare listen to that bastard, Rose," she muttered. "He clearly doesn't know the first thing about what makes a commendable woman. Let's talk about something else. Did I ever tell you the story of that time *I* had to hide away in a closet? It was all because of Lord Danby's britches and—"

Her voice couldn't drown out the conversation beyond the closet completely. "But if someone sees us," Polly started. "We have to be careful—oh!"

A zipper hissed down. "Don't you worry about that," my fiancé said. "Rose doesn't have a clue, and anyone else who notices won't give a damn."

Anyone else who notices won't give a damn. Like my stepmother? Because she knew he was committed to her scheme regardless of how often and how far he might stray along the way? I might have vomited if my lips hadn't been pressed so tight.

The bed frame creaked and gasps turned into moans. I pressed my hands over my ears. My palms muffled everything except Philomena, who'd given up on her story too.

"We can't let him get away with this," she said, her hands balled into fists. "What an utter wretch of a man he is."

"Maybe I don't have to," I said. "*Polly* hesitated a little bit. If I bring her to my father when he's back, I might be able to convince her to confess." I didn't need a conspiracy to convince Dad I couldn't marry Derek if I had the other woman testifying to his cheating.

And then what? Dad would send Celestine out to find another consort for me? Beggars couldn't be choosers. And I could just imagine who she'd pawn me off to with so little time to argue. Some other scumbag who'd bow to her scheme. Unless I found a way to reveal her too.

I bowed my head, leaning my forehead against my knees. Tears scalded my eyes, but the firm pressure kept me grounded. Kept me steady as anger rippled up over the pain.

I'd spent the last week simply trying to figure out how I could survive this, while Derek canoodled with one of our staff right here under the roof of my house, insulted me to her... Laughed about how powerless I was to do anything about it.

My fingers curled into my hair. I set my jaw. I wasn't powerless, and I wasn't alone. When Dad got home in three days' time, I'd have all the evidence I needed. Let Derek laugh. Let my stepmother think herself so above me.

It took a witch to battle a witch. And I knew how to become one, at least for long enough for it to matter.

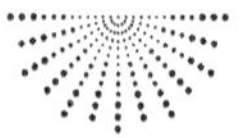

CHAPTER TWENTY-ONE

Rose

I stood by the side entrance of the scruffy split-level where Damon lived for a full minute after I'd knocked. My heart started to sink. My fingers hooked around the ribbon that circled my left wrist. I'd worn his tonight, the red one. It seemed fitting. When I'd first thought of Damon with that color, it'd been for his unshakeable daring. Now it matched his anger too.

I could understand anger. Tonight I understood it oh so well.

Shifting my weight from one foot to the other, I knocked again. The shadows were getting long, the sky turning from blue to gray. I'd slipped out of the house right after dinner. But who knew what hours Damon kept? He might not be home until after midnight for all I knew.

I could have texted him first to check, but I'd been a little worried if he'd known I was coming, he'd make sure he *wasn't* here. He hadn't even given me his address. I'd gotten that from his mom.

A pigeon cooed and hopped down to peck at a few pieces of trash scattered along the fence. The cool evening breeze teased through my hair. Then footsteps thumped on the other side of the door.

"Haven't I told you a thousand times—" Damon's rough voice said on the other side. The lock jiggled. His voice cut off when he yanked the door open and saw me.

For the first second, we just stared at each other. He was only wearing an undershirt above his jeans, revealing well-muscled shoulders and biceps—a thin line of a scar slanting across one.

I balled my hands in the pockets of my jacket. "Can I come in?"

"What are you doing here?" he said, probably aiming for snark but falling more on the side of shock.

"I wanted to see you," I said. "So. Can I come in?"

"I haven't exactly cleaned up for company."

"I don't exactly care."

He glowered at me, but when that didn't make me vanish either, he sighed and waved me in. "Fine. But don't say I didn't warn you."

If Damon ever wrote an autobiography, he'd probably make *Don't Say I Didn't Warn You* the title.

Beyond the tiled landing just inside the door, a set of creaky stairs led down to a basement apartment. A bachelor: kitchenette at one end, the narrow counter scattered with ringed glasses and a couple of pizza boxes. Bed in the far corner, the sheets rumpled and the pillow propped against the side wall to face the small TV on its cinderblock stand. A two-seater table stood between them, a deck of cards sitting on it.

The space smelled slightly earthen, like most basements I'd been in, but not in an unpleasant way. And there was no hint of nicotine in the air. No ashtray on the table or on the plywood stand beside the bed. Huh. So Damon didn't smoke down here. I'd wondered how much that habit was an actual vice and how much just part of The Badass Show he was currently attempting to star in.

"You know, normally people consider it polite to give a person a little notice before you turn up at their door," Damon said. He'd recovered his snark.

I turned to face him where he'd stopped at the bottom of the steps. "Are *you* really going to start giving me lessons on politeness?"

His mouth twitched with what looked like a grin he'd caught. His body stayed tensed, though. "Just sayin'."

I shrugged off my jacket and draped it on the back of one of the chairs, since there didn't appear to be any coat hooks around. Damon hadn't moved. "It's your apartment," I said. "Aren't you going to come in?"

"I'm still trying to figure out what you're up to, angel."

I inhaled slowly, gathering myself. Then I walked up to him, holding his gaze, and stopped just a few inches away. Close enough to make his breath hitch. My voice dropped. I was nervous as hell, but somehow I managed to keep the tremor out of it.

"A few days ago you were talking about all the things you wanted. I'm pretty sure an awful lot of them, I want too. And I'm hoping you're as done with waiting as I am."

The heat radiating off his body rose. He laughed hoarsely. "Do you even really know what you're asking for, Rose?"

"I think I've got the basics and an awful lot of the extras down. You'd be amazed what you can learn from books."

A glint lit in his dark blue eyes. "What the hell kind of books have you been reading?"

I let a smile curl my lips. "All the best kinds."

Damon shifted forward, bridging the gap between us. His chest brushed mine. His hand came to rest on my waist. A faint rasp crept into his voice. "I'm not going to give you some kind of fairy tale. If we do this, we're doing it my way. Are you ready for that?"

When he looked at me like that, talked in that low voice, I felt ready to spontaneously combust. My pulse stuttered, but I found the confidence to set my hand on his chest. And then to trail my fingers down, down, over the solid muscles of his abs, past the hem of his jeans, to the bulge straining against his fly, exactly what I'd been looking for.

He was already hard. As I cupped my hand around his erection, his eyelids dipped, lust turning his eyes almost black.

"I'm sure I can figure out anything I don't know as we go," I said. A thrill passed through me, feeling the undeniable evidence of his desire against my palm. Seeing the pleasure of my touch melt some of the defensiveness from his expression. My own desire pooled in an ache between my legs.

Damon pulled me even closer to him, trapping my

hand between us. Any nicotine smell from his outside activities had left him too, leaving only a lingering hint of leather and something richly bittersweet, like dark chocolate. His head bowed next to mine. "Have you ever touched a guy like that before?"

I swallowed hard and settled on the truth. "Only in my imagination."

"Has anyone ever touched *you* like that?"

A shaky breath escaped my lips. "No, but I figure it's about time someone did."

To my frustration, he stepped back at those words. His fingers closed around my wrist, just tight enough to be a little but not overly painful. He studied my face.

For a second I thought he was going to ask me why now, and I wasn't totally sure what I'd tell him. I didn't want to talk about Derek. I didn't want to even think about Derek. That snake didn't deserve any more space in my mind.

But that question wasn't where Damon's mind had gone after all. Or else he'd decided that part he didn't need to know. "Did you come here because you want to have sex with *me* or because you want to have sex with someone?" he said.

Oh. That was an easier one to answer. "I want you," I said. "Very, very much. But if you're asking whether you're the *only* one I want, I'm not going to pretend it's like that."

"So why pick me tonight?"

If he'd known how well that question echoed Seth's the other night, he probably would have cringed.

I gave him a little smile and the truth. "You're the

only one I know won't shut me down out of some idea about my own good. So are we going to fuck or what?"

The crude words felt awkward coming out of my mouth. But they set off a blaze in Damon's eyes. "Oh, I'll make it good for you, angel. I promise you that much."

I didn't have time to say anything about that, because the next second he was kissing me. Hard and hungry, his fingers twining into my hair and tensing against my scalp, need vibrating through his body. I gave myself over to the embrace, kissing him back. Whimpering when he tilted his head and his teeth grazed my lip. Wanting this, all of this passion and power, not just against my mouth but over every inch of me.

In the depths of my chest, my spark flared.

Damon kissed me again, walking me backward to the bed at the same time. When the backs of my legs hit the frame, he released my lips just long enough to yank my shirt up over my head. As my hair rained down around my face in its wake, he claimed my mouth again. I ran my hands up over the hot planes of his chest beneath his undershirt, and he groaned.

At his push, we tipped over together. He braced himself over me, the muscles in his arms taut. He nipped the corner of my jaw and scraped his teeth down the side of my neck, sending a jitter of bliss through me. At the same time he leaned his weight onto one arm so the other hand could wrench down my bra.

The second his fingers closed around my bare breast, pleasure rippled through my chest. I moaned. "You like that, huh?" he murmured, flicking his thumb over the tip. "What about this? Tell me how much you need it."

He twisted my nipple between his thumb and forefinger. A shock of mingled pain and pleasure jolted through me. I arched into his grasp, instinctively seeking more. The ache in my core now burned all through my body. The flame in my chest danced with it.

"I need this. I need you. Don't stop."

His laugh sounded raw. He pinched the peak of my breast again, bending down to test the other between his teeth. His knee slid between my legs, giving the slightest pressure to the spot where I was neediest.

I let out another moan, rocking against his leg. I couldn't help it. The rush of bliss and the exhilaration of my spark flaring brighter were carrying me away. Some part of me distantly remembered a plan to stay aware and in control, but it was too late. I was lost. And I didn't mind even slightly. Not once in the times I'd brought to mind the steamiest scenes from my books and let my fingers travel between my legs had I ever felt close to this good.

And there was so much still ahead of us.

Damon's fingers tugged my breast, and I gasped. He shoved his hand behind my back to strip my bra right off me. I took advantage of the temporary pause to wrench at his undershirt. With a smirk, he peeled it off.

He held himself still for a minute as I explored his chest. My thumb traced another scar that ran from just below his nipple to his sternum. "Such a tough guy," I murmured.

He glowered at me. "Don't you forget it."

With that, he heaved me farther up the bed and grabbed the waist of my jeans. Anticipation tingled across my skin just below his fingers. I lifted my hips as he yanked the zipper down. He sucked in a breath, tugging the jeans off me. Then his hand slid over my panties to cup my sex.

My eyes rolled back as a wave of pleasure coursed through me. It urged my spark higher, hotter. "Damn," Damon muttered, trailing his fingers over the dampness in the fabric. He slid them right under to test the wetness pooled at my core. "You are ready, aren't you, angel?"

A giggle escaped me as I started to pant. "Not much of an angel anymore."

Something tensed in Damon's face. His hand stilled against me. He bent down until his nose touched mine.

"You'll always be an angel, Rose," he said.

Before I could come up with an answer, he kissed me as hard as before. His forefinger curled up into my opening. I moaned against his mouth. I didn't know how to do anything anymore but quiver with bliss and ride his hand for all I was worth. My spark twirled and danced.

More. I wanted even more than this.

As he stroked me, I found the wherewithal to clutch at his jeans. Damon grunted and kicked them off. I reached for him again, the hard length of his cock beneath the thin cotton of his boxers. He shuddered as I pumped my hand. With a groan, he wrenched off the boxers too.

"Enough playing around."

He stopped to cast his arm toward his bed stand. It took me a second to realize what he was groping for.

"We don't need it," I said. Even if I hadn't been

taught as much, I could feel the protective heat of my spark flowing through me.

Damon glanced at me, startled. A growl reverberating in his throat, he pushed me back on the bed, urging my hips up to meet him. A gasp escaped me as the tip of his cock grazed my opening.

"My way," he said gruffly, catching my eyes.

I nodded, with a brief flicker of fear that was quickly wiped away by the ache of my desire.

Damon plunged into me so fast and hard that the pain radiated out of me almost as quickly as it had come. Somehow the burn as he stretched me only fed the glow of my spark and the pleasure singing through every nerve.

He held there for a moment, a tremor passing through his shoulders as I clutched them. "So good. God, Rose."

Then he started to move. He met me with slow, even thrusts that seemed to build and build, faster and rougher, hitting deeper inside me with each buck of his hips. I clung to him, every nerve aflame. The ache inside me grew and grew until it filled every pore, until I felt ready to burst with ecstasy. But I couldn't quite reach that peak.

Damon lowered his head with another groan. Sweat dampened his skin. He kissed me roughly.

"Damon," I said. "Damon, please." I wasn't even sure what I was asking for. Only that I *needed*.

"Oh, angel." His breath stuttered over my cheek. "I don't want to just fuck you, Rose. I want to own your fucking heart."

The words slipped out. "You've got it."

He made a choked sound and buried his head in my shoulder. "I loved you. I loved you so fucking much." His fingers tangled in my hair, gripping hard as if to emphasize his point. "Don't you dare even think about leaving here. Not without me. Not ever again."

As if I could conceive of leaving while he had my body on the verge of shattering apart with bliss. "I won't," I said. "Not because you told me to. Because this is where I belong."

"Yes. Yes, you do." His hand slid over my ass, raising me even higher. Letting him hit a point inside me that set off every kind of spark imaginable. He thrust and thrust again, each pump of his cock shooting pleasure through my core. "Come with me, Rose. I've got you."

Something about those words released the final wave. Pleasure crashed over me, my body shaking with it, a cry breaking from my lips. The light of my spark washed through me from head to toes in turn. As I soared on it, Damon's hips jerked. He came with a stutter of breath. His thrusts slowed.

He tugged me to meet him for another kiss. Then he slumped onto the bed, half on his side, half still covering me. I turned to nestle against him, needing to feel him against me everywhere I could. My eyelids drooped. All I could feel was the glow trembling through my body and the heat of Damon's skin embracing mine.

Nothing was carved in stone or bound with magic, but a sense of finality settled over me all the same. There was no coming back from this.

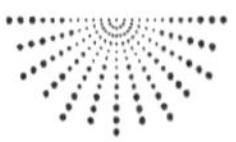

CHAPTER TWENTY-TWO

Damon

Rose's arm slid against my side. Her fingertips pressed into my bare back as she hugged me tighter. The movement pulled me out of the satisfied haze I'd been drifting in, half asleep, for Lord knew how long. The soft murmur of her breath tickling over my chest suggested she was all the way asleep.

Asleep here in my bed.

The haze in my head faded. The rest of the room came back into focus. The sheets with their stains that wouldn't wash out. The mess in the kitchen. The periodic plinking of the dripping tap I could never totally fix. The chill that seeped through the exposed concrete walls.

This wasn't the kind of place where Rose belonged. What the hell was she going to think when she woke up and saw what she'd done?

And what had I said to her? God, in the heat of the

moment, with her sweetness all around me, so many stupid words had come tumbling out. I'd told her I fucking *loved* her—

No, only that I used to. That was a little better. But still pathetic.

My gut clenched. I pulled away from her and pushed myself off the bed.

Rose's arm hit the mattress. She startled awake and blinked at me. A brilliant little smile started to curl her lips, and the twisting sensation inside me wrenched even tighter.

"Okay," I said, grabbing my boxers. "You got what you wanted. Time to go."

How to kill a smile in less than ten words. The light faded from Rose's face. I tugged on my jeans and tossed her clothes onto the bed beside her.

"Damon," she said, quiet and even, "what are you—"

"Did you think we were going to spend the whole night cuddling and I'd make you breakfast in the morning? Not really my style. Anyway, don't you need to fly back home where you belong, angel?"

Rose closed her mouth. She looked at me for a long moment—long enough that my skin started to prickle. Then she reached for her clothes and got herself dressed, one piece at a time, that gorgeous angel's body disappearing bit by bit. I turned to grab a shirt, to act as if I didn't care about the view. I'd seen it all already, hadn't I?

She got up to step into her shoes. The soles squeaked against the floor.

"You don't have to do this," she said to my back.

"Nothing you say is going to make me regret what we did."

My throat closed up. I swallowed before I swiveled toward her. "I don't know what you're talking about. We got off. Now I want my apartment back. You knew what you were getting into."

Her dark green eyes held mine, pained but unwavering. "Yes, I did."

She stepped forward, set her hand on my chest, and brushed a kiss against my lips, so soft and so fast it was already over before I could react. She backed away, scooping her fallen purse off the floor. "You know where I'll be," she said, and started up the stairs.

I didn't want to follow her up, so I stayed where I was, watching her disappear. When the door thumped shut behind her, the clenching inside me eased—but a dull ache remained. I sank onto the edge of the bed, running my hands through my hair. With each breath, the ache crawled deeper. I gritted my teeth.

I'd taken Rose's virginity, when I'd lost mine seven years ago and hooked up plenty of times since. I'd taken some little part of her innocence, when I sure as hell didn't have any left.

So why did I feel as if she was the one who'd taken something from me?

* * *

"I can't believe Silvio took you aside the other day for a private powwow," Brad said, shaking his head with his version of awed disbelief, even though this was the fifth time he'd brought it up since the weekend. "Impressing the big boss! We're moving up."

"I don't remember *you* doing anything," I said. More sharply than I meant to. I'd hardly slept last night, and my nerves felt all out of whack. We were standing on one of our usual corners, just passing the time, but somehow I couldn't relax.

"Hey, I pull my weight." Brad took a swig from the silver flask he took such pride in carrying around and passed it to me. I tipped a shot of today's offering down my throat.

The sour liquid hit my mouth with a pungent burn. I almost gagged. Instead I just grimaced and handed the flask over to George. "What the hell did you put in there this morning?"

"I was getting low," Brad said. "There wasn't enough of anything to fill it, so I put in the rest of the gin and the rum."

"It tastes like you mixed piss and lighter fluid," I muttered.

George took a sip. "I don't think it's that bad."

"Well, your taste is shit."

He gave me a look that was almost wounded. As if I was here to cater to his fucking feelings.

I kicked a dented can someone had dropped on the sidewalk. It rattled into the middle of the road. A woman who'd been walking on the other side flinched at the sound. Normally I'd have felt a little victorious, getting a reaction, but when she darted a glance at us and hurried on, all I felt was a different but equally unpleasant burn.

She looked kind of like Rose, dark-haired and pale-skinned. And she looked at me like I was a mutt she didn't trust not to give her fleas. Her glance hadn't been scared or cowed, just disdaining.

I tugged at my jacket, but the worn leather suddenly felt less like a shield and more like a scuffed-up rag. Was that and a scowl really supposed to impress anyone?

How pathetic were we? Spending the whole day talking about nothing, drinking shitty alcohol, acting like big men just because we moved stuff around in a warehouse a couple times a week. This was my life.

"Come on," I said. "Let's *do* something."

"Like what?" George said, looking blank. "Is something going down?"

"There's never anything to do in this town," Brad said with a roll of his eyes.

I sighed and opened my mouth, but nothing came out. I didn't have any ideas either.

The aftertaste of the alcohol turned even more sour in my mouth. That was the worst part, wasn't it? How was I any better than these dipshits? What the hell had I ever done to deserve a chance with a girl like Rose?

What the hell had she ever done to deserve the good-bye I'd given her last night?

Nothing. Nothing at all except being what I hadn't thought I could ever have.

My throat tightened. "I need to take a piss," I said. "Maybe I should top up that flask of yours."

George guffawed. Brad huffed and grabbed the flask from him. "Maybe I should stop sharing my booze with you, asshole."

"That's okay. *I* can afford to buy my own." The cheap

shit, anyway, but at least enough not to mix it in awful combinations.

I headed down the street to the one bar in town that opened right at noon. When I pushed past the door, the bartender was just wiping down the counter. "Give me a minute," she said.

I nodded. "That's fine. I need one anyway."

I ducked into the bathroom and closed the door to one of the stalls. As I sat down on the closed toilet, I pulled out my phone. This wasn't a good setting for this. This wasn't a good setting for anything. The floor stunk like puke and spilled urine no quick cleaning could completely erase.

Or maybe that was completely fitting for how I was feeling right now.

I brought up Rose's number. Stared at it for a while with my arms braced against my knees. It shouldn't be this hard. Just *say* something.

This was what a tough guy I was. Couldn't even find the courage to reach out to the girl who'd given me a tour of heaven.

Her face, the expression on it when I'd told her to leave, flashed through my mind. My fingers tightened around the phone. Did she even care—did it even matter to her—?

I forced myself to take a long, slow breath of the bathroom air. She'd come to me. She'd picked *me*. Hell, she'd even kissed me before she'd left, despite how much of a bastard I was being.

I could blame a lot of people for a lot of things, but the only one I could blame if I shut Rose out was me. She couldn't have been more clear that she was willing to take me however I decided to present myself.

The words still didn't come to me, but I moved my thumbs over the keypad anyway. Pressing the symbols to form a heart. <3 I hit send and leaned back against the tank, feeling as wrung out as if I'd just scaled Mount Everest.

I went back into the bar before the bartender could start wondering if I'd drowned in the toilet, and ordered a drink. I was halfway through the beer when my text alert went off. My pulse skipped a beat as I reached to check my phone.

Rose's response was as brief as my offering had been, but it was all I needed: a matching heart, offered back to me.

CHAPTER TWENTY-THREE

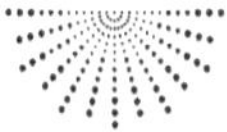

Rose

"Is she gone yet?" Philomena whispered, craning her neck toward the window.

I cocked my head. The rumble of the chauffeured car's engine was just fading into the distance. My heart started to thump. "I think so." I paused. "And I think I'd better do this alone."

The only good thing that had happened in the manor since—well, since Kyler had climbed through my window that first night—was that my stepmother had a work appointment this afternoon. Celestine would be gone for at least three hours. With Meredith fired and only the weekend staff around, there was no one left to notice if I made use of the fading but still heady flame of my spark.

With my spark not properly kindled, its heat had been diminishing from the moment I'd left Damon's apartment. I had to do this soon, or I'd lose my chance.

And I'd have to be very careful how I expended the energy I had left.

I padded past the common magicking room to the private one for the lady of the house's sole use. The power inside me picked up the quiver of a spell laid across the door.

Celestine hadn't wanted to take any chances of anyone breaking in. This was the only point of access to the windowless room. But she hadn't counted on anyone trying to enter who could draw on magic anywhere close to hers.

I turned my body slowly and deliberately, sliding my hands down through the air. Picturing a wall around this end of the hall that would encourage anyone who came this way to change direction. No interruptions, please.

My spark wavered and dipped a little lower. My chest tightened. The magic wouldn't slip through my fingers anywhere near this quickly after I was consorted. If I was consorted in time.

I put that thought out of my head. The spell on the magicking room door was a more difficult problem. I didn't want to *remove* it, because I couldn't perfectly replicate it for when Celestine returned. So I needed to convince it to let me somehow... slip through.

Her magic was focused around the lock midway up the completely smooth surface. Where a knob would have been if non-witching folk had been meant to ever open this door. I held my hands over that spot and curled my fingers toward the lock, testing the pulse of the spell's warmth against my skin.

Come with me, I thought at it. *Just ease a little over to the side...*

I dragged at it with my own power, gently and then with more force. Heat flared between my hands. I winced, but the spell moved in the same moment. It eased, inch by inch, until I left it quivering off to the side of the lock. Then, with a twitch of my fingers, I popped the deadbolt.

A giddy laugh bubbled up my throat. I forced myself to swallow it. Using magic like this felt amazing, but my spark had already dwindled to half the level it had burned at a few minutes ago. I had more left to do.

I nudged the door with just the power of my muscles. It swung open silently, revealing the shadowed space on the other side. I eased the door shut behind me and felt along the wall for a light switch. The crystal globe of a light fixture gleamed on overhead.

Compared to Celestine's office, her magicking room was spartan. Polished wood floor, a cabinet at the back for supplies, no other furnishings. The walls were bare and a neutral shade of gray.

My heart started to sink. I'd assumed if she had some evidence of the spell she was planning anywhere, it'd be in there. It *hadn't* been in her office. Or Master Cortland's house. Where else could she be hiding things? But there wasn't much of anything in here.

The brush of my socked feet sounded horribly loud as I crossed the floor to the cabinet. The hinges sighed as I opened the door.

It was packed full—boxes and jars and other objects too big for either: a large bowl made of polished shell, a sword that stretched the whole length of one shelf, a bundle of folded silk that glimmered with shifting colors, the skull of some animal I couldn't identify at a glance.

None of that was inherently suspicious. But if she'd taken notes, written down the procedure she was planning like Master Cortland had with his ideas...

I tugged out one box and then another. The first was full of feathers of various sorts. The second a jumble of semi-precious stones. The third had a heft that made my spirits leap, but when I opened it the books inside where clearly older than Celestine's time. One of them was stamped with the name Brixton, another Redfield—volumes she'd inherited through her family's line and her first husband's, I guessed.

I opened a couple of the books just in case, but the pages were old and dry. The ink was growing dull. Nothing had been written in these in decades. The stale smell of the box suggested she hadn't consulted them recently either.

As I pushed the box back onto the shelf, it jostled a small cloth bag I hadn't noticed at first. I retrieved it and eased its mouth open.

A curl of black hair stood out starkly against the white fabric. I stared at it for a long moment, my stomach clenching.

I was the only one in this family and Celestine's former one with black hair. What were the chances this lock belonged to someone important I'd simply never met, and not to me? Anytime in the last fourteen years since Celestine had come into our lives she could have snipped it—when I was sleeping or distracted.

With a part of a person you could work any sort of magic on them from afar. Track them down if you needed to find them. Cause them pain.

My fingers curled into my palm. I wanted to hurl the bag and its contents away. But the plan had been to leave this room as undisturbed as possible. Until Dad came home, she had to believe everything was completely normal.

If I took it, she'd just acquire herself a new sample. It wasn't as if I could do much to stop her even with the brief bursts of magic I'd gained.

Grimacing, I tucked the bag back into its place and reached for the next box.

This one held a heap of smaller silk scraps. The one after, sticks of various lengths and woods, striped of their bark. Then I opened one to find a stack of paper waiting for me.

My pulse thumped faster. Magical contracts. Each one held a date and two or more signatures, glinting with a faint hint of the magic that bound those names to their written oaths. The one on top was old, from twenty years ago when Celestine had engaged the services of a tutor for my younger stepsister.

I pawed through the stack, checking the dates and the gist of their content. There was her marriage contract with Dad, promising her equal authority over the estate until it passed to my hands. There was her contract with the witch she'd hired to courier messages to a business client. Immense and mundane, all the commitments of her magical life were mixed in together.

As I neared the bottom of the stack, the edge of one

page nicked my fingertip. With a hiss, I stuck my finger in my mouth. A dribble of coppery blood tingled over my tongue. I glanced into the box quickly to make sure I hadn't smeared any inside—and my gaze caught on the word *consort* on the contract just below the one I'd turned.

As carefully as I could, I raised the stack of papers and slid out the contract I'd noticed. I propped the other sheets against the side of the box so I'd know where to replace it. Then I laid the contract on the floor in the full glow of the overhead light.

My eyes shot to the names first. Celestine Hallowell and Derek Conwyn. My stomach balled. Bracing my hands against the floor, I glanced up at the date.

Almost three months ago. Three *months* ago, two months before we'd even come here, they'd finalized this agreement.

Derek Conwyn hereby declares that he shall govern Rose Hallowell as his consort in accordance with the requests of Celestine Hallowell. He may not act against Celestine's will or impose his will contrary to her intent. Where she has no stated intent, he may proceed as he pleases. He agrees to keep the Hallowell elders fully informed of the state of his consort and speak no word of this contract to said consort or any other outside party, including his benefiting family.

In return, Celestine Hallowell declares she will supply the elder Conwyns with fifty thousand dollars on the signing of this contract, and another twenty-five thousand each year thereafter provided all other conditions are fulfilled. These payments will be presented as dividends from an investment of Derek Conwyn's. She will also do her utmost to ensure that Rose Hallowell remains pliant to her consort's will, by means magical or otherwise as necessary.

Then their names, scrawled side by side. My stomach was churning now. I pressed my hand against my belly as if that would suppress the nausea.

Here it was. This was all the proof I needed and more. The second Dad laid eyes on this...

I had to make sure he did. I couldn't take any chance of Celestine hiding it somewhere else, if I made the slightest slip and she realized what I'd found. And it needed to be the real thing, not a photo on my phone she could claim I'd doctored.

How often would she be checking on the contract anyway, buried down there in this box? She had no reason to believe I was even capable of getting past her magic. Dad would be home in just a couple days.

A small risk against a big one. I had to take it.

Breathing slow and even and trying not to think about what I'd just read, I set the stack of paper back in the box and replaced the lid. Then I slid the box onto its shelf exactly where I'd found it. Derek's contract I carefully folded until it was small enough to fit in my jeans pocket. I wasn't going anywhere without it on me, not until I could show it to Dad.

I walked back to the door on wobbly legs. Shouldn't I be relieved? I had what I needed. I'd gotten what I'd come for.

But reading the terms of my stepmother and my fiancé's agreement so starkly laid out had hit me harder than any suspicion could have. The way they'd written about me, as if I were just a tool for them to use as they liked... A shudder rippled through me.

I had two more days to get through, two more days of pretending I didn't know, to protect myself.

And underneath both of those concerns, the dread that had been nagging at me from the first moment I'd suspected Celestine squeezed around my gut.

I had my proof. I had the means to convince Dad to break my engagement and see that Celestine was banished from our lives. But I still had no idea what happened after, when I had no consort and no real hope of finding another to properly kindle my magic.

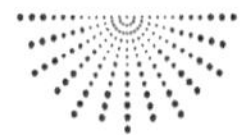

CHAPTER TWENTY-FOUR

Rose

Pulling Celestine's spell back into place over the lock took almost all the magic I had left. I pressed it steady against the deadbolt and paused, bowing my head. My breath was coming quick from the effort, a light sweat cooling my skin.

Despite all those practice exercises I'd done, all those forms I'd propelled my body through, nothing completely prepared a witch for magic usage. In time, I'd find it came easier and easier.

If I kept my spark.

The tiny glimmer that remained sent a tickle of sensation down to the base of my belly. A memory flared up, as hot as my spark had been last night. Damon touching me there, then filling me so completely...

Even if being with him hadn't lit my spark, I'd have wanted to do that again. Oh, yes, indeed.

And not just with Damon. What would it be like to

come together with Kyler, or Seth, or Jin? Or all of them, all at once? A flush washed through me as I headed down the hall.

Philomena would have called me a wanton for thoughts like that. But she'd have said it with a smile and a wink, like a compliment.

I had been planning on going downstairs and into the gardens, to bask in the sun a little and pretend that any warmth coloring my cheeks was coming from the outside. But just before I reached the stairs, I spotted Derek on his way up. My heart lurched.

Derek Conwyn hereby declares that he shall govern Rose Hallowell as his consort...

A man has needs...

"Rose," he said with his usual smile, as if nothing could possibly be wrong. By my light, he was such an actor, wasn't he? I guessed Celestine must have been looking for that quality when she'd chosen her accomplice.

I made myself smile back, but my heart was still jumping like a trapped frog in my chest. The folded contract in my pocket might as well have been burning a hole through my thigh. "Hey! I actually just— I promised one of the records people I'd get some info to them—"

I motioned toward my bedroom. Maybe I should just not talk for the next hour... or day... or century.

But Derek bought my weak excuse. "Of course, don't let me stop you. I thought maybe we could look over the seating chart before dinner?"

The seating chart. For the wedding. The wedding that was absolutely never going to happen. A slightly hysterical laugh twitched in my chest. I managed to hold it down.

"Yes, sure, that sounds good."

I ambled over to my room even though every muscle was urging me to bolt. *That* wouldn't look suspicious at all.

The second I'd closed the door behind me, I walked to the bed and collapsed on to the mattress.

"Does that mean your covert mission went well or poorly?" Philomena inquired from where she was standing over me.

"Both," I muttered. I pushed myself into a sitting position. "My stepmother and my fiancé are scheming to turn me into their puppet. I can prove it to Dad now, but I have to play along with them until he's back."

"Can't you just disappear until he returns?" Phil suggested.

"And go where?" Anywhere I tried to hide, Celestine could track me to. If not with that lock of hair in her cabinet, then only slightly more slowly with a piece of my clothing, a cup I'd drunk from—there was no way to wipe my essence from this house completely. And the very fact that I'd gone into hiding would tell her that I knew enough to be a threat.

"I can't beat her or escape her right now," I said. "Not while she has full use of her magic and I don't. The second she realizes I know what's going on, I'm screwed."

"What about those official type people who were here before?" Philomena said. "The marriage interrogators. Can't they do anything about it?"

"When I can get them involved, they can. They won't

trust just a photograph. They'd need to see the actual contract before they took action against the current Lady Hallowell." I could make a run for Seattle to present it to the Assembly... but what were the chances I'd make it there before Celestine caught up? She'd bring all her power to bear to stop me. Her whole life, her power, would be at stake.

I knew how desperate that idea could make a person feel.

No. It was safest to wait. "When Dad is here, he'll know how to handle it," I said. "She's got contractual obligations to *him*. She can't use her magic against him. Once he's seen what I have, she won't be able to cover it up."

In the meantime... An impulse propelled me off the bed. I nudged the base of my bookcase and fished out my phone.

Nope, no new messages. The last one, from Damon, floated there on my screen. My lips curled into a real smile as I looked at that silly little heart. How much had it cost his pride to send that?

I hoped he'd get his head on straight. I wasn't looking forward to any repeats of the emotional whiplash he'd given me last night. But when he let down his guard... Now that was its own kind of magic.

The flutter in my chest turned into an ache as I brought my thumb to the delete button. But I had rules. Nothing that would lead the way back to my boys.

With everything I knew now, that precaution no longer seemed like paranoia.

"Well, there," Philomena said, teasing her imaginary fingers over my hair. "You're not alone even now."

A lump rose in my throat. No, I wasn't, was I? Not completely. Maybe not at all. If only I knew...

I'd been going to ask Meredith to help me investigate the records, but I had other options. I had the contacts I'd worked with while I was digitizing records. There was that whole database of witching historical aficionados I had access to for cross-referencing facts as needed.

But if I was going to ask about a historical fact so obscure and in defiance of everything taught by today's witching society... I was going to need an oddball.

I opened my laptop up my desk and dug into the file the historical society had sent me. This was perfect. On the off chance anyone was monitoring my computer usage, they'd assume I was just looking up people for a job or for my book.

Most of the listings were esteemed academics or professionals like lawyers and doctors who dabbled in witching history in their spare time. But down toward the bottom of the database I found exactly what I was looking for.

Margo Elands. A witch living out on Staten Island who ran a literal New Age shop while also collecting supposed "historical artifacts" as an avid hobby. The database's notes said, *Elands may contact you hoping to acquire information on your projects or offering her own insights. Our recommendation is to disengage. Many of her sources are questionable, and her enthusiasm outweighs her care.*

That was code for *She believes a bunch of wacko*

things we'd rather you didn't hear about if I'd ever heard it. But it would be an awfully big coincidence if she'd just happened to hear about the wacko things I could say unquestionably were going on in my life right now, wouldn't it? A coincidence too big not to give some credence to.

The database, of course, didn't give any contact information for Ms. Elands. We weren't meant to be seeking out her advice. But it wasn't hard to look her up via her shop on the internet.

Wouldn't Kyler be impressed if he saw me now? Well, no, probably not, given that Google was pretty basic compared to hacking into banks. But I was impressed with myself. So there. I even wiped my browser's history just in case.

I wrote out a quick message to Ms. Elands on my secret phone, pausing over every second word to consider my phrasing. *I am one of the sparked. I'm sorry I can't tell you more than that right now. I've heard that you've investigated areas of witching history beyond what our community might consider appropriate. Could you tell me if you've come across any mention of unusual practices when it comes to taking consorts? With humble thanks.*

I grimaced reading it over, but I could live with it. Breath held, I sent it off.

My computer dinged with an email alert before I could close it. I blinked at it, my first thought behind to wonder how Margo had managed to reply quite that quickly. Then I remembered that she wouldn't have been replying on my laptop.

It was an email from the Consorting Advisership at

the Assembly. From the woman who'd come to interview me and Derek, I thought, from how familiar her name looked. I maybe hadn't been paying quite as much attention to that meeting as I should have.

Ms. Hallowell, the email read. *Thank you again for your time answering our questions last week. This is a standard letter, but rest assured that if you have any questions, you may reach out to our advisers at any time. The transition a young witch faces when claiming her spark is a time of high emotion, and a little confusion is almost to be expected.*

We like to remind witches on the verge of consorting of three key points:

-Any spark you gain before your initial consorting ceremony will be only a pale version of what you will experience afterward. If you have engaged in some physical intimacy with your consort-to-be, don't let that limited taste of magic worry you. This is exactly why we discourage much intimacy among young witching couples prior to becoming official consorts.

Yeah, I would have been awfully worried if my only experience had been with Derek. That was, no effect on my spark at all.

The email went on: *-The most important factors in a good partnership with your consort are developing a strong emotional and physical bond with trust, respect, and mutual regard. In the time leading up to your consorting ceremony and afterward, approach your partner with open and positive intentions, even if tensions arise. This will ensure harmony and the strength of your spark.*

I wondered if they'd sent Derek a note reminding *him* of that. He was trampling all over my trust, and he sure as hell didn't respect or regard me very well. My jaw tightened. I read on.

-When you're uncertain, look to your parents as a model for a strong witching relationship. Think back on how you've seen them resolve conflicts over the years. Take your guidance from your elders, and they will help you find the right path.

Celestine as my model? No, thank you. And my actual mother...

My gaze drifted to the photo hanging near the foot of my bed. A family portrait of my father, my mother, and me as an infant. My mother beamed at me from the image. With her black hair, pale skin, and large dark green eyes, she looked like a slightly older, slightly curvier version of me. The only way I took after my father to look at us was his lankiness and height.

Dad had never talked about my mother very much. By the time I'd been old enough to form solid memories, he must have gotten over most of his grief at her death. But he'd gone years before he'd looked for a new wife. The occasions he had talked about his first wife, it had been with a tenderness I usually only saw directed at me.

Theirs had been a love match, I knew that much. My mother had been part of a prominent witching family in New York, but she'd left abandoned any claim to her family home and name in order to marry my father and become part of the Hallowell legacy. Her family had never really forgiven my father for that transgression, according to him. At least, that was how he'd always explained why we didn't see or speak to them.

I dragged in a breath, my heart suddenly heavy. All the factors the Assembly talked about, all the elements Meredith had told me a good match needed, I had them not with Derek but with my unsparked men. If the guys had been from witching families... If I wouldn't have felt I needed to choose between them...

Maybe Dad would understand, if I tried to talk to him about this once Celestine and Derek were dealt with. He knew what it was like to love someone you weren't supposed to.

A knock rattled the door. I startled in my chair. "Rose?" Derek said. "Are you ready to come down? I've been told dinner isn't far off."

Had I been mooning around in here that long already? My chest constricted. I still didn't feel quite ready to see my unknowingly-former fiancé. "I, ah—" I started, and an alert lit up the screen of my prepaid phone.

I grabbed it, tapping through to read the full message. Margo Elands had come through. *I can see why you're keeping your name secret when you're asking questions like that. Let me see if I can help you. Accounts of consorting ceremonies more than a couple hundred years back are few and far between. I've had to dig very deep for what I have come across. The most intriguing scraps I've found—nothing official, you have to understand, only fragments of texts I'm obliged to tell you may be fictional —have mentioned—*

"Rose?" Derek repeated.

Damn. "I'll be there in a minute, I promise," I said. Anything to get him away so I had a moment to read this.

—wilder ceremonies than we see today, on untamed grounds, with a symbolic structure nearby at times to ground the proceedings. I've come across one mention of a witch consorting with a completely inhuman being, although that may very well be fancy. Also a couple of vague mentions that seem to indicate the taking of unsparked men as partners, in one case to extend the witching blood. As I'm happily consorted already myself, I haven't had occasion to try that one out.

My breath caught in my throat. So it might be true. Not just because I wanted it to be—someone, somewhere had made note of it.

My hands trembled as I typed out a quick response. *I've seen pictures depicting witches with multiple consorts. Is that something you've encountered in your research at all?*

Her reply was quick and clearly amused. *Oh, an ambitious one, are you? The only time I've ever tried to raise that matter in a remotely public way, I lost my job, so you might want to tread carefully there. But yes, I've seen the sort of pictures you've described. Few and far between, maybe because they have a habit of getting themselves destroyed as soon as anyone takes note. But I make no claims that they're anything other than symbolic. Just to be clear.*

Covering her ass in case I passed her reply on to anyone else? Well, I'd be deleting her messages in a moment anyway. I'd be in so much more trouble than her if anyone saw what I'd been asking.

My heart was outright thumping now. So what if she couldn't guarantee anything? What she'd given me was still so much more confirmation than I'd had an hour ago. Maybe following my heart wasn't quite as hopeless a risk as I'd feared.

Of course, that was just my end of the equation. I still had no idea what any of the guys would think if I laid out the full truth of my situation and what I hoped would happen.

It was about time I found out how they'd respond, wasn't it? With a shaky inhale, I brought my thumbs to the phone and started writing a new message to the four of them.

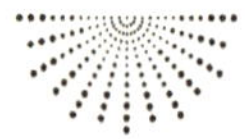

CHAPTER TWENTY-FIVE

Rose

Jin's apartment looked like a replica of the gallery below if the artwork had bled from the frames. Nothing hung on his walls, and the unmarked sections were the same pure white as those downstairs, but he'd obviously gotten into the habit of doodling on them whenever inspiration struck.

A marker sketch of a sunset beyond a tall, spiky building rose from behind the plush sofa. A dappling of flowers followed a vine around the window frame. Smears of red and gold paint ran together across the open space beside his bedroom door. They formed no object I could decipher but left me feeling oddly stirred all the same.

The smell of fresh paint hung in the air. His actual working studio was up here, maybe behind that other closed door.

I rocked on my feet on the soft shag rug, which was a

deep orange that somehow worked perfectly with the lime green of the sofa. Jin had suggested I sit down when I'd gotten here, but I felt too restless. Too much like I might need to work what I had to say out of my mouth through movement.

Kyler had already been in the apartment, sitting at one end of the sofa with a just-opened beer, when I'd gotten here. "How did you put off questions about where you were going this time?" he asked with a devious gleam in his eyes.

"I said I was looking through some more archives in the town museum," I said. That excuse had covered a couple of daytime trips already. The little building near the town hall did have a file on the Hallowell estate, so it wasn't totally unbelievable. "And I actually stopped there, in case anyone checks. I mentioned I might grab lunch. That'll give me enough time."

Jin came over with the glass of water he'd poured me. "For the lady," he said with a grin.

"Thanks." I gulped the cool liquid and immediately wished I'd taken it slower. The water plummeted down into my stomach like a stone. My gut started churning. I fidgeted with the glass and set it on the glass coffee table.

To my surprise, Damon turned up next, right on time. He gave Jin a curt nod and hesitated for a second when he saw me. I could practically see longing warring with bravado in his expression.

I knew which one I wanted from him. I held out my hand in offering. His stance relaxed by a fraction. He stalked over to take it, raised the other to my chin, and kissed me so soundly my knees went wobbly and my breath hitched. My spark gleamed into being with a rush of desire.

Damon drew back with a smirk and an affectionate squeeze of my hand. Ky let out a whistle. "Damn. I wish I'd thought of that."

A giggle tumbled out of me. "Who says it's too late?"

"Hey," Damon grumbled. But at the same time he stepped to the side as if to make room. Ky's eyes widened. Jin cocked an eyebrow like he was considering coming over and joining the fun himself. Ky shifted his weight onto his feet to stand up—and another knock sounded on the door.

I might have reached out to Ky anyway, but my stomach clenched tighter at the thought of the conversation ahead. I pulled back from Damon, swiping my hand across my temple as if that would settle my nerves.

Damon settled into the armchair next to me, leaving his jacket on and sprawling out his legs. Seth came in with a quick but warm smile at me. His gaze took in the whole room. We were all here. "What's going on, Rose?" he said.

Jin settled into the armchair opposite Damon. I motioned to Seth to sit down too. He gave me a concerned look, but he crossed the room to take a seat on the sofa next to his slimmer twin.

I hadn't given much explanation for why I'd called this get-together. Or why I'd wanted it to be somewhere more private than the café's back patio. At least if anyone had noticed me coming in here, they wouldn't think any more of it than that I'd wanted to check out the gallery.

I took a breath. "I wanted to talk to all of you because I feel like, after everything you've done for me in the last few weeks... you deserve to know exactly what's going on. And because I'm hoping that when the worst of this situation is over with, maybe you can become more a part of that side of my life."

"You don't have to tell us anything you feel more comfortable keeping to yourself," Seth said.

"I know. And I'm not supposed to be telling you any of this, of course... but I want to. I want to more than I care what anyone else would think." My hands closed at my sides. I uncurled my fingers and clasped them in front of me. "It's going to sound kind of bizarre, though. And I've never had to explain this to anyone before. So it might take me a little while to figure out a way of telling everything so it makes sense to you."

Kyler leaned forward, resting his elbow on the arm of the sofa. "It's all right. I think we've all known for a long time that there's something, ah, different about the Hallowells. We'll believe whatever you have to say."

I laughed weakly. "We'll see. It gets complicated. So." I wet my lips. The glimmer of my spark was still dancing faintly from Damon's kiss. "You've all seen a little of this."

I raised my hand, spreading my fingers in the same motion. Summoning the energy inside me to my palm. I shaped it into a flame to match the feeling of the spark inside me, filmier but bigger, so they could all see it.

The light inside me dwindled to feed that illusion. The guys sat silent, watching. Jin's expression was calm but awed, Seth's almost... proud? Kyler's eyes had lit up with an eagerness that matched the flame. Damon had schooled his face into its usual studied nonchalance, but his jaw twitched as he stared.

"That's magic," I said. "It runs in my family. It runs in... all the families I'd normally be supposed to associate with. It's what my stepmother used on you to stop you from interfering when she caught me hanging out with you by the hunting cabin all those years ago. We call ourselves 'witches,' and I guess the way you'd think of that word fits what we are well enough."

The flame petered out with the last of my briefly lit spark.

"So you're a witch," Damon said, with a hoarse chuckle. "And your stepmom's a witch. Your dad? What about the other people on the estate? That Cortland guy—"

I shook my head. "The thing about the witching blood is the spark—that's what we call the source of our power—it only lights in the women. My dad and Master Cortland are witching men, but they aren't *witches*. They don't have any magic of their own."

Jin raised his eyebrows. "I'm guessing they do something useful or you wouldn't keep them around," he said. His tone was teasing but his dark gaze was intent on me.

"That, um..." My gaze slid to Seth. I'd already pretty much told him. The corner of his mouth quirked up as he waited to see what I'd say. The rest of his expression stayed serious.

"You know the whole 'birds and the bees' talk parents are supposed to do for their kids?" I said. "Well, in witching society we're taught about how a man and a woman can come together in... emotional and physical intimacy, and that lights the spark inside the woman. The more they come together, the stronger it gets." I swallowed and looked at Damon. "I couldn't have magicked that flame from my hand if you hadn't kissed me."

He blinked. His shoulders tensed. "So the other night—"

"The other night," I said quickly, "was mostly about being with you. The fact that it kindled my spark temporarily was just a convenient side benefit."

My face heated a little, knowing I'd basically announced to the entire room just how intimate Damon and I had gotten. He seemed to chew on my answer for a moment. Then, to my relief, he shot me a crooked grin. "If you needed that kiss right now, what we did before mustn't have lasted you all that long. How much do you witches have to be hooking up to keep that fire going?"

My cheeks burned hotter. "Not *that* much," I said. "I mean, we do need to keep a good relationship with our partners... The witching men aren't at a total disadvantage. If one feels he's being mistreated, he can simply refuse that intimacy. The way it works..." I took another breath. "We take a consort. There's an official ceremony. What I get from being with any of you, the way things are now, that spark fades fast. With an actual consort, it'd flare brighter, and it wouldn't dwindle unless I used the magic."

"Your fiancé," Kyler said. "He was going to be your consort too. That's why you felt you had to marry him?"

"That's part of where it gets complicated," I said. "The way the spark works—they say it's to ensure the line isn't passed on if something about a witch is such a problem no one is willing to take her... If I haven't taken a consort by my twenty-fifth birthday, my spark will never kindle again. For anyone."

Silence settled over the room. Jin broke it. "Your birthday is in July, isn't it?"

"Yeah," I said quietly. "I've got about two months left. It's my own—my own fault. I took so long deciding. None of the witching men I met were quite who I wanted to spend the rest of my life with. In the end I just picked the guy who seemed like the best of my options."

"And he turned around and made some deal with your stepmother," Seth filled in, his voice dark.

"I have full proof of that now." My fingers brushed over my pocket with the folded contract. I'd slept with it in my pillowcase under my head last night. "When my father is back tomorrow, I'll go to him. My stepmother—I don't even know what she'd do to me if she realized I knew, to stop me from telling—but if I can bring it to him, and as her consort, he's the one person she *can't* use her magic to harm. The question is what happens then."

"You're obviously not marrying that asshole," Damon muttered.

"No," I agreed.

"So then you need someone else as your consort," Kyler said. "Back to the same problem you had before. And only two months left to find someone who'll commit to you like that..." He frowned, looking at his hands as if he might find a way to grab hold of the problem and piece it together with them.

Looking as if he wasn't totally sure he'd want to.

"That's why I asked to meet all of you today," I said.

The ripple of tension that had been running through the room between the guys abruptly stilled. I could feel, almost like a hum in the air, their attention focusing on me with a shift toward anticipation.

"What do you mean, Rose?" Seth said.

My hands twisted in front of me. "Well, obviously I've found out it isn't true that only a witching man can affect my spark at all. I don't know for sure if a full consorting will work with someone who's not of that blood, but from what I've felt, from what I've been able to find out, I think trying would be worth the risk."

Damon laughed sharply. "You're asking if one of us would take that spot."

I ducked my head. "No, actually. I was thinking... I've seen evidence that maybe this wasn't even uncommon sometime in our past..." Why was this part harder to come out with than all the taboo information I'd already shared? I squared my shoulders and lifted my chin again.

"The group of us, we've always felt like a family to me," I said. "Like a complete unit, meant to be together, to play off each other's strengths. I know that's kind of fallen apart since I've been gone, but we've come together again, haven't we?" All of us except Gabriel. But we'd found a new equilibrium of sorts even without him.

"I want us to stay together," I went on. "There's no one in the world who means as much to me as you all do.

I couldn't pick one of you. I guess it's selfish of me, but if I can have you, I want all of you."

"Rose," Kyler said, his eyes wide. "You mean— How would that work? In the long run, I mean."

"I don't know," I admitted. "There's a lot I haven't figured out yet. I don't even know how hard it's going to be to work around my father's approval and the pressures from the rest of the witching community—but I don't need their blessing. I'm my own witch. There's no *law* against this. And I think I *do* need you."

I stumbled onward before any of them could speak. "I'm not asking for an answer right now. I know you have your own lives, and committing to me in some kind of permanent relationship could upend everything. I just wanted to talk to you, now that I know that's what *I* want, so you have as much time as possible to think about what you want. And to let you know how much you mean to me. The logistics, I can work on once I don't have my stepmother to worry about."

As the last words spilled out, I felt suddenly drained. What more was there to say? I'd put my heart out there. It was up to them what they did with it.

Kyler pushed himself off the sofa. He walked straight to me and wrapped his arms around me, pulling me to him. As I leaned into his thin but solid body, Jin joined our embrace, and then Seth, and then Damon, until I was surrounded on all sides by their overlapping warmth.

"I do need to think about it," Kyler said. "It's a lot to take in. But you have no idea how much I want to just say yes right now even if that means diving in blind. It's the most incredible fucking honor of my life that you asked at all, Rose. You have to know that."

"Same here," Seth said roughly.

"No argument," Jin put in.

"You know how I feel about you, angel," Damon said, his voice low.

I exhaled in a shudder that was almost a sob, but more one of relief than anything else. "Okay. I want you to be sure, whatever you decide. We have two months. There'll be a lot of details to work out. I just needed to start somewhere."

* * *

The guys left one by one. I watched from Jin's front window, keeping to the side of the curtain, to see if anyone seemed to be paying attention to the comings and goings from the gallery. A few people passed by in the early afternoon sun, but no one lingered. My guys vanished in their varying directions.

Jin, who obviously wasn't going anywhere, came up behind me. As I turned toward him, he rested one hand on my waist and used the other to tug the curtain closed. He nudged me against the wall, ducking his head close to mine. Under the tangy smell of paint that always seemed to cling to him, I caught a prickle of something warm and savory, like wood smoke.

"You know," he said with a smile, "it just occurred to me that you asked me to marry you, or as close to as you can get, and I haven't even had the chance to kiss you yet."

My heart leapt. I licked my lips, practically tasting him already. "I assume you're planning on correcting that horrible oversight?"

His smile grew. "Less of a plan, more of a 'let's see where this takes us.'"

He tipped his head and brushed his mouth against mine. Barely a ghost of a kiss, but it woke up every nerve in my body. It woke up my spark, only just dulled from Damon's kiss.

But Jin didn't kiss like Damon at all. He didn't do anything like Damon. He took his time, easy and languid, kissing a little harder, a little deeper, building my longing without touching me anywhere except my waist and my mouth.

By the time his tongue teased over mine, I was already breathless with wanting. I kissed him back hard, gripping the front of his shirt, as if I could pull him into moving faster. But there was something exquisite about the slow, sure escalation. I was so sensitized just from his kisses that the moment his fingers eased up my side, every inch of my skin quivered with excitement.

"No need to rush," he murmured, the heel of his hand grazing the side of my chest. "I want you to enjoy every second of this."

"Oh, believe me, I am," I said in a voice so husky I barely recognized it.

Then he palmed my breast, and I moaned.

CHAPTER TWENTY-SIX

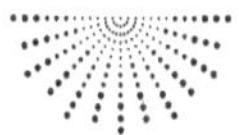

Jin

Rose's eyelids fluttered. I loved the way the flush in her cheeks deepened when I stroked my thumb over her hardened nipple. I loved the little noise she made in her throat when I nibbled the corner of her jaw.

Even better than all of that, though, was knowing that with each shiver of pleasure I gave her, I was lighting that fire of magic inside her. Joy and power all in one.

"Jin," she murmured, tilting her chin to give me better access. I moved my mouth down the side of her neck with a flick of my tongue for good measure. God, she tasted as gorgeous as she looked, sweet and flowery.

My thumb swiveled with steadily increasing pressure around the peak of her breast. She whimpered, her hips arching toward me. Our Briar Rose had woken up, all right. And I wanted her welcome to be the headiest experience of her life.

I released her breast just for a moment to slip my hand up under her shirt and unclasp her bra. As the cups fell loose, I nudged them up, caressing her sensitive skin directly. Rose's breath stuttered against my mouth as I caught her lips for another kiss.

I kissed her until I felt drunk from the taste of her, like some kind of rose wine. High from the gasps she made as I stroked her nipple to an even stiffer point. I dipped my head, slicking my tongue over the tip of her neglected breast through the textured fabric. Rose quivered and moaned.

Her hips swayed toward me again, hungrily. I didn't want to rush through this interlude, but I didn't want to leave her unsatisfied too long either.

I fondled her breasts until her breath had turned into panting. One of her hands had balled against my shoulder. The other had tangled into my hair. She whimpered in what sounded like protest when I straightened up, but only for a moment. Then I kissed her again, lingering but deep, as my fingers trailed down her belly to her jeans.

She trembled at the loosing of the button, pressing her mouth more insistently against mine. I eased my hand down. First teasing over the soft skin of her lower belly. Then the silky curls of her mound. Then that little nub that made her cry out the second my fingertips brushed it.

I pulled back to watch her as I explored even lower. Her delicate folds were so slick with arousal my cock hardened painfully. As if sensing that, Rose reached down my chest. I caught her wrist.

"No," I said, brushing a kiss to her cheek. "This, right now, is all for you."

I curled one finger inside her hot, tight center, and then another. The heel of my hand rubbed against her clit. Her hips bucked. We found a rhythm together, between the rocking of her body toward me and the pulse of my fingers inside her.

Her breath spilled, jerky and searing, over my chest. Her head had tipped back against the wall, her whole face flushed now, her lips parted and eyelids low. An ache filled my chest. I pumped my fingers faster, wanting to give her the release she was craving so badly.

"You're beautiful, Rose," I said under my breath. "Absolutely stunning. No matter what happens after today, I want you to know that. You don't deserve anything less from anyone than how I'm making you feel right now. So never, ever settle for it."

"Jin," she mumbled. "I almost—oh. Oh!"

Her body outright quaked. Her core clamped around my fingers. I wrapped my free arm around her, bracing her against me as she unraveled. Her limbs went limp against me, her head sagging so her forehead rested against my shoulder. A sigh tumbled out of her.

After a moment riding out the last tremors, I slid my hand out of her panties. She touched the side of my face and drew my mouth back to hers. Her kiss sucked me in, making my head spin. It took all my willpower not to press her back against the wall with my hips and release some of the pressure straining inside my pants.

Her arms tightened around me. "I don't want to go back," she said.

I eased away far enough for her to see my smile. "Just one more day, right? Tomorrow you can tear down their plans and kick them to the curb."

"Yeah," she said, determination flaring in her eyes. But the worry still lingered there.

"If you think you'd be safer hiding out here," I started to offer automatically.

She shook her head. "If I don't come home, Celestine will panic. I don't want to find out what she'd do then. To me and to anyone she finds me with." She sucked in a breath. "It's fine. I can do this. Like you said, just one more day."

I had said that, but as I waved her off, my throat felt even tighter than the crotch of my jeans.

At least one of those things I could fix. I ducked into the bathroom and brought myself over the edge with just a few strokes of my rigid cock and the thought of Rose moaning beneath me.

When I came out into the living room, the whole space felt more vibrant somehow. As if Rose had left some lingering brightness behind. Worry still nibbled at the edge of my mind, but otherwise my nerves were singing. My fingers itched to hold something a little more constructive than my dick.

I pushed past the door to my upstairs studio, what was meant to be the master bedroom with the largest of the second-floor windows. A piece that was only half-finished stood on the easel in the middle of the room. I'd been poking at the image last night but hadn't managed to pull it together.

Now, stepping through the doorway, the blank space on the canvas struck me with a rush of revelation. In the back of my head I could suddenly see exactly how—if I brought the orange tones across here—deepened the purple that swirled through the lower edge—where was that clay I'd thought I might mix into some new work? Yes, yes, that was exactly what it needed. A smear here, a slap there. Rake the paintbrush through it. Building out and toppling down...

When I stopped, my tacky hands falling to my sides, I was breathing hard. Fumes of oil and earth saturated my lungs. Staring at the picture I'd brought together made my heart squeeze.

I hadn't even known this wrenching beauty was what I'd meant to capture. The buildings I'd drawn roughly along the banks of a river bulged and melted down the bank. The sun burned through the haze to sear the water. The scene was ruined and breathtaking all at once.

When was the last time I'd created something that made me feel this much?

My gaze drifted through the room, to the canvases leaning against the walls, ones I hadn't chosen for display yet, others I'd been holding back for a larger auction. All work I *had* been proud of.

In comparison to the image I'd just pulled into being in the space of half an hour, all those pieces looked dull. Hollow. They showed the picture I'd tried to paint... and that was it. I'd been happy enough with them. I'd known I'd get compliments, buyers. But did they really stir anything in me?

Maybe they had when I'd constructed them. But not like this. Nothing like this.

How had I started coasting on talent rather than pushing it harder, without even realizing?

Rose had helped me find my way back. I swallowed hard, swiping the back of my arm across my damp forehead. A tug of longing in my chest nagged at me to get her back here. Hell, to get her right in *here*, to see her amid my work, to see what stirred in me then. I never let anyone come into the studio with me, but her...

I closed my eyes. I was getting too caught up. Rose was spectacular, I'd never doubted that. But I couldn't make a decision about tying myself to another person—to four other people, really, if the other guys took her offer—for the rest of my life based on one ecstatic painting.

I had time. There wasn't any need to rush in. We could take more moments to... explore each other. Enjoy each other. I could see how I felt, how she felt, after more of that.

By the time I'd finished washing the paint and clay off my hands, the sink was streaked nearly as bright as the canvas was. I was rinsing the porcelain clean in turn when my phone rang where I'd left it in the living room. I gave my hands a hasty rub with the towel and jogged to get it.

It was my dad. "Hey," I said. "How's the recording going?" He'd been holed up with his latest rock star client laying down bass tracks for the last couple weeks.

"Almost done," Dad said in his usual jovial voice. "That's why I'm calling. I just got a fantastic offer. One of the bands I worked with last year is hitting a bunch of the spring music festivals in South America and they want me along for the ride."

And he was so excited about that he'd needed to call me right away? "That's great," I said, not totally sure what to add. We might have had artistic temperaments in common, but sometimes I didn't totally understand my dad.

"That's not the point, Jin," he said with a laugh. "It's a very relaxed schedule, eight shows across a month. Lots of time to see the sights and enjoy the local scenery in between. I thought you might want to come with me."

"Oh," I said, with a weird twist of my gut. "When is this?"

"We'd leave next week. I figured, the loose schedule you tend to keep, the short notice wouldn't be too much of a problem? They only just asked me." He paused, and his next words tumbled out faster. "It's been a while since you hit the road with me—and we never did South America. It'd be good to spend some quality time with you again, kid."

It had been a while. I should have been excited by the possibility. New places and cultures to absorb and pour back into my art—that was what I lived for.

But all I could think of in that first instant was Rose. Rose and a month away from her, a month that might mean I lost her completely. I glanced back toward my studio, toward the work that had come to me in a burst of inspiration more intense than anything my jaunts with Dad had ever provoked.

Maybe I hadn't been coasting at all. Maybe Rose

simply woke up something deeper in *me* than I would ever be capable on my own.

"Well, I..." I started, struggling to decide what to say.

"If there's some kind of conflict, let me know and maybe I can help you sort it out," Dad jumped in. "I'll be home for a few days before we'd need to take off on the tour anyway."

It hit me then: the desperate note in his voice. Dad was lonely. He wasn't offering this only for my benefit—he was begging for the company.

Why wouldn't he be lonely? He spent more time running around catering to his famous clients than tending to his relationship with Mom. They seemed to get along well enough when he was in town, but I couldn't tell how much they even had in common anymore. They had more like a series of quick flings than an actual marriage. He'd been a cool but erratic older friend to me more than an actual father.

Was that what *I* wanted for the rest of my life, with any girls who came into it? Was that what I'd take, just to avoid the thought of commitment, when I'd been offered something so much greater?

My chest clenched. "Dad," I said, "I'm sorry, and I'm looking forward to seeing you next week, but I really can't leave. Not right now."

We went back and forth a few more times, and in the end Dad said we could talk more when he got home. After I'd hung up, I sank down on my back on the couch. Somehow exhausted and excited and terrified out of my mind all at once.

This opportunity was what I'd been waiting for,

wasn't it? Even if I hadn't let myself admit it. To find my way back to the dynamic that had sparked between the six of us when we were younger, that had changed everything about how I saw the world.

But what Rose had offered had only been hopes. What were the chances we could make them real?

CHAPTER TWENTY-SEVEN

Rose

Philomena sprang at me the second I came in the manor door. "So how did it go?" she asked, her skirts rustling as she hustled with me up the staircase. "What did they think of your stunning proposition?"

"They're thinking about it," I told her. "Which they should." As much as part of me longed to claim the guys completely as mine this instant, I knew I didn't really want that. "It's a risk for them too. Probably even more than it is for me. It won't really count unless they've thought the risks through and decided they're all in anyway."

"I've seen the way they look at you," Phil said. "All of them. I don't think there's anything in this world that could tear them away from you."

There had been, once already. And her name was Celestine. I touched my pocket, feeling the faint outline of the folded papers there: the contract, and the hasty photocopy I'd made while I was in town.

Dad should be home mid-day tomorrow. I had less than twenty-four hours left before all this could be over. Spark take me, I wished I could bury myself in my duvet and not come out of my room until he was here.

The first thing I did when I reached my room was open the wobbly bit at the base of my bookcase to stash the photocopy. If Celestine noticed the contract was gone before Dad got back, she could track it down easily enough, but there was no magic in that ordinary piece of paper for her to trace. It wouldn't be as solid proof as having the original, but it'd be enough to convince at least Dad, I thought. A little extra precaution never hurt anyone.

My hand slid into the narrow space to nudge aside the phone—and touched only the cool wood of the floor. I frowned, pushing my fingers deeper. Had I shoved it in farther than I usually did the last time I'd used it?

My groping hand encountered nothing but dust mice. Pulling my arm back, I squinted into the dark space. I couldn't see anything in there either.

My pulse started to thump. I stood up and glanced around my room. Had I forgotten to put the phone away after I'd confirmed today's meeting with the guys last night? I'd been so careful with it up until now. And surely if I'd left it out last night, I'd have noticed it in the morning before I left?

"What's wrong?" Phil asked, her forehead furrowing.

"The prepaid phone I used to talk to the guys," I said. "It's gone." And I couldn't see it by my bed or on my desk or anywhere else I might have set it down if its disappearance had just been an accident, either.

Phil's eyes widened. "What does that mean?"

"I don't know." I grabbed my purse and dumped its contents onto the bed. My heart sank lower as I pawed through them. Only my regular phone, the one Dad had gotten me as part of our Family Plan, was there. If the prepaid one wasn't anywhere in the room or anywhere on me...

I dropped onto the bed, pressing the heels of my hands to my temples. "Rose?" Phil said tentatively.

"Someone found it," I said, the words coming roughly even in my head. "Either I left it out and someone saw it, or someone searched my room for anything I might be hiding."

"Your stepmother."

"If it wasn't her, it'd be someone who'd have taken what they found to her."

The loss of the phone wasn't a total catastrophe. I'd deleted all the message threads as they'd come in. Kyler had given it to me with the numbers programmed in, but I'd deleted those contacts as soon as I'd memorized them. Celestine couldn't know what I'd been using the phone *for*.

But she knew that I'd had a secret phone for some purpose. That I must have been communicating with people I didn't think she or my father would approve of. And she'd taken it away from me.

I still had my regular phone. I could still—

I groped for it and brought up my account information. Was there any way I could keep a message or two totally private, even with the linked plans? She'd be monitoring anything I did with this phone even more now.

A window popped up on the screen informing me that my account had been temporarily disabled. I stared at it for a second, my fingers tightening around the phone.

My computer? I darted to my desk and flipped open the laptop. But even that brief hope was squashed a second later. The icon for the internet connection was crossed out. I tried to reconnect to the house's network, and an error message popped up. Incorrect password.

"Is that bad?" Philomena ventured.

I straightened up, my stomach knotting. "Yeah. I can't talk to the guys at all."

Celestine wasn't taking any chances. I was surprised she hadn't tracked me down in town the second she'd come across the other phone, if she was resorting to this.

Maybe she simply hadn't had a chance yet. Where was she right now? In her magicking room, already working some spell to trap me here more?

The heat of my spark quivered inside me, bright from Jin's attentions not that long ago. I focused on it as I padded to my door and eased it open.

There was no way of telling whether she was using the magicking room or not, not without opening it up and looking inside. Unless... Maybe I could use my own magic to sense where she was, at least if she were nearby.

I ducked back into my room. My hand shot back to my pocket with the contract. I didn't have time to find a perfect hiding place, but for now... I glanced around and shoved the photocopy behind a row of books on one of the bookcases. Better than nothing.

Moving back to the middle of the room, I inhaled deeply and spread my arms out at either side. Then I turned in a slow, smooth circle, gently rotating my hands.

A trickle of magic flowed from my spark through me and out into the house. Seeking out the essence I'd recognize as my stepmother. There was a figure bent over the desk in his bedroom—Derek. There was one of the cleaning staff in the bathroom. A kitchen helper loading the lunch dishes in the rooms below. The—

I felt her, with a cold prickle that rushed over me. She was close—she was coming into the front hall and heading up the stairs.

I dropped my arms, hugging them to me. After a moment, Celestine's shoes tapped softly past my door. I edged up to it and pressed my ear close.

She stopped. There was a pause, and then a quiet knock. The squeak of a door hinge. And my former fiancé's voice. "Yes?"

My stepmother spoke in such a hush I only made out the words by straining my ears. "We need to talk."

Derek didn't say anything else, not right then. The hinge squeaked again—the door clicked shut. Then I couldn't hear anything at all.

Philomena clutched her skirts. "We must find out what they're saying. They're conspiring against you right now."

"I know." My heart was outright racing now. I clenched my hands.

I could do this. I had magic now, even if it wasn't as much as she had.

The spark inside me danced. I closed my eyes, picturing that hard closet floor, the press of the clothes with Derek's spruce-y cologne, where I'd crouched when I'd heard him with Polly. His room was only maybe forty feet away. Not that far at all. I'd have rather my first attempt at this sort of magicking had been an even shorter distance, but I didn't have a whole lot of choice, did I?

I gathered the heat and the light inside me, and then I spun on my feet, whipping my arms around me at the same time, following the form of teleportation exactly as I'd been taught.

A chill and a crackle snapped around me. Everything went black. Then I was reeling against the hanging pants in the closet I'd imagined, my head spinning. All the magic I'd held in my chest snuffed out as I caught my balance.

I braced my hands against the floor, stilling any sound, clamping my mouth shut against a hitch of breath. I'd been lucky I'd had enough vigor in my spark to carry me this far. My chest was totally hollow now. I *really* needed not to get caught.

The closet door was slightly ajar. I shrank deeper into the shadows, away from the thin streak of light that cut across the floor. I could make out the back of Celestine's form where she stood in the middle of Derek's room, the curve of her silver-blond bob and the sharp lines of her dress suit. The faint rasp of metal wheels shifting against wood suggested Derek had gone back to his desk chair.

"Are you sure she hasn't run off?" he said. I couldn't tell from his flat tone whether the idea concerned him.

"One of my staff saw her returning from town a short while ago," Celestine said. "I laid down a spell when we arrived here last month to alert me if she traveled more than a few miles beyond our property. And I've just finished a magicking that will prevent her from leaving the boundaries of this estate, at least until tomorrow. So I'm not worried about that."

My lungs constricted. I really was trapped here then. But Celestine couldn't keep a spell like that up once Dad returned.

Derek sighed. "What if she doesn't even know what we're planning?"

"She knows something," Celestine snapped. "Someone's been poking around in our business. That's enough. We can't risk delaying any longer."

"And her father—"

Celestine's shoulders went rigid. Her voice took on an iron edge. "Should remain undisturbed. We can have the matter settled without him knowing there was any trouble."

What was she talking about? How exactly were they planning on "settling" this "matter"? I bit my lip, wishing I could see their expressions. Wishing I could ask them what the hell they meant.

"Well," Derek said. "I suppose if you think it's best. All this subterfuge has been tiring. We might as well get the gist of it over with."

"Excellent," Celestine said. "All you have to do is meet me by the old ash tree just beyond the back gardens at midnight. I'll take care of the rest. I have everything we need for the ceremony. And I can handle Rosalind."

The ceremony. A chill shot through me, so sharp my whole body stiffened. My pulse thumped.

That was what they were talking about. The gist of it. Settling the matter. They were going to force me into the consort ceremony with Derek tonight.

Of course. There'd be no chance for me to go to Dad then. No chance for me to find any other way out of Celestine's magic. They'd found the perfect solution to their problem.

How the hell was I going to stop them?

The chair's wheels rattled as Derek shifted it. "She isn't going to want to come. You might have a fight on your hands. What if she comes to me looking to light some of her magic? She'll be suspicious if I put her off. Or does that not matter anymore?"

Celestine guffawed. "It'd take a lot more than some inexperienced chit with a half-kindled spark to overpower me. I've been preparing for this day for years. Why not let her have a little taste if she comes to you wanting it? She might as well enjoy that brief freedom while it lasts. When we're done tonight, she won't be able to so much as twitch that spark of hers unless it suits us."

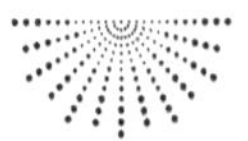

CHAPTER TWENTY-EIGHT

Rose

Derek tried to work for a few minutes after Celestine left before he grunted to himself and pushed back his chair. My body deflated as he walked out of the room. I waited until his footsteps had treaded away down the hall, and then I unfolded myself from the floor of his closet.

My legs wobbled under me as I slipped to the door. I couldn't pretend the weakness was only from staying crouched on the floor. My whole body felt shaky, as if I'd just come out of a rough bout of the flu.

But the rough times weren't behind me. They were ahead.

My breath only steadied slightly when I'd darted into the hall. I dashed for my room and shut that door behind me firmly, turning the lock—as if that would do me any good when Celestine came to collect me. A shudder passed through me. I sank onto the side of the bed, clutching my stomach.

Midnight. I had about ten hours left before my fate was sealed. Spark help me, I had no idea how to change that fate.

Celestine was right. There was no way I could challenge her. Even if I'd come with my spark freshly flaring after that tryst with Damon, the magic I had couldn't compare with hers, fully kindled. She must have stoked her own inner flame high before my father had left.

Ugh, thinking about that even vaguely made me feel even more sick.

It didn't matter. It wasn't as if I could reach the guys from in here anyway. I was trapped like a mouse in a cage.

My hand rubbed over the ribbon I'd wrapped around my wrist this morning. Blue today—bright blue like Gabriel's eyes and his confidence as limitless as the sky. I'd always thought he was the one who'd held us all together all those years ago, but today I'd been coming to the guys to see if I could take that role now. So much for that. I couldn't even send them a simple message...

My fingers stilled against the silky fabric. My gaze rose to the window. The memory swam up of Kyler standing in front of it that first night when I was back, holding up my white ribbon to return it to me.

In case you need us, and you can't reach out any other way.

My pulse skipped. My beautiful brilliant boy. Of

course it'd be Ky who'd thought of a solution to a problem that hadn't even happened yet.

I went to my jewelry case, my breath catching for a second before I opened it. But there they all were, the other five ribbons. My stepmother hadn't thought to steal away *this* method of communication.

I probably could have used the blue one to the same effect, but I slid out the white instead. The one I'd used before. The clearest message. The brightest signal I could offer against the dark bars of the gate.

The only question now was how to get it out there without Celestine noticing.

What reason could I have to go out to the gates if I didn't want her to think I was up to anything suspicious? Ah.

I balled the ribbon in my pocket and made myself amble down to the front door as if I had nothing all that urgent on my mind. Outside, I headed toward the garage. One of the workers who'd been polishing the hood of Celestine's Jaguar glanced up.

"Miss Hallowell. Do you need to go somewhere?"

"No," I said. "I just noticed when I came in today that the gate's hinges are getting a little squeaky. Figured I'd take care of that before my dad gets home. I know you Sunday staff are always extra busy."

I shot him a sympathetic smile, and he grinned back. He was probably the only one on duty in the garage today. "Much appreciated," he said. "If you're sure you don't mind..."

"Oh, it's nothing."

A strange pressure wafted against me as I approached

the gate. My stepmother's spell. I stopped by the hinges, my chest tight. All at once I felt very, very certain I did not want to pass beyond these walls. I suspected if I'd tried to, my feet would have turned me right around of their own accord.

That was fine. I wasn't here to leave anyway. I could work around her spell.

I dripped the oil onto each of the hinges. Then I paused for just a second to snag the ribbon on one. Against the outside of the bars, where it would barely be visible from this side.

There. I'd put out my call.

I'd just have to hope that one of my guys saw it in time.

* * *

The window's screen made a faint grating sound as I tugged it out of the frame. I winced and stopped to listen for any movement outside or in the rooms around me.

Crickets chirped in the dark yard below. The warm evening breeze teased through my hair, carrying the scent of the garden's hyacinths. Faint strains of the jazz music Derek was playing on his computer filtered from his open window to mine. That was all.

I let out my breath and set down the screen. I'd claimed I was going to bed with a headache right after we'd finished dinner, so I didn't *think* anyone would bother me until Celestine came calling at midnight. But I'd needed to wait until it was dark enough that even the weekend staff had been sent home, other than the few who lived on the property. Dark enough that I could expect the shadows to properly hide me.

The cloth bag I'd tucked my supplies into bumped against my back as I climbed onto the ledge. I'd raided the common magicking room before dinner. The simple linen dress I'd changed into had come from there too.

I hitched the loose skirt up to my thighs. The rough bark of the oak tree bit into my fingers as I grasped the oak's branch and clambered all the way out.

It was a nerve-wracking descent, clinging to the trunk and easing my way down from branch to branch as quietly as possible. Finally I was close enough to the base to lower myself to the ground. I crept across the soft grass along the side of the house, ducking beneath the level of the windows.

At the back corner, I stopped and peered around the side of the manor. My pulse skittered. In the hazy light of the solar lanterns that hung around the patio, Celestine's man Douglas was strolling through the back gardens. His gaze swept the shadowy grounds.

But he was positioned to catch someone sneaking out the back doors. I backtracked a few steps and dashed for the tallest hedge that bordered the outer boundary of the gardens. There, I dropped to my knees. The sharp evergreen smell of the hedge filled my nose as I listened.

No running footsteps, no shouts of alarm. He hadn't noticed me.

My heart kept thudding. I slunk along the hedge until I reached the last short grassy stretch before the darker sprawl of the forest. I peered through the brambles, trying to make out Douglas's position. Only a bit of the light from the patio penetrated the dusk this far out, but I didn't want to take any chances.

There. He ambled a little farther to the left, and then he turned on his heel to face the patio. I pushed forward, my bare feet pattering across the grass and onto the uneven ground of the forest floor.

I ran several paces through the trees and stopped in the thicker shadows. There, I listened again for any sign of pursuit.

None came. Exhaling in a rush, I pulled my flats from my bag and tugged them onto my feet to give me a little protection against the pebbles and roots. Then I hurried onward.

Speed mattered more than silence now. If the guys had come, I didn't know how long they'd been waiting— or how long they could keep waiting.

The bridge Kyler had picked for our emergency meeting spot lay about a twenty-minute walk northeast of the manor. I hit the stream first and treaded along its rocky bank. The burble of the water was faintly soothing as it guided me on into the deeper woods. The moon was rising, but its pale light barely touched the forest floor.

The trees parted where the stream widened to almost a river at the bridge. The arching structure was built of stones now so worn and lichen splotched you'd almost think they'd grown right out of the stream.

Four figures were standing around it. A choked noise of relief broke from my throat as I scrambled the last several feet to meet them.

Kyler reached me first, pushing off the side of the bridge and striding forward to catch me in his arms. He kissed me hard, and for a second it almost felt as if everything was all right now.

He drew back, his hands resting on my shoulders, his eyes dark in the dim moonlight. "Are you okay? What happened? You have no idea how worried we've been."

The other guys gathered around us. I dragged in my breath. Everything wasn't all right yet. It might not ever be. And the time I had to try to make it right was slipping away with every thump of my pulse.

"My stepmother knows I'm starting to figure out something's wrong," I said. "She found the phone you gave me. I don't know what else she might have noticed. She decided—she decided they have to do the consort ceremony tonight. To make sure I'm already bound to Derek and under their control before my father gets home."

Kyler's eyes widened. Damon swore. Seth stepped closer, his brawny shoulders tensed. "We won't let them hurt you. Do you need us to get you out of here?"

"You can hide out at my studio," Jin offered. "I have plenty of room."

I shook my head. "I can't. She's put down a spell around the estate—it'll stop me from leaving. And even if I could break through that, as soon as she comes for me and sees I'm gone, she has ways of tracking me down."

"So what do you need from us?" Ky said, swift and solemn. "Just say the word. We're here."

They were. Like always. My throat choked up again. It took me a second before I could speak.

"I don't want to ask this," I said. "Not when I promised you we'd have time—not when there's still so much I don't know about how we'd get by, afterward. But the only way I can think of that I'd be able to challenge her and win… is if I'm already consorted. My spark fully kindled. I don't even know if just one—but maybe, with all of you—"

I stumbled over my words. The guys were staring at me. I made myself barrel on. "You don't have to. I wouldn't blame you for feeling it's too fast, too much. It doesn't have to be *permanent*—the standard consort partnership can be severed—but only after at least a few years have passed. It's still a huge commitment. I know that. If I could see any other option—"

"Rose," Damon broke in, his voice raw. He stepped up beside me. His jaw clenched and then released. "I'm in. You've got me."

My heart flipped over. I hadn't known if any of the guys would agree, but Damon was the last one I'd have expected to offer first.

"And me," Kyler said without hesitation. "No way am I sitting this out. We can worry about the fine print later."

Jin chuckled breathlessly, raking his hand through his blue-streaked hair. "Oh, to hell with it. Yes. I'm ready. You're the best adventure I've ever been a part of, Briar Rose. I'm in until the end."

My heart swelled with so much joy and affection I didn't know what to do with it. But Seth was still standing silent beside his twin, his mouth tightly slanted.

I grasped his hand. "You don't have to. It's all right."

His eyes met mine with so much emotion it nearly rocked me on my heels. "It's not that I don't want to," he said roughly. "You have no idea how much I want you,

Rose. All I'm trying to figure out is what's right for you."
He squeezed my hand back. "I love you. Don't you doubt
that for a second. We all love you."

He shot a pointed look around our little circle.

"Yes," Ky said with a giddy laugh. "So much, Rose."

Jin's expression turned unusually serious. "I do. More
than I wanted to admit to myself."

Damon scuffed his sneaker against the ground and
glowered at Seth. But when his gaze slid to me, it
softened. His voice came out with a rasp. "Sometimes I
feel like I've loved you my whole life, angel."

My eyes had welled up. Our group still didn't feel
quite complete, but it was whole enough and already
bound together by more trust and emotion than I could
imagine sharing with anyone else. I wished I could
somehow hold them all at once.

"I love you too," I said. "All of you. I always have."

They closed in around me, embracing me like they
had this morning in Jin's apartment. I breathed in their
mingled scents: Ky's musky mint, Seth's warmed bronze,
Jin's paint-tinged sweet smoke, Damon's leather and
bitter chocolate.

"Let's do this," Seth said. "Don't wait on my decision.
I'll watch out for you either way."

"All right," I said. "Come with me."

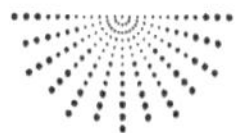

CHAPTER TWENTY-NINE

Seth

Rose took the lead, and the four of us fell into step behind her. Her pale gold dress made her look like a wraith, but a lovely one. She crossed the uneven ground with steady, determined strides, one hand clenched tight around the strap of her bag, fallen leaves crunching under her feet. The cooling breeze flicked her black hair across her pale shoulders. I couldn't look away.

What was I doing? Part of me was hollering at me to throw myself at her feet and pledge my eternal loyalty to her already, and another part was full of the gnawing sensation that I shouldn't be here at all.

I hadn't lied when I said I loved her. Oh, God, how I loved this girl, sweet as lilac and fierce as flame. And I'd fallen so quickly back into seeing her as the center of my world.

It'd been one thing to live for the next time we'd gather around her on her estate when we were kids. For a guy who was almost twenty-six years old—could *this* level of devotion really be healthy?

But the fact was I'd never felt the same sense of purpose as in those old days when we'd roamed through these woods by Rose's side. Nothing in my life since had felt that sure or right until the moment she'd walked back into it. What was fixing a sink or building a fucking backyard shed when I could be holding up this woman and her magic?

If it had been just about me, I'd have thrown in my lot with her in an instant tonight. It wasn't, though. What Rose needed mattered more than what I wanted. Would I really be supporting her when I needed her so badly myself? What if the weight of that need just dragged her down?

The thought made my gut twist and locked my mouth.

Damon came up beside me, his eyes narrowed. "Why are you still here if something back there matters so much more to you?" he said, his voice sharp.

My brother's head jerked around. "We all helped Rose before any of us even knew about consorts," Kyler said. "There's no reason we all have to take that step to keep helping. If Seth's not ready—"

"It's all right. It's a fair question," I broke in. Damon's comment hadn't even rankled me. I met his shadowed eyes. "Nothing matters to me more than this."

His lip curled partway into a sneer. "Then what's stopping you?"

The fact that nothing mattered to me more than this. But I didn't think saying that would clarify things for him. Damon was the last person who'd understand holding back when your instincts were propelling you forward. How often did he think more than a few days into the future?

Ky's attention had shifted back to Rose. Longing was written all over his face. Was that how I looked when I watched her too?

Jin was beaming as he tramped along, as if he'd left every hesitation and concern he'd had behind when he'd accepted her proposition. Were *any* of them really thinking?

It wasn't just me ready to throw my whole life in with her, was it? Maybe all of us were more invested than was really wise. It could be that what Rose needed right now wasn't wisdom but exactly this incredible devotion, this passion. To hold her up. To kindle her spark. To help her overcome everything ahead of her.

And if later on that dedication became too much... Would it make any difference if I wasn't adding to her burden? Whatever Ky said, after this was done, it'd be the other three guys she turned to, not me. I'd be left on the sidelines if I wasn't a part of this all the way through.

A memory rose up in the back of my mind of the night when Rose had come to me, flustered and shy but just as determined as she was now. Wanting my touch and the security I could give her with it.

I know if I get too caught up, you'll be looking out for me at least as much as I should be. Probably more.

I was supposed to be the strong one, so why was I so fucking afraid? Not even afraid of her, but of me, of how well I could stay in control. As if I hadn't always been the one of us best at keeping my head and heart in check.

What could I really do about her stepmother and that asshole she'd been supposed to marry if I hung back now? What could I do to keep her steady through whatever came afterward?

Resolve filled me as I picked up my pace to catch up with Rose. I could give her all that, all my attention and love and all the power she could take from me, and be strong enough not to lean on her too much, couldn't I? If even I couldn't... we were all careening toward disaster anyway.

Rose's pace had slowed. The branches leaned more densely together up ahead. I walked faster to push one aside before she reached it. Like the old days, clearing a path for her. Making her way easier however I could.

Rose glanced up at me and smiled, so brightly it lit my heart. "Thank you."

Yeah. That felt right.

My hand dropped to take hers as we walked on. Damon muttered something behind me, but I ignored him. I could weather his attitude. I could weather just about anything when I had Rose.

I eased another branch aside, and we emerged into a clearer patch of woods. In front of us, amid a stand of trees draped with vine, I caught a glimpse of stone blocks. The rim of a tower.

My breath caught. Oh. We'd only come out this far once when we were kids, but the feel of the place had stayed etched in my memory. The stillness and the aura of some kind of significance. Almost like magic.

Not almost. We could acknowledge it now. This place *was* magic. Why else would Rose have brought us here?

"All right," she said with a hitch in her voice. "Here we are. Let's see if we can do this. I think the three of you—"

"Four," I said. "You've got me too."

Her lips parted. "Seth..."

I touched her cheek and bent to kiss her. A pleased murmur escaped her. She tilted her head to kiss me back more deeply, looping her arm around my neck. When we eased apart a few inches, every nerve in my body was quivering—with a little apprehension, sure, but mostly with happiness.

Yes. That was exactly where I was meant to be.

"I'm sure," I said. "I promise you, I've never been so sure of anything in my life."

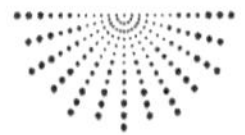

CHAPTER THIRTY

Rose

"All right," I said. My voice sounded quiet despite the stillness around us. As if the towers absorbed some of the sound with their latent power. A quiver of anticipation passed through me, looking at my guys who were looking back at me in the darkness of the forest.

I was really going to do this. I was going to take not one consort but four. And I couldn't have loved the men I was linking my heart and my magic to more.

Assuming this worked. I'd spent the afternoon reading everything I could about the consort ceremonies, figuring out which elements seemed to be necessary and how they were typically combined. In any normal case, a witch who wasn't involved in the consorting would have directed the ceremony, like Celestine had been meant to for mine with Derek. But I hadn't seen anything that indicated a witch couldn't call on those forces herself.

A spark wanted to be kindled. It only needed all

parties involved to show how committed they were, to form those magical bonds between us that would last the rest of our lives if we let them. To appeal to the greater Spark that ran through all of us and through life itself.

The eccentric amateur historian had mentioned structures in the wild where the ceremonies had once been held. Considering the etchings I'd found inside the one tower and the symbols of connection and loyalty marked on their outer walls, I had to guess this arch might be one of those. It did feel right standing here near all their history, with all this natural life around us.

"I think we should stand beneath the arch," I said. "Or as close to that as we can get."

Seth moved forward to push between two of the saplings that blocked the way. "The vegetation isn't too dense in here." Now that he'd decided, his eagerness to see our plan through radiated off of him.

The rest of us clambered into the space. The towers stood about ten feet apart, the stone arch maybe five feet wide, high above our heads. The ground beneath it held only grass of varying lengths, a few patches of flowering weeds, and a log where a larger tree had fallen beside the structure. The air there had a cooler edge, but it couldn't penetrate the warmth building just beneath my skin.

I opened my bag and got to work arranging the rest of my supplies. A crystal bowl that I lay on the ground in the middle of the small clearing. Five sticks of charcoal, each the length of my hand. And the five ribbons to match the white one I'd tied to the gate.

Kyler fished in his pocket when he saw those. "I

brought it back for you again," he said with that brilliant smile.

"Thank you." I wrapped it around my wrist like I so often did, but left half of the length hanging. Then I handed out the sticks of charcoal and the ribbons, each color to the guy it fit. Yellow for Ky. Green for Seth. Red for Damon. Purple for Jin. The blue one I left in the bag. The ceremonies I'd read had used rope or twine, but they'd also emphasized that symbolism that harmonized with the consorts' emotions was the key. I couldn't think of any better material than this.

The guys had settled into a natural circle around me. I stood with the bowl at my feet and breathed in deeply. Taking in their scents, the quiet of the arch, and the energy of the forest around us.

My spark flickered dimly in my chest, partly lit by the kisses I'd gotten from Ky and Seth. I was going to need more magic than that to begin the ceremony.

Damon had offered himself first, so I turned to him first. "I need a little help kick-starting my powers," I said.

Desire lit his eyes. "You don't have to ask twice, angel," he said, and tugged me to him, shoving ribbon and charcoal into his pocket.

He kissed me hard and hungry, sliding his fingers into my hair and tilting my head for better access. As his tongue tangled with mine, my spark flared brighter. His other hand slipped up my side to caress my breast through the soft fabric of the dress. Lust spiked between my legs as he tweaked the nipple like he had that night in his apartment.

Then another presence pressed against me from

behind. Kyler, I registered, just before Damon claimed my mouth with an even deeper kiss. Ky lowered his lips to the crook of my jaw, kissing a trail down the side of my neck. His arm circled my waist. His fingers traced over my ribs and up to stroke the curve of my neglected breast.

The glow of my spark spread all through my chest. I gasped into Damon's mouth. He took the opportunity to plunder it even more thoroughly. The combined heat of their bodies enveloped me. Ky's thumb swiveled around my nipple, and my hips swayed between his and Damon's. I'd thought getting it on with just one of my guys had been pretty spectacular. This? This was paradise.

It would have been easy to get lost in the moment, in the rush of our rising desire. But my magic was smoldering behind my sternum now, ready for my use. I had to stay focused, to direct this ceremony as well as succumbing to it.

I eased my head away, and both Damon and Ky immediately drew back. Ky was breathing hard, Damon grinning fiercely. A thrum of arousal seemed to course all through our circle. I knew without having to look that all four of the guys were as hard as my panties were now damp.

"Fuck," Jin said, sounding awed.

"Later," I said, with a slightly hysterical giggle. I gathered my breath again, sucking the night air deep into my lungs. The flame inside me steadied, still burning hotly. "Follow my lead. It all starts with me. First I have to show that we mean to honor the light that brings life. When I come to you, offer your mouth to accept."

I slid my foot across the grass. The ground I stood on was a far cry from the smooth boards of the magicking rooms where I'd done almost all of my practice, but my muscles adjusted, finding the right tension, the right speed. I weaved my hands through the air, from my chest where my spark licked at my ribs up into the air and then down my body from belly to core. All the magic in me, for the world and for me. My blessing to the great Spark that brought life to us all.

"The Spark that guides us, bless this partnering," I murmured.

I'd never performed magic on this scale in front of the guys before, nothing but a few little tricks. I couldn't risk checking their expressions in case they distracted me from my casting. But the atmosphere around me—a breath drawn in, the stirring of feet—held only wonder.

In a fluid movement, I swooped my arms down and scooped up the bowl from the ground. I turned as I raised it toward the arch and the sky above it. My feet swiveled on the grass at the same time, whirling me in a slow circle. My spark seared to the edges of my body and tingled up my arms.

The gesture was only symbolic. I tipped the bowl as if dribbling the magic I'd sent into it over my mouth. Then I held it to Seth. He raised his head like I had, his lips parting. A tiny jolt of energy passed from him to me. His essence touching my spark directly. The connection starting to form.

I turned to Jin next. As I tilted the bowl, he tipped his face just as Seth had. Another electric tingle passed through my chest. Then Damon. Then Ky. My spark was starting to jitter. An eager quaking, as if something at its center were waiting to snap free.

I set the bowl down and spun around it again, expelling magic through our ring. Sending it out to each of my guys, opening myself to them and calling them to me.

When I came to a stop, I was facing Jin. I stretched out my arm to offer my stick of charcoal. He copied my gesture, holding out the stick I'd given him. I touched the tip of mine to his and propelled a flash of magic through me.

A flame leapt up from the joined sticks. Jin's face glowed with pleasure and the flickering light.

"With you I would kindle my spark," I said. "Will you join me?"

"I will," Jin said, a smile stretching across his face.

I let the flame simmer down. Then I held my stick to Damon's. He touched his to mine without any further prompting. I expelled another quaver of magic toward them. Another flame, dancing with passion, ignited between us.

"With you I would kindle my spark," I said. "Will you join me?"

Damon smirked at me, the light gleaming in his dark eyes. "I will."

I lit the flame and made my request to Kyler and then Seth. The magic inside me was dwindling with the effort, but it was heating up at the same time. The shrinking spark seared against my heart.

Even as my spark contracted, magic sang through the stone blocks around us. The power was growing in the air, wrapping around us like an echo of the arch overhead. But I had to finish this ceremony before I lost enough power to complete our bonds.

Holding on to that energy as tightly as I could, I lifted my hand with the charcoal into the air. The guys did the same. "We will honor the Spark with our bond," I said, and nodded to them.

"We will honor the Spark with our bond," they repeated, their voices mingling together. I twisted my other hand in a spiral. All the sticks flared a second time, streaking light through the darkness. The vibration of energy in the air prickled over my skin.

The connection wasn't finished. I'd honored it and I'd opened it and turned our devotion into light, but I hadn't sealed it yet. I brought the charcoal to my other hand, snuffing it against my palm. The flames on the guys' sticks blinked out in the same moment.

I drew the glyph for joining across my palm. This part they couldn't do themselves. I stepped to each of them in turn, cupping my hand over theirs, guiding their fingers through the looping shape. I stopped at Ky and caught hold of the loose end of my ribbon.

"I, Rosalind Hallowell, take Kyler Lennox as my consort," I said, placing the ribbon on his glyph-marked palm. His fingers closed around it. Magic rippled through my words and through that symbolic cord between us. My chest pinched. Did I have enough? "I will light my spark by him and never let it burn him."

My spark flickered out with that last press of power. It radiated into Ky. "Now you," I said quietly.

He glanced at the yellow ribbon he held and offered one end to me. I curled my fingers around the strip of silk.

The magic I'd given him quivered through Ky's words. "I, Kyler Lennox, take Rosalind Hallowell as my consort." The corner of his mouth quirked. "I will light her spark with my heart and never do her harm."

My throat tightened. He hadn't needed to add that last part, but it fit.

The magic I'd sent to him tickled back over me with his words. It sank into my chest. And then my spark burst like a firework.

Light and heat exploded through my body. It blinded me from behind my eyes, stealing my breath, scorching my throat. Kyler inhaled sharply. A sob fell from my lips, but it was a sob of joy. The magic raced through every nerve, through every pore, as if my spark and my body were one.

The woman from the Assembly had been right. Even after the intimacy I'd already shared with these guys, I couldn't have imagined this exhilaration. The way every particle in my body rang out with the sweep of power.

I clutched Ky's hand, yanked him to me, and planted a kiss on his mouth. A little of the magic rushing through me cascaded on into him. He gripped me harder.

I wanted. Oh, I wanted, with an ache already painful at my core. The ceremony's potent energy urged me to fulfill that need. But I had three more consorts to complete my bond with.

Tearing myself away from Kyler, I turned to Seth. He held his hands out to me, ready to accept my ribbon and to offer me his. My heart squeezed. It took barely a sliver of the magic coursing through me to imbue my words to him.

"I, Rosalind Hallowell, take Seth Lennox as my consort. I will light my spark by him and never let it burn him."

He set his ribbon in my waiting hand, clasping his fingers over mine. Magic streamed back from him to me. "I, Seth Lennox, take Rosalind Hallowell as my consort. I will light her spark with my heart and never do her harm."

Another giddy wave coursed through me. I leaned in, and Seth was there to meet me. He kissed me so hard tiny echoes of my spark danced behind my eyelids.

When I swiveled to face Jin, his eyes were bright with unspoken words. I gave him the end of my ribbon. Emotion and energy quivered through my chest. "I, Rosalind Hallowell, take Jin Lyang as my consort. I will light my spark by him and never let it burn him."

My artist's voice rang out rich and steady. "I, Jin Lyang, take Rosalind Hallowell as my consort. I will light her spark with my heart and never do her harm."

The third deluge of magic made my legs wobble. Jin caught me by the waist. I gripped his shoulders and kissed him until the ache of need became unbearable.

One more. One more, and then I could satisfy that desire.

Damon accepted my ribbon, looking down at it as if he couldn't quite believe it was really there in his hand. Then he clenched his fingers over it. His gaze seared into mine.

"I, Rosalind Hallowell, take Damon Scarsi as my

consort," I said, my voice quivering now with the magic swirling through me. "I will light my spark by him and never let it burn him."

His voice came out low and rough. "I, Damon Scarsi, take Rosalind Hallowell as my consort. I will light her spark with my heart and never do her harm."

The final joining hit me like a thunderclap. I tumbled into Damon's arms, my lips crashing into his, but the ache inside me split open with the flow of magic, letting loose a flood of longing. To hold and be held, to touch and be touched. To take all my consorts in every way I possibly could.

The flood swept us all together. As Damon kissed me back, other arms came around me. A mouth brushed my shoulder. Another nipped my ear. Fingers trailed across my breasts and down between my legs. I whimpered, my hips swaying to meet them.

Damon pulled his lips from mine. He teased the edges of his teeth down my throat to nip my collarbone. His hands dropped to my thighs, hiking up the skirt of my dress.

"I won't be greedy," he said, looking like hunger incarnate. "But I'll get you ready."

He dropped to his knees and tore my panties off me. Seth's strong arms closed around me from behind, his solid chest supporting me. He kissed the sensitive spot right behind my ear. Kyler leaned in to claim my lips and Damon—

Damon slicked his tongue right over my clit.

I moaned, my hips bucking. Damon held my thighs, and Seth supported the rest of my weight. "Best thing I ever tasted, angel," Damon muttered, and pressed his mouth to me as if to devour me.

A different sort of sparks careened up from my core. Seth's hand rose to cup one of my breasts. Jin was there at my other side, bending to lap the other nipple into a stiffened peak. And oh, Damon's lips and his tongue, the flick of it over my clit again and again.

I was so ready for release I barely had time to savor it. Damon suckled me harder, his tongue tracing my opening and the edge of his teeth grazing my clit. I shuddered in Seth's embrace. An orgasm ripped through me, feeling as if it'd set all the magic in me ablaze. Bliss quaked through my muscles.

Somehow I still wasn't sated. I made a sound of protest as Damon stepped back. His cock bulged against the fly of his jeans, but he shook his head. We both knew I had three other consorts I was burning to join with.

My fingers caught the front of Jin's shirt. I yanked him to me. As he kissed me hard, I reached for the button of his slacks. He groaned.

"Yes, Rose. Fucking yes."

As if we were one being with a single purpose, the five of us moved to the edge of the clearing, to the log. Someone stripped off my dress and laid it on the mossy surface for me to sit on. The cool air felt shockingly electric against my naked body. My guys still had on too many clothes.

I kissed Jin again, tugging down his zipper. At the same time, I hauled at Seth's shirt with my free hand. He chuckled hoarsely and wrenched it off. Then he was holding me from behind again, his bare chest against my back, his hands rising to massage my breasts.

My fingers closed around Jin's erection. It twitched against my palm. "Rose," he murmured. He kicked off his pants and knelt between my splayed legs. As I stroked him, he pushed closer. The head of his cock rubbed over my clit, making me gasp. The need inside me burned. I guided him to my opening.

He sucked in a breath as he slid inside me. His hands settled on my thighs, holding them in place. With a heft of his hips, he pulled back and sank into me even deeper. The blaze inside me flared like a wildfire.

Seth kissed the side of my neck, still fondling my breasts with sure, skilled strokes of his fingers. Ky bent between his brother and Jin to press his mouth to mine again. I tipped my head back against Seth's shoulder, opening myself more to his twin. Oh, Spark help me, even with Jin's thrusts setting me on fire from my core and Seth's hands stoking the flames through my chest, I wanted even more.

I grasped Ky's pants and tugged. With a startled breath, he yanked them and his boxers down. His cock sprang free, long and slim to match his body and stunningly erect. I couldn't imagine doing anything in that moment other than urging it to my lips.

Ky groaned as my mouth accepted his cock. His hips bucked, pressing it deeper inside, almost to my throat.

I sucked him in and swirled my tongue around his salty skin at the same time. He clutched my hair. His hips jerked again. "Fuck, Rose, I'm so close already."

I was close and far and everywhere in between. The

pulse of Ky's cock in my mouth and the caress of Seth's hands over my breasts and the rhythm of Jin rocking in and out of me. The pants of Damon's breath somewhere beside us where he was stroking himself in time with the rest of our maelstrom of passion. My body thrummed with pleasure and my spark roared like an inferno, both sensations threatening to swallow me whole.

Ky broke first, spilling himself in my mouth with a ragged gasp. I slid my lips off of him and swallowed. Then he was there again, kissing me mouth to mouth, not caring about his taste on my lips.

Seth squeezed my nipples between his fingers, making my nerves jump with a shock of bliss. Jin plunged deeper, faster, our bodies growing slick with sweat where we joined. He arched to let the base of his cock bump my clit. Again, and again, and—

Ecstasy blasted through me as if my spark had detonated. I cried out, clinging to Seth's arm, to Ky's shoulder. Jin thrust another few times, propelling me even higher over the edge, and then he tumbled over with me. He spent himself inside me with a groan.

Damon tugged my chin, tearing me from Ky's mouth to claim mine with his own. His hand jerked over his cock. He came with a sharp inhale, his teeth scraping my bottom lip.

My body had gone limp, the muscles sagging even as magic crackled through every limb. My head had nestled against Seth's chest. I peered up at him. "Seth?"

"I'm good," he said before I could expand on that question. He eased me up so he could kiss me on the mouth. "I have you," he murmured. "The rest can wait. Unless you need…?"

There wasn't a particle in my body my spark wasn't scorching. If any more magic lit me up, I was pretty sure I'd explode.

"No," I said, pulling all of my guys closer. "You've already given me everything I need. Everything I could ever have wanted." My boys. My consorts.

That last thought sent a heady rush of possessiveness through me. Jin nuzzled my cheek. Damon looped his arm over my belly. Kyler pressed one last kiss to the inside of my elbow. Seth brushed his lips against the top of my head.

It wasn't just magic that flowed between us. I could feel the love that shone from all of them and from me in return, a giddy tingling everywhere we touched.

I'd returned to the only house I'd ever really thought of as mine a month ago, but now… Now I was truly *home*.

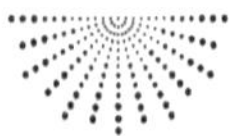

CHAPTER THIRTY-ONE

Rose

The tick of the grandfather clock carried through the otherwise silent house. I pulled my duvet higher over my head, my eyes open in the darkness underneath. Not that it was any less dark in the room around me.

Celestine needed to think I was asleep. Magic was still rushing through my veins, my spark ignited enough to fill my whole body. The twined bonds of my consorting held it steady in my chest.

This power wouldn't fade. But I didn't know yet how much my stepmother might hold. If I was going to get through tonight, I needed to use every possible advantage, including surprise.

Alongside the thrum of the magic, a dull throbbing ran through me, sharpest low in my belly. I was pretty sure certain parts of me were going to be physically sore tomorrow, but that didn't dull my longing. My pain at being apart from the guys I'd only just partnered with.

Normally consorts didn't leave each other's presence for at least a week after the original ceremony. Both to solidify the emotional and physical bond, when often they hadn't been that intimate beforehand, and to avoid this discomfort as the strands of magic that joined us were so newly formed and unused to stretching. Could the guys feel it too, this twang calling out for us to come back together?

The rush of our first coming together, all five of us, had been so explosive... Heat rose in my cheeks as I remembered it. The magic of the ceremony had unleashed all our passions. I hadn't expected to come quite this far in just a few weeks from the knowledgeable-but-virginal Rose I'd been when I arrived here. But I definitely wasn't complaining.

My lips curled with a brief grin. Actually, I was very much looking forward to more moments like that one. Maybe with a little more time to savor the experience when we didn't have the ceremony's urgency whirling around us.

Fulfilling my longings would have to wait until tomorrow, at least. After my father and I had finished dealing with Celestine and Derek... What was Dad going to think of the choice I'd made? He'd agreed with Celestine that it was best for me not to get too close to the boys all those years ago.

But he couldn't have been worried we'd do *this*. He wouldn't have thought this was possible. He'd wanted to spare me the broken heart of falling for them and not being able to have them.

The consort bonds couldn't be severed, not so early. He'd just have to find a way to accept it. As strange and unexpected as it would seem, he'd at least be able to appreciate that I was happy. I was still his daughter. I was still a Hallowell.

And I'd be the lady of this estate now.

It'd been just shy of eleven o'clock when I'd scrambled back through my window. It had to be almost midnight now. I repressed the urge to squirm with impatience. Chatting with Philomena might have helped pass the time, but I didn't want to be distracted either.

The noise reached my ears so faintly at first I didn't quite notice. A soft rasp from the direction of the door. My pulse hiccupped.

My lock was turning over. I'd set it before I went to bed both to make sure no one without magic came barging in and found me gone, and because that was what Celestine would have expected. Now with her magic she must be releasing it.

The door whispered open. The air shifted against the top of my head, the only part of me not covered by the duvet. Footsteps padded across the floor to the bed. If I'd had any doubt about who had entered, it would have vanished at the sound of my stepmother drawing in her breath. That was enough to recognize her.

With a rustle of her clothes, she bent and rested her hand on my shoulder to shake me awake.

My heartbeat thundered in my ears. I whipped out

my arm, tossing aside the duvet and whipping magic through the air in the same movement.

I caught just a glimpse of Celestine's pale face contorting with shock before the magic I'd hurled at her struck her across the calves. She stumbled backward, thrown off-balance. I swept my hands toward her again, summoning enough power to smack her right onto the floor.

She hit the floorboards on her back with a thump. I twisted my fingers, and coils of magic formed around my stepmother's wrists and ankles to hold her in place. Holding her from throwing any magic back at me.

She jerked her head, directing some spell at me that way. I clapped my hands together and it dissolved.

"No more," I said, the glow of my spark radiating into my words. I traced a sheet in the air and cast it toward her. No tutor had ever taught me to sculpt magic to this specific purpose, but the energy inside me sang out so clearly I saw exactly how to move with it, exactly what to say to it. "Your power will stay in your body."

The barrier closed around Celestine's form. I stepped closer, poised over her.

My stepmother stared up me in the dim moonlight from the window, her blond bob askew, her pale eyes glossy with shock and alarm. As she stared at me, a flicker of a deeper horror darkened her expression.

"Rosalind," she said, her voice tight. "What have you done?"

"What have *I* done?" I said. The anger I'd been holding in since I'd first uncovered her scheming seared up through me. It crackled into my throat. "I've done what I had to do, to survive *you*. What I want to talk about is what you've done, and everything you were planning to do next."

Celestine's lips pressed flat. She kept herself propped up on her elbows, braced awkwardly against the floor but unwilling to give in and slump down. Somehow she still had enough elegance in her tailored blouse and dress pants to look as if she'd meant to be lying there. I gritted my teeth.

"You can't get out of this by staying quiet," I said. "I know everything. I know you were coming in here to force me to take Derek as my consort tonight, whether I wanted to or not. I know you were going to pervert the ceremony so he would have more control over my magic than I do. I know he's taken an oath to follow your orders when it comes to me. I don't even know how many laws of the Assembly that's already breaking. It can't get much worse."

"Then why are we talking about it?" Celestine asked.

I glared at her. But the truth was, I didn't know everything. There was something I wanted to hear from her. "Why? Why would you do that to me? I know we've never really gotten along, but I didn't—I've never tried to *hurt* you."

A lump rose in my throat through the anger. What could possibly justify my stepmother, the woman who'd acted as my mother for nearly twelve years, turning me into a virtual slave?

Celestine shifted as if testing the bindings I'd placed on her, but they held firm. Her jaw clenched. "Your spark will shine bright. Clearly it already does. That sort of power is better kept in check."

"Says who?" I snapped. "You've got plenty of power. Should someone be pulling your strings?"

She chuckled a little hoarsely. The glint had come back into her eyes. A shine that looked more like terror than anything else now. "Oh, Rosalind. You have no idea yet. Look at you with your spark just kindled and no experience at all wielding your magic. The Hallowell line runs strong in you, and your mother's blood mingled with that..." She shook her head. "It isn't safe to give a witch like you free rein."

There had to be more to it than she was saying, but I was tired of hearing her make up excuses. I drew myself up even straighter, reveling in the magic still pulsing through me with all the strength of my consorts and my spark. "That's not a decision you get to make. And you'll be sorry you did. When my father gets back tomorrow, you and my 'fiancé' are going to tell him everything you planned, every horrible detail—"

Celestine started to laugh. Real laughter, strained but loud enough to cut off my words.

"You think I can't make you?" I said. "I found the contract. I have the proof even if you don't say anything. And I have enough magic to keep both of you here long enough to face whatever retribution will be coming."

"From your father?" she said, catching her breath. "Rosalind, this was all his idea. He's even more a part of it than I am."

My mouth snapped shut as if the words had been a chilly slap across my face. I wouldn't have thought there was anything that could have dampened my anger, but she'd found it. For a second I could only stare at her in a daze.

"You're lying," I spat out. "You're trying to confuse me. Why would he trap his own daughter?"

"He knows the power you're coming into even better than I do," Celestine said. She even smiled, small and sharp. "You're his little lamb, and he wants you on a leash."

No. There was no way that could be true. "It's your name on the contract," I said. "You met with Master Cortland to discuss it. You tried to do it while Dad wasn't here to find out."

My stepmother raised her eyebrows. "All the practicalities went through me because I'm the one with the magic. And because after he gave his instructions, he didn't want to think about the details too much. He does love you, in his own way."

She said the words with a mocking lilt. My hands balled at my sides. "And tonight?"

"Do you think I want him to come home to our plans potentially on the verge of exposure? He entrusted me with the responsibility to get this done. I meant to do it."

My stomach had knotted, my dinner threatening to come up. I fought down the nausea. "Why should I even believe you? You could be making all this up just to deflect the blame. To try to stop me from going to him."

"I suppose I could be," Celestine said, "but I'm not. If you've read the contract, you know it refers to the Hallowell 'elders,' not just to me. It was drawn up right in his home office, you know. I'm surprised you didn't recognize that linen paper he's so fond of."

I wasn't going to pull the contract out to check it now. "That doesn't mean anything," I said. "You could have taken a piece of paper from his office easily enough."

"But why would I write in a clause that gives him any authority over the matter if I was trying to do this behind his back?"

I didn't know. I just hadn't had enough time to think it through. I wavered on my feet, uncertainty twisting through my magic—and my stepmother lunged.

The bindings holding her wrists and ankles had faded with my confidence. She wrenched free with a sizzle. Slamming into me, she tackled me to the ground. The barrier I'd placed against her magic crumbled too.

My tailbone jarred against the floor. I shoved away from the slam of her elbow and a smack of magic from her hand. With a sweep of my arm, I propelled her backward.

Celestine skidded on her feet and spun around. A wave of magical energy crashed through the room toward me. Books tumbled from my shelves. My bed frame rattled. On instinct alone, I waved my hands over my head and huddled in a protective ball.

Her magic shook me but bounced off my shell. The family photo of me and my parents fell from the wall. It hit the floor with a cracking of broken glass.

I scrambled up before Celestine could attack again and hurled a blanket of magic at her with all my strength. It slammed tight around her, pinning her arms to her sides and her magic back inside her chest to smolder with her spark. She froze in place.

Celestine's gaze smoldered too as I walked up to her. My chest squeezed with my ragged breaths, and not just from the effort.

I didn't know if she was telling the truth. But even as my heart ached at the thought that Dad might have orchestrated this scheme, I couldn't rush ahead blindly. I'd gotten this far, protected myself this much, by waiting and watching until I understood. What if I *did* turn her over to him, and he only turned on me? What if I brought her all the way to the Assembly and came home to find him waiting with some other trap I wouldn't see in time?

I could get my own sort of retribution. And I could make sure Celestine never interfered with my life again.

"These are my conditions," I said to my stepmother, pressing every ounce of power I had into the words. Pressing those words into her, into her mind, into her will. A blunt hammering, an illegal magicking—but she was the one who'd crossed that line first.

"You will gather your things and go within the hour. You will not speak—no, you will not communicate in any way about me or my family to anyone. You will not communicate *to* anyone from this household or come within a hundred miles of it or anywhere else my father or I might be, unless I allow it. *Do you agree?*"

Her eyes narrowed, but I wasn't giving her a choice. She nodded.

"Say it," I demanded. "Show me that you mean it."

I didn't need to explain what I wanted more than

that. She spoke with a thready voice that carried a hum of magic. As binding as the contract she'd signed.

"I, Celestine Hallowell, will leave this estate in the next hour. I will not convey any information about you or your family to anyone. I will not communicate with anyone from this household or come within a hundred miles of your properties or where you or your father travel without your permission. I agree."

She grimaced. "I wouldn't want to anyway," she added in her usual voice. "Not when I know how angry your father is going to be when he finds out what a catastrophe this has turned into. You know, I wouldn't be surprised if he would have made me swear the same thing and banished me just as quickly. Like father, like daughter?"

The words were sneering, but her chin wobbled, just for a second. Her eyes twitched when I studied her. And in that second I believed her a little more than I wanted to.

"You're afraid of him," I said. "With all your magic—"

"There are forces other than magic in this world, Rosalind," my stepmother said. Her stance had started to deflate, her shoulders sagging. "You'll find that out soon enough. Now will you release me? My hour is passing."

She didn't look like the powerful, haughty witch I'd always seen her as anymore. She looked like a sad, beaten woman.

My stomach churned. "Go on," I said, motioning to dispel the magic holding her. "Don't forget you're not allowed to speak to anyone. And I want my phone back."

Celestine bowed her head and slunk out the door. I

followed her into the hall, watching to make sure she went to her room. She emerged a moment later to give me the prepaid phone she'd taken. Then she ducked back in. A suitcase thumped onto the bed. Clothes hangers clinked.

I'd put everything I had into that last, psychological binding. My spark still danced in my chest, but the roar of its earlier fire had dimmed. I'd needed to be sure that the magic I'd woven with hers to bind her to the oath would last for a long, long time.

Derek must be out by the garden, waiting. Well, he could stay there until he gave up. I expected he'd wait until well after Celestine left, but even if he saw her, she wouldn't be able to tell him where she was going or why. Let him wonder if it came to that.

I'd thought I was going to go back to my bedroom and pretend nothing had happened that involved me. But my feet carried me in the other direction, to the office Dad kept here in the manor.

I stood outside the door for a long moment. Then I flicked my fingers by the knob to release the lock with my magic.

The office was the same as I remembered it from my childhood: the tall shelves packed with books and charts, the big mahogany desk, the looming leather armchair. The smell of polished wood and black licorice, from the candies Dad liked to chew on when he was thinking an issue through.

How many nights had I slipped in here when I was little, before Celestine, before even my boys, to curl up on his lap and beg him away from his work?

He'd always come. No matter what else he'd been doing, he'd always come when I'd asked him. He'd always been there for me. *My little lamb.*

My fingers dug into my pocket as I approached the desk. Dad had taken his laptop with him on his trip, but the printer sat in its usual station in the corner. I laid the contract on the desk, unfolded it flat, and tugged open the printer's paper drawer.

The page I drew out felt exactly the same to my fingertips as the paper the contract was written on. I set it right beside. The ache inside me spread right through my ribcage.

The color was the same. The faint texturing of the fibers—*Real paper shouldn't be smooth as plastic,* I'd heard him say more than once. *It should look like what it is.*

The paper didn't mean anything. Celestine could have stolen it as easily as I'd taken this page right now.

But I stood there studying them for long enough that my head started to ache too. And when I left the room, I didn't have any more answers than I'd come in with.

CHAPTER THIRTY-TWO

Rose

I woke up to bright morning sun streaming through my bedroom window. I'd slept in.

No wonder, after that late, crazy night. My whole body ached, head to toe. I rubbed my forehead as I pushed back the covers.

I'd put the books back on my shelves. The family photo Celestine's magic had knocked from the wall lay on my bedside table. The glass had fractured with a dozen cracks, segmenting my face and my mother's and father's into jagged pieces. Looking at it, a deeper pain pierced through my chest. I wet my lips.

Today, Dad would be back. Today I could start to discover how true my stepmother's words had been.

Until I was sure, I had to keep pretending everything was normal. If this scheme had started with him, at least I knew she hadn't let on to him that I'd been causing her any trouble. She'd wanted to maintain the illusion that she had everything under control.

I had a month. A month until my consorting with Derek was supposed to happen, as far as Dad knew. A month to uncover the entire truth.

But he wasn't due home until the late afternoon, which mean I had the rest of the day to do what I wanted without worrying about what he'd see. The tug in my heart told me exactly where I needed to go.

Philomena sashayed over as I was pawing through the clothes in my closet. "Well," she said. "Look at you, Rose. You conquered the witch and sent her fleeing."

I restrained myself from reminding Phil that I was a witch myself. "And I have my guys," I said with a smile I suspected looked a little goofy.

"Yes." She looked down at her hands, uncharacteristically awkward. "I suppose you won't be needing my company anymore then."

My head jerked around. I stared at her. "What?"

"I mean, now that you have so many fine gentlemen offering their attentions... And I can't exactly be there the way a real friend would be..."

"Phil," I said firmly if only in my head. "You have been every bit a real friend to me. And I absolutely still need you. A girl still needs her girlfriends, no matter how many guys she's got. Now get over here and help me figure out what I can wear that says, 'I just got magically married' without *actually* saying, 'I just got magically married.'"

Phil laughed and leaned past me. In an instant, she'd laid her hand on the perfect dress.

I practically flew down the stairs on my way out. Not quite fast enough to avoid Derek, though.

"Rose!" he called out as I reached for the front door. My shoulders stiffened at his voice. I breathed into the glow of the spark in my chest and turned to face him with an even smile.

I was a witch now. I had more power in my body than he'd ever hold in one finger. He couldn't hurt me. He was nothing to me.

My unknowingly former fiancé stopped and looked me up and down. The pale yellow summer dress was like a slightly fancier version of the robe I'd worn for the ceremony last night, but casual enough that it didn't look odd for a stroll into town. "You look nice," he said, but his expression stayed tense. "Is everything all right?"

Feeling me out. Celestine had gotten him wondering how much I might know. But from what I'd heard yesterday as I crouched in his closet, she'd kept him mostly in the dark about the details. So I just kept smiling. "As far as I know. It looks like a beautiful day, doesn't it?"

He studied me, his mouth forming a slightly uncertain smile. "It does. Have you seen your stepmother by any chance?"

This morning? "No," I said truthfully. "Why?"

"I just— I haven't run into her all morning. Usually we cross paths at breakfast, at least. The staff don't seem to know where she is either."

He raked a nervous hand through his ash blond hair. How long had he waited out in the darkness last night before he'd realized she wasn't coming? That he wasn't gaining his consort and slave quite yet, if ever?

Part of me wanted to boot him out of here like I had Celestine. But her disappearance was going to raise enough questions. I could play the long game and see him brought to justice properly.

"I don't know where she might have gone," I said, also truthfully. "I'm sure she's fine, wherever she is. Maybe she went to arrange something for my father's return home."

"Yes, of course, that would make sense."

He wandered back down the hall without even asking me where *I* was going. Too much on his mind, I guessed, with his co-conspirator mysteriously vanished. Let him go soothe his worries with Polly if he wanted to.

I strode out into the warm May sunlight. The wind picked up, teasing through my hair and tickling my nose with a bouquet of floral scents. I slipped past the gate and walked as fast as my feet would carry me into town.

I'd already texted my guys to tell them I was okay and coming to meet them. No, not just my guys. My consorts. A real smile stretched across my face that even my uncertainties about my father couldn't shake. I could spend a few hours where I was meant to be, with them all around me.

We'd agreed to meet at Jin's gallery, since that offered the best balance between being a public and private space. I glanced through the first-floor window as I came around to the front door and saw all four of the guys had already gathered.

Damon was pointing at one of the paintings and

making a skeptical face, but amusement danced in his eyes. Jin was laughing and shaking his head. Kyler jumped in between them, pointing to that painting and then another across the room, maybe to indicate some connection he saw between them. Seth stood back, watching the others with his arms folded over his chest, but even he looked relaxed and happy. My heart swelled with affection for all of them.

The closed sign was showing, but the door was unlocked. I flipped the deadbolt over as I came in. Whatever the guys had been talking about, the conversation stopped the second they saw me.

Jin leapt to lower the shade over the window. "Rose!" Ky said, striding to meet me, but his twin beat him there. Seth pulled me into his arms and kissed me soundly.

I lingered there, enjoying the combined gentleness and power of his embrace. He eased back reluctantly. I turned and opened my arms to Ky, who claimed my mouth and swung me around at the same time. I giggled as he released me.

Damon caught me from behind. I tipped my head back to meet his lips. He kissed me hard, his hand stroking down my side with a hunger that promised more to come.

Jin didn't wait for Damon to let me go. When I looked to him with the other guy's arm still around my waist, my artist teased his fingers over my cheek into my hair and leaned in. His sure and steady kiss combined with Damon's determined heat behind me left my body melting.

When I'd had a proper greeting from all of my

consorts, Ky stepped forward again, his gaze concerned. "Is your father already back? Everything's taken care of with your stepmother?"

I hesitated. I didn't want to ruin this reunion with all the complications last night's confrontation had revealed. Not yet. We'd have to talk about it soon, but it could wait a little while.

"She's gone," I said. "She won't be coming back."

He beamed and kissed me again, so thoroughly I went weak in the knees. As Ky pulled back, Damon cleared his throat. "I say we take this upstairs."

"Mmm," Jin said agreeably. "I think our consort deserves a bed when we can give her one."

A flush spread over my skin. Oh, yes, I was going to enjoy the next few hours very much. "Lead the way," I said.

We were just heading to the stairs at the back when a faint sound from outside tugged at my awareness. The distant rumble of an engine. I paused and felt the tug again. Just a slight nudge in the middle of my chest. My spark jittered with it.

"What?" Seth said, following my gaze with a frown. "Do you think you were followed?"

"It's not that." But I didn't know what it was. Only that I needed to find out.

My body moved of its own accord. I hurried to the door and opened it. The sunlight spilled over me just as a motorcycle came to a stop by the sidewalk outside. My heart skipped a beat before the figure who stepped off it even reached for his helmet. Some part of me, deep down, already knew.

"What—" Ky said behind me.

The guy pulled off his helmet and slung it under his well-muscled arm. His dark red hair gleamed in the sun, falling in a loose wave to just past his ears. His bright blue eyes caught mine. He smiled, slow and easy like he always used to, and plucked a folded scrap of paper from the pocket of his motorcycle vest.

The page I'd torn from my favorite book, years and years ago.

"Hey, Sprout," Gabriel said. "Something told me I'd find you here."

ABOUT THE AUTHOR

Eva Chase lives in Canada with her family. She loves stories both swoony and supernatural, and strong women and the men who appreciate them. Along with the Witch's Consorts series, she is the author of the Dragon Shifter's Mates series, Demons of Fame Romance series, the Legends Reborn trilogy, and the Alpha Project Psychic Romance series.

Connect with Eva online:
www.evachase.com
eva@evachase.com

www.ingramcontent.com/pod-product-compliance
Lightning Source LLC
Chambersburg PA
CBHW061323190726